Advance Praise for
SOMETIMES THE GIRL

"With gorgeous prose and a setting so real you can smell the boxes in Elsie's attic, Jennifer Mason-Black crafts a story that's part-mystery and part-odyssey. Through her complicated, layered relationship with Elsie, Holi unboxes secrets, deep wounds, and a longing for the kind of healing that comes with human connection."

—Carrie Firestone, author of *The Loose Ends List* and *The Unlikelies*

"*Sometimes the Girl* is a book so powerful and tender that you just want to hold it close, knowing it will help you weather your own hard times. With enormous skill, Jennifer Mason-Black crosses the generation gap to plumb the pain—and poetry and transcendence— that unite two women writers of two wildly different eras. This is a metafiction every bit as addictive as the bestselling novel it's about."

—Margot Harrison, author of *Only She Came Back*

"Mason-Black never shies away from the hard questions and harder answers in this devastating, engrossing puzzle of a story. I can't stop thinking about it."

—Mary McCoy, author of *I, Claudia* and *Indestructible Object*

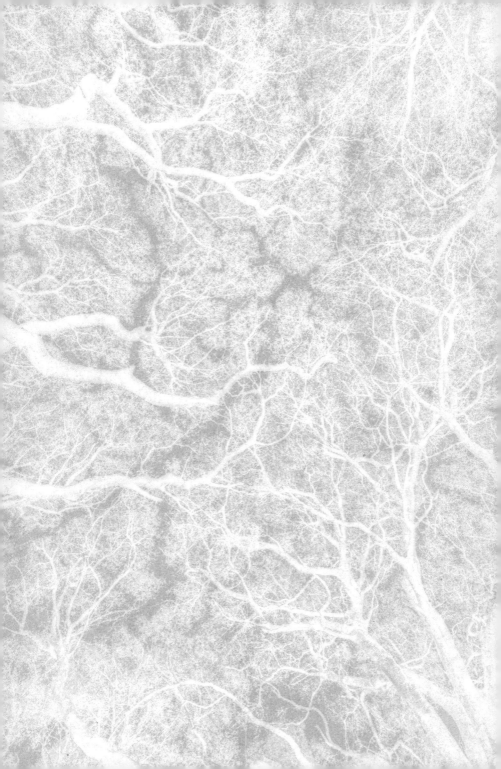

JENNIFER MASON-BLACK

SOMETIMES THE GIRL

Carolrhoda LAB
MINNEAPOLIS

Text copyright © 2025 by Jennifer Mason-Black

All rights reserved. International copyright secured. No part of this book may be reproduced, stored in a retrieval system, or transmitted in any form or by any means—electronic, mechanical, photocopying, recording, or otherwise—without the prior written permission of Lerner Publishing Group, Inc., except for the inclusion of brief quotations in an acknowledged review.

Carolrhoda Lab®
An imprint of Lerner Publishing Group, Inc.
241 First Avenue North
Minneapolis, MN 55401 USA

For reading levels and more information, look up this title at
www.lernerbooks.com.

Cover photo: Design Pics/Shutterstock. Design elements: adisetia/Shutterstock; Nenilkime/Shutterstock; Nataliia K/Shutterstock; andreashofmann7777/Shutterstock.

Main body text set in Janson Text LT Std.
Typeface provided by Adobe Systems.

Library of Congress Cataloging-in-Publication Data

Names: Mason-Black, Jennifer, author.
Title: Sometimes the girl / Jennifer Mason-Black.
Description: Minneapolis : Carolrhoda Lab, 2025. | Audience: Ages 14–18. |
    Audience: Grades 10–12. | Summary: "When eighteen-year-old Holiday, an
    aspiring writer, gets a short-term job sorting through the attic of an acclaimed
    ninety-something author, the author's secrets change how Holi views art and life"
    —Provided by publisher.
Identifiers: LCCN 2024010411 (print) | LCCN 2024010412 (ebook) |
    ISBN 9781728493299 | ISBN 9798765650844 (epub)
Subjects: CYAC: Authors—Fiction. | Secrets—Fiction.
Classification: LCC PZ7.1.M3764 So 2025 (print) | LCC PZ7.1.M3764 (ebook) |
    DDC [Fic]—dc23

LC record available at https://lccn.loc.gov/2024010411
LC ebook record available at https://lccn.loc.gov/2024010412

Manufactured in Canada
1-53599-51382-8/22/2024

FOR THE TRUTHTELLERS

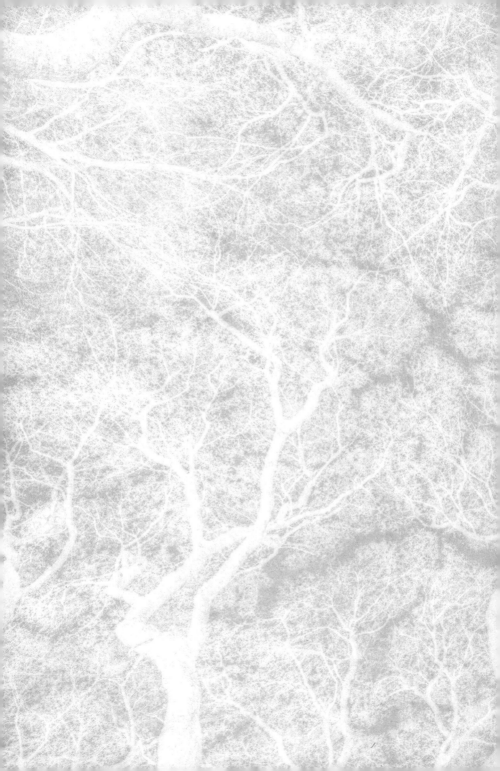

NOTE TO READERS

This story deals with a suicide attempt, addiction, death, and sexual violence. For 24/7 free and confidential support and resources, these are some places to start.

Suicide & Crisis Lifeline: call or text 988

National Sexual Assault Hotline: call 800-656-4673 or use the online chat at https://hotline.rainn.org/online

Substance Abuse and Mental Health Services Administration's (SAMHSA) National Helpline: call 800-662-4357

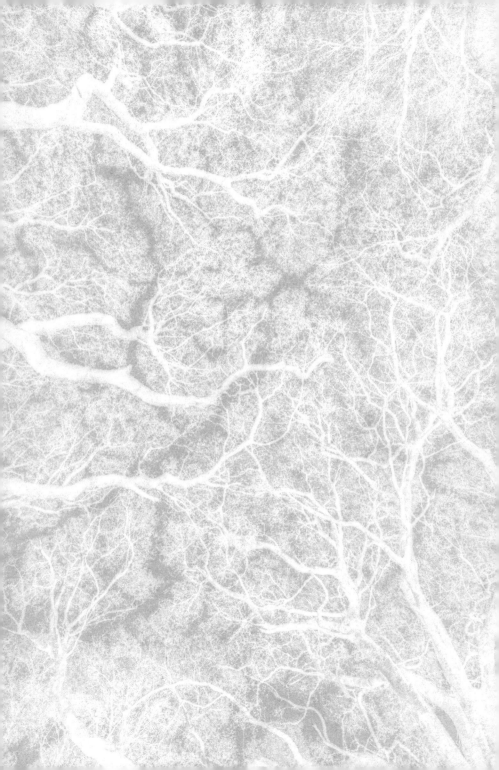

The hill is perfect.
 The hill is alive.
It's not the length—it's the curves, and the sand along the edge, and the cars dusting by. It's the hot sun, and the hot wind, and the air on my face and on the hairs of my legs. It's feeling the tremor of the wheel when I slide along the edge of the sand as the wake of a truck buffets the bike and me—and that breathless sense that right here is the edge of life. Right here, on a sunny September day. One wiggle to the left, one wiggle to the right, and life changes instantly. Ends, even. Under the car wheels, onto the rocks . . .

Here, though, now, I'm not a younger sister, a daughter, a sorta ex-girlfriend. I'm not Holiday, or Holi, or even Hol. I'm not the sum of my experiences: of classrooms and clubs and pain that hurts too much to share.

I am cells and stardust, heart and hands and breath.
The hill is not the only thing alive.
I am too.

I promised I would show up to the address my mother gave me on time. I didn't promise I'd dress for success. I'd be lying if I said I didn't care whether I got this job, but nine tenths of that caring is about the money and the remaining tenth has no say over what I wear.

Mom opens the door to the white ranch house, tips her head in that *forgiving you now but must you?* way.

"Hey, at least I took my helmet off. I even wore a bra. And my mask." I grin beneath it and run a hand through my sweaty hair. I shaved it off in the spring. It grew back faster than I thought it would. I like the smoothness when it's gone; I like what I can do with it when it grows. Maya has to bleach her hair to get good color. Mine is damn close to white naturally, especially in the summer. Only now it's green.

Mom shakes her head, more of a twitch, and smiles as she leads me into the living room. An old-school rotary phone hangs by the door. A relic in the house of a relic—I've entered a living history museum of the twentieth century.

"She doesn't have much time left," Mom said when she first told me about the job. "If nothing else, she won't be able to live at home much longer. She needs help organizing her things— boxing and cataloging and such. She wants it taken care of this fall so her children aren't left with it when she's gone."

"Why *not* leave things for her kids? Or have them help her with that stuff now?" I asked.

If there were an award for looks that strike a perfect balance of sad and knowledgeable, Mom would win every year. "Time and personality. Too little of one, too much of the other."

If your mother's a hospice nurse, you hear a lot about things like quality of life and end-of-life planning. If your dad died when you were little, you've seen it up close and personal, whether you remember it clearly or not.

My dad's the reason I wear my mask now, at a point when

so many people don't. Not every congenital heart condition is significant enough to cause lifelong issues. My dad's was, and when the flu came calling when I was three, he left with it. In my house, we treat our flu shots as an annual toast to his memory, rolled up our sleeves as soon as COVID vaccines became available, and continue to follow a checklist of COVID manners. High among them: never entering a stranger's house unmasked without permission.

"She'll be a minute," Mom says. "Have a seat. Unless you're slimy . . ."

"Not me." I pull the front of my tee free of my body, flap it a few times for good measure. It's the old shirt for Robin's band, the Horse Caves, and it's been through worse.

A couch, a chair. I take the couch. The fabric scratches at my calves. It's red, almost maroon, with tiny flecks of gold. I pick at one, curious.

"Holi," Mom hisses. I stand again.

It's a tidy room filled with tidy things: coffee table, glider rocker by the window, a fireplace sealed by glass doors. Above it on the mantel are pictures that look like they came with the frames: laughing children, smiling adults in formal poses. The only one that draws me in is a stark black-and-white photo of a tree. I step closer to study it.

It's a wolf tree, branches gnarled and reaching out horizontally from a trunk too big for a single pair of arms to surround. A single dry leaf clings to an otherwise barren upper bough; a lightning scar carves its way down the trunk.

Wolf trees are witnesses. Survivors. They stand where once there were farms, where pastures came and went, where they grew strong alone and, finally, outlasted even the memory of what once was.

At least that's what I learned in my forest ecology class. And Intro to Photography taught me to recognize time periods and style and some of the big-name photographers This print opens the file cabinets in the back of my brain, but they quickly close again. All I can say is that it's really good. I lean in for a better look—some photographers sign their work.

A creak from the hall reminds me that I'm not here to grade the art. An old woman enters the living room. Wrinkled, every part of her nearly translucent—hair, skin, pale blue eyes—and dressed in a tan skirt and a white sweater, as though it isn't ninety-five degrees outside, as if she's not paying a fortune in air conditioning. Small too. Not like a doll, more like a gnome. She's wearing a cannula and pulls an O2 canister behind her.

Somehow, I imagined that someone like her—scratch that—that *she* would be instantly recognizable. She's not. Writers aren't like actors; Stephen King aside, they tend to blend into a crowd.

"Elsie, this is Holiday," Mom says.

I wipe my hands on what's left of my jeans. I cut them knee-length because I like them better than Lycra bike shorts. Maya embroidered stuff on one pair—sweet potato vines, she said—and I used fabric markers to draw a pattern in dragon scales. The vines are still there, the scales not so much.

"You've no need of a mask here. Please remove it."

There's something a touch too *royal we* about the way she says it. I take the mask off anyway, draw a deep breath free of the smell of my own mouth.

The woman stares at me. "Are you a girl?"

It appears we're skipping the chitchat. "Yes."

She examines me top to bottom: the green hair, the ear piercings, the Horse Caves tee, the chain that runs from one belt loop into my pocket, the circle of my pocket watch showing through the denim. "One never knows what young people may call themselves these days. With the name Holiday, I expected you to be . . . sprightlier."

Maybe in another seventy years? "With the name Elsie McAllister, I expected you to be . . . less easily puzzled by people." I smile afterward, to make nice.

A sigh slips from my mother. Elsie, though, she gets the message. Whatever she thinks she knows about me, I know much more about her. There are other Pulitzer Prize winners living in the Amherst area, but there are no other America's Treasures, anywhere. No permanent A+ reputations based on just one book, a book read in every high school, a book that erased all chances at anonymity for a small-town girl from Eastley, Maine.

I also know that I need to do better if I'm actually going to get hired. I point to the black-and-white photo. "I like that picture."

She comes closer, tugging her little wagon along. She smells like lilac and old-lady soap. She taps the glass with a manicured, varnished nail. "You know what it is?"

"An oak. A wolf tree."

"Is that what it's called? Wolf?"

"What do you call it?" I'm honestly curious. Probably just *oak*, or *dead tree*, or *Christmas gift*.

Those pale eyes blink up at me. "A reminder."

I should stop. I don't. "Of?"

"You're lacking in manners, Holiday."

"Holi," I tell her.

Without acknowledging the correction, she says, "The tree is a reminder of truth."

5

"And truth is dying from a lightning strike?"

"A reminder is for the person it reminds. No one else need understand." She speaks like a rich woman, like every flaw has been neatly removed and the gaps sewn up seamlessly. Of course, she is a rich woman. Very rich. "I assume you're earning money for college. You graduated this spring, correct?"

I know this question and its variations well. The first person to ask it was Mom when I told her I wanted to leave school. *But why, Holi? Is something going on that I should know about?* She meant something bad, and the answer was no. It wasn't depression, it wasn't anxiety, it wasn't plummeting grades or bullying. I didn't walk away from school because it was bad; I walked toward something better, at least for me. Coming back after a year of online classes, I realized high school was just one of many places to learn. At sixteen, I could get my GED, go to community college on financial aid, and get a jump on my future.

But life happens, sometimes in ways that knock you so far off course you're not sure you're still on the same map. Still, even though I only completed one semester of college, I don't regret my choice.

My grandfather likes to say that if you make a choice most people don't, half the people will respond with judgment and anger, a third with curiosity, and the rest with very little interest. Me—I've learned to stop everyone before they even start. "I got my GED at sixteen. Do you need someone with a diploma or someone who will show up and work every day?"

She studies me with what might be appreciation. "Are you capable of lifting boxes? Carrying them up and down stairs?"

I flex an arm in response. I've worked haying season at more than a few farms, loaded plenty of haylofts with freshly dried bales. Lugging old-lady boxes around will be a breeze.

"I'd expect you here Monday through Friday, from nine until five, starting tomorrow. The pay is twenty-five dollars an hour, plus a five-hundred-dollar bonus if you're finished by October fifteenth. And I won't stand for any sharing of my private life."

I glance at Mom. HIPAA still exists between a nurse and her daughter, but maybe that's not enough for Elsie. "I can stay in the attic when my mom's here. Or leave, if that's better."

Mom only comes by Elsie's house once a week and is in and out in under an hour. I'll have no trouble staying out of the way.

"That's not what I mean. No prying into my business. You follow my requests regarding my belongings, regardless of the task. Can you promise that?"

I can feel my mother's eyes on me.

My plan is to go to New Zealand with Maya at the end of the year. That's money I have to earn. If Mom could give it to me, like Maya's parents will do for Maya, she would, but she can't. Instead, she's found me this gig, which pays well enough to almost cover the full cost of the trip.

Of course, Mom's thinking of more than just the money. From her perspective, this is a chance for me to connect with a woman whose book made me cry when I was fourteen, to fangirl over her and to extract nuggets of wisdom about writing. Seeing Elsie McAllister in the flesh, I suspect this will be less a case of learning from a master and more like watching my grandmother putter.

But I love my mom and I love my plans with Maya. It's the beginning of September now. I can stand any job for six weeks. "Yes. Cross my heart and hope to die, I promise that I will not pry." I do cross it, for good measure.

Elsie coughs. Not a polite little puff, but a bend-over, phlegmy hack that makes her sound like a truck driver. For a moment I think she's hiding a laugh in the cough, until I remind myself that she is, in fact, not well. To be in hospice, you need a doctor's referral saying you probably have less than six months to live. Some people live longer than that, so Elsie's not necessarily on death's doorstep, but she's not far from it either.

Mom lasers in on finding common ground. "Holiday's a writer too."

She's wrong about that. I believed it for most of my life, but I know the truth now. Holiday Burton is not a writer.

And if there's anyone in the room less thrilled than I am to hear Mom say these words, it's clearly America's Treasure. She looks away. "How nice," she says flatly.

"I'm not looking for advice," I say quickly. "Just a job to pay my way out of the country. Not that I'm fleeing the law or anything. My—" *Girlfriend* is the word I want to use, but I don't think Elsie here would appreciate it. More important, Maya isn't my girlfriend anymore. "My friend Maya and I are planning to work on farms in New Zealand."

I get the feeling that Elsie is no longer listening to me. Some of the color has faded from her face, making the makeup she dusted onto the folds of her skin stand out.

"Elsie, what if we sit for a few minutes?" Mom takes Elsie's arm in the way she does, like it's not a job or an inconvenience but something she *wants* to do. To my surprise, Elsie pats Mom's hand. They shuffle to the chair together, my mother's free hand pulling the wagon. Elsie leans back, closes her eyes.

I look at my mom, mime opening the door. She holds up a stop-sign hand.

Elsie's eyes open. "Writing's not much of a job for a young woman. You're best off doing something practical. Nursing, perhaps, like your mother."

Elsie McAllister is no judge of character. If she were, she'd recognize that absolutely no part of me screams *please give me needles and thermometers and other things to insert into people's bodies.*

Also, what the hell? I didn't expect antifeminist writing advice from an iconic woman writer. Is she worried I might be competition for her? Or does one glance at me show that I have no talent and shouldn't be encouraged? Then again, she's in her tenth decade of life. Maybe, being a Product of Her Time, she honestly does believe women writers are a bad idea. Aside from her and her single brilliant book and her guaranteed place in the American literary canon, of course.

"I could interview plenty of people," she says. "If I put out an ad, I'd have many applicants." She's right. The Pioneer Valley's full of colleges, and even more full of college students desperate to jump on easy work for good pay. It's also full of writers who are eager for big connections or pearls of wisdom or a chance to up their coolness quotient.

"But it's tiring," she goes on, "and if I wait too long, my children will get involved. If you can promise me that you will do as I say—whether it makes sense or not, whether you agree with it or not—then you are hired."

So many possible replies. I could just say no—that I won't do anything I disagree with, even if doing it would get me that plane ticket. Or I could ask what she might want me to do that would require my unquestioning loyalty. Or I could challenge her on the idea that young women shouldn't write.

Instead: "Yes, ma'am. I'd be happy to accept the job."

Maya smells like no one else. If pheromones are the basis of attraction, hers draw me in like one Luna moth entices another. Which is a weird thing to say about anyone, I suppose, but weird doesn't make it untrue.

She's beautiful too. Her mother's Indian American and her father is Massachusetts Irish, and Maya's skin is a shade I've never found the right word for, and her eyes are dark enough to fall into, and her hair is black and right now it's in a braid. She's shorter than me, but our hands are the same size, and hers are equally likely to have cobalt-blue oil paint or deep dark Hadley loam on them, and there is nothing about her that I would ever change.

Except that she's no longer in love with me.

When she broke things off right after her high school graduation in May, she said she didn't know what she wanted anymore. Pretty soon, it seemed like what she wanted was a dick, because she hooked up with Logan, a lacrosse player who went to Deerfield Academy and did nothing interesting in his spare time. Sometimes things happen in your mind that make your body feel like it's attached to teams of horses all running in different directions, like you're actually being torn apart. That's what it was like when she told me about Logan.

Logan didn't last, though. Now Maya just says that she doesn't know what she wants, and that as long as she doesn't, she needs to be single. It's hard when your best friend is also the only girl you've ever been in love with and a newly painted line now exists through your heart: friend on one side, happily-ever-after on the other.

I meet her at Sweetser Park after my job interview. She's lying in the grass, the late afternoon shade from the trees stretching long on the lawn.

"Hey," she says, rolling onto her stomach as I sit down. She's wearing this gauzy tank that she sewed herself. The narrow straps show off the swirling red-and-orange flower inked on her shoulder blade. She designed it, calls it a fire bloom.

I touch it, out of habit. For luck. "Hey."

She looks up at me, one eye closed against the sun. "How'd it go?"

"I got the job. I think it's mostly because she didn't want to do more interviews. She asked if I was a girl because 'one never knows' these days."

Maya laughs. I cross my legs and lean forward, the muscles in my back unclenching.

"So you'll be working for, like, one of the most famous living writers in the US." She sits up and pulls her water bottle out of her backpack. It's got a dent on one side, from where it fell off the rocks on top of Mount Orient, and a sticker of a black cat on the other. "How does that feel?"

"Like I'm gonna get paid twenty-five bucks an hour to carry her boxes."

"But it'll be more than that, right? Getting tons of advice, finding out why she never wrote another book, ending up with a killer recommendation for a big-league writing program . . ."

That tiny part of me I've been squashing pops up to say *yessss*. I squash it again. I've had more than enough advice.

"Know what she said when my mom told her I was a writer? That it's no job for a young woman."

"You're kidding me." Maya does look surprised, mouth slightly open, beads of water on her lower lip.

"I'm so serious. Like this was Victorian times and I was trying to sneak onto a pirate ship dressed as a boy."

Maya brushes away the sweaty hair on my forehead, draws an eye there with the tip of one finger. It's like riding the hill, being here with her, her skin against mine. More—it's like being everything. Not just me, but the birds and the trees, and the little kid eating a cookie at the fountain, and the ground itself, full of things growing and moving and existing.

"So, maybe you'll win her over and her last words will be 'Down with the patriarchy!'"

Before I can come up with a witty response, I see Robin sauntering toward us. It's the only word for the way my big brother moves. He'd make fun of me if I said it, and I'd punch him in the shoulder, and it would be no big deal. Only it would, a little. Even the people close to me don't understand how I see them, how I store away little bits of their souls in vials in my mind. The ways they walk or eat, or what makes them cry, or if the sun makes them sneeze. No exceptions. Even Robin. Even now.

Despite the three years that separate us in age, he and I look alike on a surface level. Tall and gangly. He dyed his hair black over a year ago, then shaved it all off. Now it's back, as pale as mine when undyed, as straight as if it were ironed. His eyes are green, mine are brown. We're both sharp angles and pasty pale skin, but there's something about Robin that sucks people in. I scare them away, like a sculpture made of broken glass.

"Holi. Maya."

"Do I know you?" I say. He responds by sitting down almost in my lap.

I sometimes imagine that I can see the energy around everyone. My brother's stretches out so far beyond him, purple light that drifts, bumping into everyone, making them see him even when he's nothing but shadow. Around the time he shaved his head, I thought he might stay shadow, his purple light fading fading fading until it vanished into nothing. I would peek into his room at night, as quiet as the ghost he was becoming, and watch to be sure he was breathing.

Because without him my life would be a cyclist careening down a hill, bouncing off a bumper, sliding beneath a wheel.

Only here he is again. Sometimes there's magic in life. Sometimes it brings people back from the places where you almost lose them.

"Did you get the tickets?" Maya asks. If she were asking me, I'd laugh, because I'd never forget something so important. Robin, though . . . his memory wavers at times.

"Tickets? Of course. Devil's in the Details, we await your coming."

We haven't been to a concert in a long time. Not since Robin's last Horse Caves gig. If we mapped out his brain, at least two thirds of it would be music, but it's gone mostly unfed for closing on two years. Seeing Devil's in the Details is about more than live music, though. I've loved them since I first saw them—when Blue Riley surprised her runaway sister on the stage of a reality TV singing competition nine years ago. The two of them toured with their band for a while after, then faded away before COVID started and stayed away until this year. My nine-year-old self, with her enormous crush on Blue, is thrilled to finally be seeing the band live later this month.

Maya glances at her phone, groans. "It's totally not you chasing me away, Robin. They called me in to manage pickups." Maya works at a CSA farm just outside of town. She doesn't need to, not even to pay for New Zealand—her parents pick up the tab on anything she wants—but she loves seeds and she loves plants and she loves the dark rich soil.

She doesn't look at me. Doesn't need to know I'm disappointed as hell. Tuesday nights are for kicking around. It was true when we were together, still true now that we're not.

"I have the design for you, though." She fumbles with her bag, pulls out a page torn from a sketchpad and hands it to him. "Tell me if it's not right. It's just roughed out."

I lean in to see the paper. It's more than a sketch. She's worked a sapling, leafed out in the greenest of summer greens, the trunk silvery and slender, almost willow-like. The roots mesh beneath it, creating a nest. Within the nest is a dash and a dot in vermillion. A semicolon.

"Too corny?" she asks, worrying her lip. Waiting for Robin's approval the same way I do.

"Gorgeous. So much better than what I would've come up with. I owe you big time."

She jumps up as the town hall clock chimes four. "Just make sure they know I designed it, okay?" She's barefoot, and around her ankle is an expensive wisp of a gold chain. Logan's gift, not mine.

And just like that, she's yanking sandals out of her bag and hopping into them, hurrying to the stop as the PVTA bus lumbers toward it. She blows a kiss back to us just before she disappears through the doors.

I don't even have to say it. Robin rests his arm on my

shoulders, tugs me close enough that I can smell the warm Robinness of him.

"There's more to life," he says in that rumble that hits me like a mama cat's purr.

"Maybe I don't want more."

He squeezes me until the bones of my shoulders shift. "Maybe you do and you just don't know it yet."

I pick a clover leaf from the green, spin it between my fingers before slipping it behind his ear. "Let's wish," I say. Like we used to, when I believed wishes could call magic into motion. I close my eyes and make a wish about coming here, again and again, and always finding Robin.

There's a time for writing: late at night, when the house becomes just breath, when the cat taps the window screen in counterpoint to the moths that bounce there, seeking the light on my desk. Deep house music trails from the phone on the nightstand. The college students living in the rental half of our house are silent—studying or sleeping. Robin's safely in his bed. I can't focus until he's there, after he's brushed his teeth, after I've asked if he's taken his meds, after he opens his mouth and rolls his tongue to show he's swallowed. It's a joke, but it's not, too.

The tiny fan whirs in my window like a plane designed for Stuart Little, eternally taxiing for takeoff. We've never done AC, just pulled in the air at night, kept out the sun during the day. I'm so used to the sound of the fan that I keep it on in the winter as white noise, letting it blow dust bunnies across the floor while I sleep.

The laptop screen glares at me as I start again.

The dragons sparred on a hill burned barren, just soot-stained rock left behind. She knew because her father had told her of it so long ago. Once he'd climbed there, he'd said, and seen the long, scaled tail of one curled around a stone the size of a man. It hadn't moved as he'd crept toward it, and he'd touched it. He'd felt the smooth scales, one overlapping the next, the leathery skin that spread between the bony spurs at the very tip.

It wasn't until he crept closer, around the edge of the stone, that he realized why it didn't move. The tail was nothing but a tail, torn off, the ripped flesh buzzing with flies.

I stop. Highlight it all. Delete.

I can imagine it. I can feel it. I see it like a movie. It haunts me every time I open my laptop or even think about opening it. But it's like one of those dummies used to teach CPR. Breathe into it, pound on its chest as much as you want, it's never going to live. What I end up with is one word after another, when it should be like a string of fairy lights, every single one burning from the shared electricity.

I turn the desk light off. The room is lit by the laptop now. Sometimes it's easier in the dark to find the things to say. But it's not dragons that come to me.

Once upon a time, there was a girl who loved another girl very much. But somehow, no matter how much she loved her—this other girl who smelled of rich soil and carrots and didn't laugh nearly often enough and had the tiniest amethyst stud in her nose—the love never came back to her.

What is the purpose of love when you can't share it?

I close the lid.

In the morning, I agree to take the bus to work, mostly to satisfy my mother. "You don't want to show up all sweaty, Holi."

"I do, actually. I want to show up dripping, leaving spots all over the carpet."

"She does, Mom. She told me." Robin knuckles my head as I spoon hummus into a little glass container. I shove him away, but not before he snags one of the carrots meant for my lunch bag.

"Please, sweetheart. For me, if you can't do it for yourself."

"I can't do it for myself because I'm someone who rides a bike and gets sweaty and doesn't have an issue with it. But . . ." I can see the twist in her face, the struggle between wanting me to be entirely myself and wanting me to hold on to my job. "I'll take my bike with me and ride it home."

Mom's already moving, travel mug in her hand. "Great. I need to let the plumber into the apartment before I go. Love you, have a good day."

Our house, like many in Amherst, began life over a hundred years ago as a classy single-family home, and eventually was divided into apartments as the college population grew. My grandfather made a down payment on it for us because he knew the rental income would cover our monthly mortgage payment. Sure, managing the apartment is additional work for Mom, but it's less work than worrying about where to live.

Robin and I leave the house together. Most mornings he's gone at five for the breakfast shift at the diner. He cooks there a few nights a week as well. The manager loves him like he's her own kid, unlike his boss at the upscale place he works at on weekends, where he's just a cog in the machinery of a kitchen producing food far too expensive for us to eat. This morning, though, he's on his way to therapy. He's been downgraded to one appointment a week, which is great in theory, but I'd have him there every day if I could.

"Did you remember—" I begin. He taps his phone in response. No matter what I might ask about, he's already got an alarm set to remind him of it. He used to remember everything; now he relies on alarms and paper notes.

Our bus stops are on opposite sides of the road, so he squeezes my shoulder and heads across just as his bus slides to a stop. I wait another five minutes for mine, my only company a guy with a purple backpack carrying on a phone conversation in Mandarin. Grad students. They're everywhere in the summer. It's not so much that there are more of them as that there are fewer undergrads to dilute them.

When the call ends, he pulls a paperback copy of *Doctor Faustus* out of his bag. He must be in the English department because no one reads Marlowe for fun.

We still have all my dad's books, even though he died when I was three. His tiny, careful notes fill everything, including the Marlowe plays. Whenever I read them, I pretend that he's telling me all these things in the same way he taught his students. I don't remember his voice, but his disembodied hands have stayed with me, their eloquent fingers and blueish nailbeds.

The bus pulls up. I load my bike on the front and slip my

mask on. I'm the only person wearing one, but that doesn't bother me. COVID manners include wearing masks as solidarity with and protection of folks like my dad. When I sit alone in the back and count the minutes until we reach my stop, it's not breathing through the filter that bothers me. It's not claustrophobia either. I just hate trapped air. Stillness. The kind of air that likely filled Elsie McAllister's house even before COVID struck.

Think about New Zealand. Not about the long-ass flight— think about Maya instead, about being in the sun with her every day. Think about camping with her, about long roads when it'll be just the two of us. Think about what Elsie McAllister's money will buy me.

A middle-aged woman is putting a cloth bag in the back of a Subaru Outback as I walk my bike up the driveway. She pulls her hair free from an elastic as she closes the hatch. "Are you Holi?" she asks over her shoulder as she reaches for the driver's door. At my nod, she continues. "Elsie left a note for you. I have to run to my next house—can you let her know that her lunches are stacked in the fridge?"

I nod again. She hops in the car and backs swiftly out to the road.

The note is in an envelope taped to the front door. The penmanship, like something lifted from an invitation in a costume drama, says, *Please come to the back door and enter there. You may follow the hall to the closed bedroom door and knock if I am not already present.*

I stick the note in my pocket, wheel my bike to the back,

and go through the slider there. Her quiet cul-de-sac is in a pricey part of town. Maya's part, where student housing is minimal and the lawns are monoculture or orchestrated meadow and homeowners don't worry much about an unlocked slider because everyone notices an out-of-place car.

I enter the same sterile room as yesterday, as still as a rest home for introvert ghosts. Down the hall, I pass an open door to a lemony kitchen, two more doors opening into guest rooms, one to a study with a desk and a chair and shelves full of . . . encyclopedias? Finally, on the left, a closed door. I knock.

I hear nothing. I knock again, a little louder. This isn't going to turn out to be a job where I don't even make it through a day because the person I'm working for dies immediately, right? Old people can die of diseases, but also fall and hurt themselves, or have heart attacks or strokes, all sorts of things, and I can imagine them all in graphic detail as I reach for the doorknob.

It turns before I connect. Elsie is alive.

She's also so tiny. Short and pale, her makeup awkwardly bright on the soft whiteness of her cheeks. Her hair is actual white, not that yellowy-white that some elderly women have. This close, I can see that the cannula has irritated the edges of her nose, leaving them red and chafed.

"Holiday," she says. "You're prompt. That's a good start. Come." She edges past me, and I step back to make room for her oxygen. I need to ask my mom about the etiquette. Would I risk breaking something vital if I tried to pull it for her?

I follow her back down the hall. We stop at one of the guest rooms I passed a minute ago.

"We'll use this as storage space. Please strip the bed and fold everything neatly, then come out to the parlor."

Parlor. My grandparents use that word, but no one else I know.

I strip the bed, fold the cotton spread and the floral sheets. For once, something my mother insisted we learn comes in handy. The fitted sheet is a neat square when I finish with it. I leave everything on the end of the bed, the pillow on top.

First job successfully completed. I head out to find Elsie.

She's opened a door in the back of the living room. It looks like a pantry, with storage shelves on three sides. A rope hangs from the ceiling.

"I can't get into the attic myself anymore," she says, pointing up. "Pull down the ladder and go up there. Take this with you." She hands me a spiralbound notebook and a ballpoint pen. "I would like an inventory of what's up there. Boxes should already be labeled. However, I need you to check the contents to be certain the labels are correct. You may take these upstairs in case any boxes are damaged and in need of replacement." She points to a stack of unassembled bankers boxes leaning against the wall. "At the end of the day, bring down what you've cataloged. We'll schedule time for you to show me the contents so I can determine what to do with them."

"Why don't I just bring stuff down at the start and we look at it together?"

She draws herself up as much as she can. "Because this is the way I want it done. Do not argue with me. Please remember, I prefer privacy in all areas, including my possessions. I trust you not to snoop."

What kind of secrets lurk above? Love letters? Naked pictures? Thigh-high boots with toes filled with coke? The line between cataloging and snooping . . . I'm not sure I'll even recognize it.

I look her over once more. She'll never see the top of that ladder again. The least I can do is provide her with some peace of mind. I mime a zipped mouth.

The ladder pulls down with a creak. I climb. And groan as quietly as possible when I get to the top and pull the chain to light the lonely bare bulb there.

Boxes, yes. So many boxes. Stacked, three to four tall, for what looks like the entire length of the house.

I'm gonna need a bigger notebook.

The first ten boxes I examine sport black Sharpie labels. Boring things: *Christmas China, Thanksgiving Decorations, Extra Linens.* Who keeps boxes—boxes!—of extra linens? Rich people, I suppose. Old women, living alone, with beds no one sleeps in anymore. I feel a little bad for her.

I also feel bad for me. The sweat runs off my nose, my shirt too soaked to absorb more when I rub my face with it. I drain my water bottle within the first hour, sheer stubbornness keeping me from going back down to refill it.

Elsie has apparently never met a useless object that she didn't find deserving of rafter space. Still, I dutifully tread the line between examining and snooping as best I can. Somewhere between *Christopher's Hockey Trophies* and *Misc: Quilting*, a new story comes to me. One about a girl traveling across an endless desert. Two suns, maybe, or would that be too Tatooine? Just her, and sand, and heat, and maybe an eagle. Or a lizard.

A dragon.

Writing's easier when you're six. Or even ten. You write what you love. Love puppies? Write about a house full of them.

Love planes? Write about ones that talk and fly on their own. You don't think about whether it's good or bad, whether there's a reason to write.

Last year I wrote a novel. I wrote it like a little kid—without worrying whether it was good or not. It ate at me to be away from it. Everything was chaos elsewhere, but time held steady and still when I wrote. I felt every bit of fear and happiness that the characters did, but I also controlled it.

The story itself grew like a living thing in me. A girl's father abandons her to be raised by their village as he travels deeper and deeper into the lands of the dragons, returning less and less often. Until, finally, he no longer returns. She decides she has to follow, because what else is there to do for someone like her, someone who doesn't really belong anywhere or to anyone? Only, the farther into the dragonlands she goes, the less and less human she feels, the less and less she wants to. Finally, she becomes scales and leathery wings and nothing like the creature she began life as, powerful and utterly alone.

I could feel the scales and the muscles under the skin, feel the wings as they beat. The flames too—not like a bonfire at all, instead blue, almost clear, and smelling nothing like ash. Writing it didn't feel like work. It was like stepping out of the rain and into a warm cabin, a fire in the woodstove: just right and good.

A phone rings downstairs—the rotary one, judging by the ring. It keeps ringing, on and on. I scoot to the ladder, afraid for the second time that day that America's Treasure has died on my watch.

I'm halfway down when the sound stops and I hear the soft murmur of her voice. It's gone by the time I reach the living room. She's there, though, as if she's been waiting for me.

"Water," I say, holding up my bottle.

She follows me to the kitchen. A heel of plastic-wrapped bread sits in solitude on the counter, surrounded by acres of Formica. It doesn't smell like a kitchen, or much of anything. A sliver of light streaks in from beneath the shades over the window. From the other room comes the tick of a clock.

"Oh, I forgot. The woman leaving when I got here said she left your lunches in the fridge," I say.

"Paula. The housekeeper." Of course. I doubt Elsie makes much of a mess, but she's in no shape to clean whatever she leaves behind.

When she moves, I do smell something. A whiff of cigarette. America's Treasure still smokes, even now, when her lungs are so crap that she has to lug oxygen everywhere she goes. I wonder whether she leaves the oxygen somewhere else while she smokes. Is my short life going to end with me trapped in an attic as the flames rise from a Virginia-Slims-fueled explosion?

"You should think about getting some plants," I say. "Might help with your air quality."

When I was ten, my friend Mouse gave me a baby ficus plant because I was frustrated I couldn't have a puppy. "It's boring to look at," she said, "but it will live for much longer than a dog, won't make anyone allergic, and will supply you with oxygen. And you can pet it all you want." She was right: it's required almost no care and I still rub the leaves between my fingers when I'm nervous.

Elsie glares. "Did I ask for your advice?"

"Nope."

She watches me as I fill my bottle. I drink half of it, fill it again.

"You drink like a boy."

New Zealand. Think of New Zealand and swallow the words that rise first. I shrug. "I'm not."

"Do you like girls?" Maybe being old means you get to say anything. Maybe being famous does.

I screw the water bottle cap on. Tightly. Carefully. Like maybe the future of the world depends on whether that cap is on good and tight. It's a simple enough question she's asked. It's just none of her damn business. For someone obsessed with her own privacy, she doesn't care much about other people's.

I glance at the wall clock. "You have a lot of boxes."

"Yes, I expect I do. It's been a long time."

She doesn't follow me when I head back to the trapdoor.

It's not until late in the afternoon that I find any evidence of her having written a book. The last box I reach for doesn't have a handwritten label like everything else so far—*Lampshades* or *Cutlery* or *Mouse Nests*.

Instead, there's a packing slip taped to the outside when I rotate it. I open it anyway, as required, to make sure that it really does contain twenty-four copies of *Tongues as of Fire*.

It's a strange title. In ninth-grade English, Mr. Cooper explained that it came from the Bible and had to do with Pentecost. Not that this cleared anything up. But the title didn't stop me. I read the whole book in two days, then started again, this time more slowly so I could savor the language. At least half the class skipped it completely, relying on the Wikipedia summary instead.

The copy I pick up is pristine. No creases, the dust jacket free of any signs of wear. I open it. The pages make that crackling sound of a new book springing to life.

Only this one isn't new. This one is almost fifty years older than I am. I turn to the first page.

The night the world burned, my mother woke me from sleep with the light of her lantern and the touch of her fingers.

I can hear Elsie reading it. Not how she sounds now—the way she sounded on the old vinyl Mr. Cooper brought into class, a scratchy recording of a reading she gave in the late '50s. Her voice was strong. No nonsense. At least that's how I remember it. I could probably find it on YouTube if I wanted.

Sticky fingers isn't my vice, but right at this moment, I want one of these books. The box is complete, all twenty-four copies. Even if I could stuff one down my shorts and carry it out, it would be obvious later that one's missing.

Why would she have done that—left the entire box untouched? I put the copy back, run a hand over the stack of spines. Then again, why did she stop writing after one book?

"Some people have just one thing they want to say to the world," Mr. Cooper told us. "Maybe when you write something that good, that true, that captures something so essential, then you don't feel you need to write more."

It sounded reasonable at the time. I pick up the copy again, look at the back flap. The author photo, surprisingly, isn't a glossy posed one. Someone caught young Elsie with her head turned, her bob ruffled by wind. Something short of a smile rests on her lips. She wasn't hot, exactly, but still, something about her makes you want to look again. And again.

I try to imagine that woman laying down her pen or typing *The End* on the paper in her typewriter, pushing away from her desk, and . . . quitting. Saying *been there, done that*.

I suspect that's exactly the kind of thing she means when she tells me to respect her privacy and not snoop.

But this attic is both vast and very full. Pack rats don't pack-rat everything *except* their writing. Odds are, the answer to why she stopped is here.

The box contains one other thing, laid under the top two books. A single sheet of paper, a single line centered on the page:

A yellow sweater with mismatched buttons.

A coded message? Line for a story she never got around to writing? Clue to a treasure hunt she once designed and then forgot about?

I grab a box containing three costume sombreros and stick the paper in with them. It's not exactly snooping. Just curiosity. It hurts nothing.

Right?

My phone buzzes at 4:30. Robin. **Stop by work and I'll feed you fries.**

Gonna stop by the farm first. See what Maya's up to.

He doesn't respond. I know what he's thinking. He loves Maya too, but he believes she's being unfair. That she should let go, give me space. To do what—that's the part that's never clear to me. She's my best friend, not just my girlfriend. Former girlfriend.

I finish upstairs at 4:45. Once I've carried the cataloged boxes downstairs, it's clear I've hardly made a dent. At this rate, my plane ticket is guaranteed.

Elsie takes the notebook and pen from me as I exit the attic. "I'll pay you on Fridays."

I nod, listening for some sign that she's the person I heard on that old recording, the person in the author photo. But she's just a white-haired lady with a faded voice who smells of lilac and cigarettes.

"Please leave me your phone number in case I need to reach you," she adds.

My eyes drift past the wolf tree photo to the ancient rotary phone on the wall. "Do you have a piece of paper? And a pen?"

Do I even remember my number? "Or should I write it in the box notebook?"

There's a funny look on her face. It's almost . . . I could swear she's holding back a giggle. She reaches into her pocket and pulls out an iPhone, latest model. "I'd prefer if you just enter it in this."

Oh. The ring tone I heard earlier must've come from her cell, not the dinosaur on the wall. I gesture toward the rotary phone. "So is this just the setup for a joke or does it work?"

She gives me a *none of your sass* look. Still, she's enjoyed this thoroughly. "Ah, that reminds me." She goes to the rotary phone and tugs at the front. It swings open on a hinge to reveal three hooks, keys dangling from each. She takes out one on a keychain of tiny blue beads. "You may have this for your own use, though the back is always open. In case of emergency."

I pocket the key she holds out. "Did you actually want my number?"

"Of course." She hands me her iPhone. "Put it in the contacts and text yourself so you have my number as well."

For the first time she feels like a person to me, not a queen in a costume drama. I've been telling myself that I don't want to talk with her about writing, but right this minute, I kinda think I do.

My phone blings with a text from Mom, followed by a knock at the door from a neighbor who's come to help Elsie with groceries. The moment passes. By the time I'm on the road I can't imagine asking her anything more than where she'd like her old books stored.

Maya's working in the pickup shed at the CSA farm. The chalkboard on the wall lists what produce is available today, what can be picked in the fields. Maya's stacking lettuces. She smiles when she sees me.

She loves this—seeing the starts in the greenhouses, and the cover crops being plowed under, and the long row of sunflowers. She loves the kids eating beans while their parents pick, and the filled cloth bags with greens sticking out the top. She'll brush carrot fronds across her face, rub herbs between her fingers so that the scent of lemon balm clings to her.

New Zealand is for her. I never would've thought of even leaving the country if she hadn't suggested it. That's always been there between us, even though we never talk about it. Her mom is a vascular surgeon. Her dad is a professor and department head at Amherst College. Dinner at their house includes asides like "when we were last in Paris." At my house, it's more along the lines of "when we were last in Trader Joe's."

For Maya, New Zealand is taking a year off before heading to a college education that will cost more than the house I live in. Her parents will pay her way. I can't go with her there, but I can go on this trip. Love means being willing to follow, right, wherever you need to go?

Today, love means handing her lettuces from a crate while people mill around us. She's wearing long silver earrings that dangle lower than her hair and make a tinkling sound like wind chimes when she moves. She has a faded green apron on over her shorts and tank top.

"Good day?" I ask.

"Kinda. I need to get home quick after work. We have to go to a faculty dinner thing."

I've always joked that I'm the girl from the wrong side of

the tracks, only it's not really that much of a joke. Logan fit that whole liberal-in-a-blazer-that-promises-not-*too*-liberal scene much better than I ever could. My problem isn't the gay thing, or the appearance thing—it's much less tangible and rides in on a thousand inbred social cues that separate the wheat from the chaff.

I shake water from a head of lettuce. Maya smiles at a middle-aged woman who has walked over holding a bunch of carrots. "These seem small," the woman says. "Do you have larger ones somewhere?"

Where I would've told her to suck it up, Maya patiently launches into a full explanation. By the time she's finished, the woman will be ready to go home and lecture her family on biodynamic farming as she feeds them delicate and delicious steamed carrots.

I wander to the cooler and check out the fruit popsicles. I'm about to grab an elderberry one when I hear my name.

I turn slowly. The man is a shiver shorter than me, streaks of silver along his carefully styled, trendy-long hair, nerd glasses balanced on his nose, a sleekly trimmed beard. There's a woman behind him—a student, I'd guess. She's giving me the once-over in a less than friendly way.

"How have you been?" He steps forward, arms rising to hug me. I don't move. He grasps my shoulders instead. "I was bummed that you couldn't come back to work over the summer."

"I have another job. With Elsie McAllister."

I know that look. It's not *you're so interesting*; it's *you've got something I want*.

"Wow, that's great! Good for you. Maybe she can teach you some things about writing." He turns to the woman with him. "Holi here wants to be a writer. I gave her pointers last year when she was doing some office odds and ends. Perks of the job, right, Holi? She's not at your level, of course."

The last bit's a gift to the woman. There's something in the creases between her eyes that suggests jealousy. Hunger. Wanting the whole meal to herself. The whole meal being John Allen, former student of my dad's and now director of the creative writing MFA at UMass.

I could've told her that I have no interest in anything on that table if it would've made a difference. But it also stings, what he said. I keep expecting it to go away, to heal over. I can feel his hand on my shoulder every time I sit down to write.

I shrug. "I'm only eighteen. An MFA is a long way off."

His laugh is a hair shy of being real. We're the only two who know it. "Of course. But you act so much older, Holi. You make it hard to remember just how young you are."

The woman edges closer to him. She's a cat who's wormed her way onto a lap and has begun to preen. I look her over, because there's a fist balled up inside me and it wants to do some damage. She's got a tattoo of a wreath of flowers on her wrist, what looks like two lines of poetry in tiny script on one bicep. Her brown hair is in two short braids, and she's wearing a paisley sundress. She's very thin, her ribs a bony staircase up her chest.

She's not the one I'm mad at. We're not competing, whatever she thinks. I want to press a popsicle into her hand and tell her she should walk out into the sunlight and leave John Allen behind, because she's worth more than that.

"I'll remember that—not to act too old."

"Right, it's been really great to see you, Holi. We should catch up sometime. Stop by my office. I'd love to hear about what you're doing for Elsie. And your writing, of course."

"Yeah. Later."

He doesn't even leave yet. They pick out vegetables like each item is priceless, the woman giggling at everything he says. He gives Maya a hug when she sees him. A hug. Maya only knew him because I was working for him. Does he really need to hug her?

But that shouldn't surprise me, should it?

No harm, no foul.

I get to the diner right around old folks' dinnertime. There's a steak special and they're piling in for the chance to eat meat and potatoes, just like back in the day. I sit at the counter, away from everyone, and Robin draws me a ginger ale before ducking back into the kitchen.

There's a new server on the floor. Yet another college student, most likely. She's wearing tan pants and a faded blue tee with a little icon above the left breast that I can't quite make out.

She stops by me. Pulls the shirt out to make it easier to see. I guess my staring was not as discreet as I hoped. The image is a pair of butterfly wings with an eye resting above them.

"Tomorrowland!" I say.

She smiles and nods.

Four years ago—even two—I would've given anything to go to Tomorrowland. It's a huge electronic music festival in Belgium, drawing hundreds of thousands of people and all the biggest DJs. I wanted to go the same way I wanted to go to Disneyland when I was ten, and just like with Disney, the appeal waned as I got older. Unlike Disney, however, I've never met anyone who's been to Tomorrowland, and in a weird way I'm starstruck.

Before the girl can respond, Robin sticks his head out the

kitchen door and spots us. "Hey, Holi, this is Noa. Noa, my sister, Holiday."

Noa wipes her hand on her pant leg, holds it out. I take it. She has dark green polish on her nails. Her straight hair is pulled back in a ponytail, with a small metal barrette on either side to hold the wisps.

Robin adds, "Noa's working here while Mel's away. She's from the Netherlands."

"Holiday? Interesting name." Her accent's not very strong. If I were relying on my Spanish, people would know it wasn't my native language instantly. It would take time for me to recognize the same with her.

She's taken her hand back. Her stare is intense, like she's secretly prying all the data from my head and storing it away to be used later.

And she's waiting for me to respond in a normal human way. "Funny, right? Our dad was a big Truman Capote fan—do you know his stories?" I don't stop to find out. "Dad wrote a novel about him. It wasn't published," I rush to add. I can feel the blush coming on. "Anyway, Holiday Golightly. *Breakfast at Tiffany's*. That's where my name comes from."

"And yet you're just Robin," she says to my brother. Once upon a time, before things got messy, girls loved him. He loved them right back. Now he lives like a monk and Noa looks at him like she understands that.

"Just Robin," he says.

"Robin Goodfellow, actually," I reveal with little-sister speed. "AKA Puck from *A Midsummer Night's Dream*." As the story goes, my dad took one look at Robin, mere minutes from the womb, and turned to Mom and said, "Puck." To which Mom said, "Yes, but every kid everywhere knows what that rhymes with," so they named him Robin Goodfellow instead.

Noa has just joined the elite circle of people who know Robin's full legal name. Which I have no good reason to have shared.

Robin lets it slide. He says to Noa, "I lured Holi here with fries. Do you mind snagging them in a minute? I'm getting a little backed up with orders."

"Of course," she says.

"Going straight home from here?" Robin asks me.

"Yep. Maya's working. Nothing else to do."

"Sorry, I won't be home till eleven or so."

And I will be awake to make sure he comes home.

He taps my knuckles and returns to the kitchen.

Turning to Noa, I point again at the Tomorrowland graphic. "Did you go?"

She takes a seat on the stool next to me. "I did, when I was sixteen."

"I would've loved to go when I was sixteen."

"Why didn't you?"

She asks it as though there's not an obvious answer. It makes me feel like a peasant, the world outside the valley so far out of reach as to be unimaginable.

"No money. And no passport, though that should be coming soon. I'm saving money to go to New Zealand. With my girlfriend—my friend."

She blows at a few strands of hair that have escaped her barrettes. "She's your girlfriend or not?"

"She was." It still feels like splinters under my fingernails to say it. "It's maybe more of a break? She met someone else."

"Ah." She looks around the diner, my drama nothing at all. A bell dings in the kitchen. She's up immediately, heading back there. After a minute, she returns with my fries. "You want mayonnaise or ketchup? Or vinegar?"

"Mayo? Is that a thing?"

She wrinkles her nose at me. "Not in the US, I guess. At home, yes."

"I'm into ketchup, thank you."

"Perhaps our mayonnaise is just better." With a tug at her ponytail, she's off again.

I stick my earbuds in and pull out the tiny notebook I keep in my back pocket. It's ridiculously small. I use it to make lists. Things I want to do in life. Things I have to do. Stuff I can cross off later in the week to feel like I've accomplished something, anything. I keep track of how much money I've made and subtract it from what I've planned out for New Zealand. I write down things I notice, tiny bits of life happening around me. Lines that keep getting stuck in my head, ideas for stories that I don't have time to write.

Well, no, it's not time that's lacking. Last night my writing lay in front of me like a dead bird until I deleted it. I suppose I shouldn't delete any writing, but I hated the way it looked, so I had to get rid of it. I didn't even want it near me.

So, I'm the saddest kind of writer: a pretend one. It would be great if I could make something out of the contents of my notebook. Only, my list novel would be something like this:

1. *A girl has a father.*

2. *Talk with Robin about birthday present for Mom.*

3. *Look at Robin's pill bottle to make sure he's taking them.*

4. *The father hunts a dragon.*

3. *Do I ask Maya to design a tattoo for me too?*

2. *The dragon is dead.*

1. *So is this story.*

Today, my notes are focused on Elsie's attic. A benefit of the notebook is that it makes me look busy, which means that no one comes up to talk to me. More so since I cut and dyed my hair. When I had blond hair to my shoulders, I never intimidated anyone. Soon as the hair came off, so did half the people, including a lot of the creepy dudes with "hey baby" routines dialed to literary style. The ones who still talk to me either are old or think I'm badass. They ask me what I'm listening to, or if I'm a student, or—clueless newbies from out of town—if I can help them score.

Not a student, never gonna help anyone find drugs. And if I tell them what I'm listening to, they're almost always disappointed.

Before everything—when Robin and Alex and Hedy were together all the time—we'd go to Secret House whenever word came that a location had been picked. We'd pile into Alex's mom's Subaru and hit the road, dance almost all night. Robin and I would get home as the light began to change toward morning. We'd lie on his bed, the breeze blowing through, the curtains shifting back and forth, and could still feel it— the music—beating beneath us, around us, connecting us. It sounds silly, I know, but that's how it felt.

Anyway, that's what I listen to a lot of the time now. The music we danced to in abandoned factories and old warehouses and midnight fields. I suppose I'm hoping the echo of the music will jumpstart the heart that beat for us all. The one that broke eighteen months ago.

Today, "P.S. You Rock My World" sneaks into the shuffle. The night we brought Robin home from the hospital, we all snuggled close on Mom's bed, Robin between the two of us, and we listened to that on Mom's stereo, the vinyl hissing a little. Robin buried his face on Mom's shoulder, and she knit her fingers through his hair, and I could feel the shudder of him as he cried silently. I cried too—*not* silently—and Mom gripped my hand in hers and said "Babies, babies," softly, as the song slipped over us.

That night, all Mom's hugs and all her blankets still couldn't fend off the icy grip of fear clutching me. Today, the late summer heat blows in as the door opens and closes. Lily the hostess greets the newcomers. She graduated from UMass last spring and here she is, working at a diner, because undergrad degrees spawn debt more than they do good jobs.

I continue my list of the most boring boxes in the world. I've just written *Christmas Placemats (for real!)* when Noa returns.

"Are they secret notes?" she asks, pointing at the notebook.

Yes, I'm a spy waiting for my European connection. Is it you? "Not really. I'm working in this author's attic and it's just a list of labels on her boxes. It's silly but doing this—writing—keeps people away."

"Like me?" She grins, and I notice the gap between her front teeth. I used to have one too, before years of orthodontics.

"No, like strangers who want to talk about things."

"Like me," she says again.

I smile. Does she want to talk about things? With me? And why? "How long are you staying in Amherst?" Holi Burton: purveyor of thrilling conversation.

"My Airbnb rental is until the middle of this month, so not long."

A crowd of college kids comes in, changing the energy of the diner just like that.

Noa wrinkles her nose again—is that also a Dutch thing, or just a *her* thing?—and tugs the ends of her ponytail apart to tighten the elastic. "Enjoy your fries, Holi," she says as she walks away. "Come to Amsterdam someday and try them with mayonnaise."

I return to my notebook and write *Misc: Awards*. I opened that box wondering what it was like to have so many awards that you could toss them in a box labeled *Misc*. The contents were literally tossed in there, an assortment of smoky glass ovals and tarnished metallic points and wooden bases with *Elsie McAllister* engraved on their plaques.

What made America's Treasure despise the candy store of fame? I'm still thinking about it twenty minutes later when I lean against the swinging door and catch Robin's eye in the kitchen. He tips his head at me, a spatula in his hand, and I salute him. I'm thinking about it as I ride home too, the *why why why* in time with my heart, my hair damp beneath my helmet.

Was it boredom? Is it possible to be so bored with fame that you would toss all evidence of it in boxes, hide it in the attic, and never write again?

6

Mom's sitting at the table reading the paper when I get home. This—her relaxing—happens once in a blue moon, now that she's working toward a master's degree on top of doing her job. She's changed into cutoffs and an ancient Cordelia's Dad tee with a hole in the armpit. In the secret language of Mom, that shirt translates to her missing Dad. It still happens, even after sixteen years, but why tonight?

"Hey," I say as I hang my helmet on the coatrack. I join her at the table. "What's happening, old lady?"

She gives me a roll of her eyes. "You are, my monster child."

I tug the newspaper out from under her hands and fold it up. "You do realize that you're not supposed to kill trees anymore, right? You can just look at a screen to get all this. Or not look at all."

"First of all, I can't not look. It's my job to look, as your mother. Second, my eyes are old and tired and screens make it worse. And third—" She shakes her head. "And third, sometimes it hurts to change."

Her eyes have that glassy look that tells me she's choosing not to cry. They looked that way almost all the time before the sapling that is Robin's mind finally showed green growth again.

Tonight, though, it's not about that. I should've remembered.

"It's his birthday," I say. Would've been. Dad stopped aging a long time ago, but his birthday still hovers in time, just as much as his death day.

"It is." Her eyes shine a little more. I put my hands over hers. Mine are bigger, harder, with calluses at the bases of my fingers. The skin on her hands is looser than it used to be. Eventually she'll be Elsie-old and alone, me and Robin off doing whatever we do when we grow up. If we grow up.

She stands, pulls her shirt's hem down to cover her soft belly. The tee was always a little small on her, but now, her body rounder than it used to be, it stretches tight. "How did it go with Elsie today?"

"I wrote down the labels of boxes in her attic. It's easily the most boring job I've ever had." That includes ice cream scooper (too many people), summer camp assistant (too many kids), and *organizational assistant* to a UMass professor whose clutter regrew faster than a hydra's heads. At least Elsie's box stash isn't increasing.

"Yes, but she needs your healthy body to do the things hers can't."

"You make it sound like possession. I didn't sign up for that."

She gets a jelly jar out of the cupboard and fills it with water. "I want you to treat her well."

"You really think I'm going to treat an ancient woman dragging an oxygen tank around *badly*?"

"I don't know, Holi." She makes little birdwing movements with her hand. "I don't know why I'm this way tonight. I'm sorry."

I wish . . . I'm not sure what I wish. I've grown up as a girl with an empty space for a dad—unlike Robin, who was five when Dad died and remembers so much, good and bad. I know Dad's death affected me, I know the experience is part of who I am, but his life did too. And I can remember almost none of it. Don't get me wrong, I've always had family—Mom, of course; my grandfather, who helped when we were little and Mom had to work; Martín, Mom's best friend who's always been a part of our lives. Just not my dad.

I don't want the pain Mom's feeling tonight, but I wish I had some of the memories.

Her phone vibrates on the table. I look over at it. "It's Martín."

She reaches and I pass it to her. When she says "Hi," I give a little wave and head up to my room.

Mom's known Martín since he and Dad were in grad school together. He teaches at Hampshire now. His friendship with Mom—Robin and I sometimes wonder if it's something more. No surprise sleepovers, or secret extra toothbrushes, or any of the things you see in movies about single parents moving on. Just Martín and Mom on the couch some nights, her feet in his lap, their minds tangled together in passionate discussions about modern poetry of the sort he writes. Tomorrow he's flying to Puerto Rico to visit family. Mom's driving him to the airport.

Upstairs the heat is a hand pushing against me, preventing my lungs from filling. I open the window and turn my fan on. On hot summer nights like this, Maya and I used to draw alphabets, entire poems on each other with ice cubes. Never at her house, where the AC is set at 65 degrees. Just here, on my futon. Some nights Robin would stop in before heading out, sometimes to take us with him. By the time I was fifteen and the world was starting to open up again, we all had fake IDs to get into clubs. I never drank, while Robin would pick drinks in vibrant shades of blue or green, garnished with onions or cherries skewered by plastic swords. Ironic drinks, chosen to entertain Alex and Hedy.

Once they were a trinity: Robin, Alex, Hedy. Now they're two disconnected people and a patch of violets and daisies under a skinny sugar maple in a pasture repurposed as a green burial cemetery.

While the drugs went with clubbing—right up until they went on without it—the alcohol was more like wearing a funny scarf or a smoking jacket. Or so Robin said. An experiment. "It's like we all have a well inside. There's this well and until you start tossing things in, you don't know how deep it goes, or what should fill it, or if it's even empty."

Back then. What would I say to my sixteen-year-old self if I had the chance? *Hold tight*, maybe. *This boat of yours isn't made for high seas.*

Once more I face my laptop.

She'd heard their scales shone like the sun, but she'd never seen one until the day she opened her father's secret box by mistake.

And John Allen's face pops up in my mind like a fucking balloon. Him and his hungry student who he'll convince needs only him as sustenance.

No harm, no foul.

I close my laptop and watch a moth bump against my screen while I think about the things that can never be erased, no matter how many times you hit delete.

Martín is waiting for Mom in the kitchen when I come down to pack my lunch in the morning. He looks like your standard middle-aged poet: expressive hands, rumpled dark hair graying along the temples, metal-framed glasses with oval lenses. A frame backpack and a laptop carrier are all he has for baggage. No kids of his own to pack for, though he was married once.

At Hampshire, Martín teaches poetry and postcolonial writing, while at home he writes at a desk tucked within a labyrinth of bookshelves. I've caught him writing here as well, on paper from the ancient printer or on recycled one-sided flyers. One minute he's talking about how to scramble eggs correctly, the next he's dived into an ocean of free verse.

"How are you this morning?" he says. He's dressed in the more upscale of his two modes: tidy business casual vs. chill gardener. He could likely pull off dockworker's gear at Hampshire with no questions asked, but he sticks with neatly ironed button-downs and khakis.

"Just fine, thank you." That's the rhythm of our exchanges, tongue-in-cheek formality. It's started to feel strained, though.

"How is your job?"

"Lots of lampshades and fancy plates and sheets. Kind of a tidy landfill."

He nods. "An archeological study perhaps?"

"How so?"

"What is kept. What is hidden. What is valued. A microcosm of a civilization to be unearthed." He smiles at me. "Or perhaps just a lot of things for you to carry."

"Not to burst your bubble, but it's totally the second."

Martín put Band-Aids on my knees when I fell off my first bike, and taught me to cook rice and beans correctly, and dragged me to poetry readings that I secretly loved and once cried at. He's not Dad—has never pretended to own any of that space—but if Dad were open fields, Martín would be the river running alongside them.

Lately, though, it's like someone dumped chemicals in that clear water. I lean away from his hugs, keep conversations superficial. He may still be himself, but I'm no longer me.

"Hey, I'm finally ready," Mom says as she comes into the kitchen. She looks rushed, as always, and happy, which is good to see. "Holi, I should be back by early afternoon, but then I need to work. I'll text to let you know I'm back in town."

"Okay. Have a good trip," I tell Martín.

"Thank you," he says. He looks at me like he understands my distance but still wants my explanation. Instead, I snag a pear from the fruit bowl as he picks up his bags and away they go.

The Chinese grad student is at the bus stop again, lugging the Riverside Shakespeare in his arms. Some books are not designed for backpacks, or backs, or anything short of a wheelbarrow. He must be teaching summer session. The classes the faculty don't want to deal with.

This could've been my dad. Waiting for the bus on a sunny summer day, thinking about his defense, that doctorate so close he can almost taste it. Only he would've looked dog-tired from two kids up all night with a stomach bug. He wouldn't have carried the Riverside, because he wouldn't have been able to.

He would've smiled at the mockingbird in the lilac by the bus stop, though, the way this grad student does. He too might've whistled back.

When I arrive, Elsie's in the living room, wheezing. Not bad, not like call 911 and look for an EpiPen—working at summer camps teaches you a few things—but enough that I sit across from her so that she doesn't try to stand.

"Some nights are harder than others," she says. In her hand is a handkerchief, and her skin is roughly the same shade of white.

"Ain't that the truth," I say.

"For an aspiring writer, you do not choose your words, or your diction, with care."

Okay, she's sucking in more than enough oxygen. I stand up. "For a woman on life support, you smell curiously like a cigarette."

The look she gives me reminds me of Bette Davis in an old movie, the one with the "buckle up" line. "Does it give you some pleasure to point it out? There are things you can say no to in life, and things you cannot."

Sure. Exes your skin just can't forget. Novels you've destroyed that long to be resurrected.

That's enough morning angst. "Same thing as yesterday?" I motion toward the trapdoor. "If so, I'm going to fill my water bottle."

"You mustn't spill it," she says.

"It's so dry up there that any spill would dry up instantly. Just like my desiccated corpse if I have nothing to drink."

Her laugh sounds like a large rusty hinge. I've made America's Treasure laugh. The courage that fled as I rode home yesterday comes charging back. Now or never.

"Did you write a little bit every day? When you were writing it?" 'Cause there can be only one *it* in this house.

She gives me another look, one that goes over my head,

honestly. It's like if you put annoyed and curious and sad in a blender, with a dash of salt thrown in. "I've hired you to help me. Not to act as my biographer."

I shrug and head to the kitchen. She hasn't moved when I come back through with a full water bottle. I open the closet and reach for the trapdoor cord—

"I wrote in a flurry." Her eyes are closed. "When it takes hold of you, there is nothing else. The rain could be coming through the roof and . . ."

I know exactly what she's saying. I'm . . . embarrassed? The intensity of what she's said feels like nakedness. Mine, hers, both.

"There's nothing else," she repeats. I think of the picture on the back of her book. Of her at a desk, the clatter of typewriter keys as she tries to catch the words before they escape. Of how much I want to say *me too*.

"I'll be down for lunch," I say and escape.

According to everything I've read—from her Wikipedia page to the intro of the edition I read in ninth grade to the library research I did for my paper on the book—she wrote *Tongues* slowly, back and forth with her editor for several years. The original draft, though—perhaps she wrote it in as much of a rush as I wrote mine.

See? Common ground. Mom would be impressed.

I pull a box at random. It's labeled *Misc: Correspondence, unanswered*. Inside are cards. Fancy cards, handmade cards, tastefully monogrammed stationery. I open a few, expecting birthday wishes or holiday tidings.

Instead I find thank-yous and congratulations, hundreds of them. There are handmade ones from kids, mostly from school classes. From adults there are store-bought cards and crisp stationery.

Dear Miss McAllister: I read your book and I'm so glad you won the Pullet Prize.

Dear Miss McAllister: Congratulations on your win! It is well deserved.

Dear Miss McAllister: Congratulations on the Pulitzer! Quite a trick for a girl.

Dear Elsie: I hope you won't think me forward, but I see you're single and expect you could use a man to help manage your business affairs.

Dear Miss McAllister: Or should I use Ms.? Are you one of those girls always on about your rights? I would hope not.

Dear Miss McAllister: Why did the brother die in your story?

All that need, soaked into the papers. Was it that she had only one story to tell, or that she couldn't stand all those people assuming she'd written something just for them—and expecting her to do it again?

She won the Pulitzer for fiction almost seventy years ago. I know because I looked it up. The kids who wrote to her are all adults now. Not just adults: parents, grandparents, happily childless senior citizens. The others? Dead, I'd guess. I'd *hope*, even, in the case of some. I can't help but shred a few of the cards. Ones that told her girls should be in the kitchen, not stealing men's glory; one suggesting she needed a man who wasn't afraid to knock her down when she got too uppity; or one that flat-out—well, fuck that one in particular.

Perhaps those hateful letters scared her into silence. I mean, these days you get death threats online for saying science is real, for liking one flavor of ice cream more than another. Anything at all, and ten times as many if people know you're a woman. On bike forums, I'm JuniorG, with a picture of an open road for an avatar, location: Nowhereville. Safety first.

Back then? This hate arrived as a tangible thing, fueled by a fury that not only wrote it out, but bought a stamp and found an address and stuck that evil in a mailbox. Hardcore misogyny.

But now I'm imagining, not working. I write it down in Elsie's notebook: *One box of fan mail.*

The next box is smaller. Inside are stacks of business correspondence. Accounting letters on her publisher's official letterhead, typed, not printed. I run my fingers across the imprints left by the keys. More zeroes in the numbers tallied there than any person ever really needs.

It's only when I dig down that I discover it's not all finance. At the very bottom are other letters, on different letterhead.

Dear Miss McAllister: While I appreciate the obvious care and enthusiasm with which you write, as well as your skill in depicting a full palette of characters, I find the subject matter of Of Wild Things and Flame *to be highly inappropriate and of little literary merit. Indeed, it reads like pulp fiction, without the genre's sense of pacing. Moreover, I find the choice of topic personally offensive. For that reason, I am declining the request to act as your agent in this and all future literary matters.*

I take out my other notebook, write down the name at the bottom of the letter. I'm curious whether Chester P. Mayweather ever made it as a literary agent. Seriously, how many times do you kick yourself in the butt for turning down Elsie McAllister's book? Is it like four times? One hundred? Every day, multiple times a day, until you die?

There are others of the same type in there. *Tongues* must've started life as *Of Wild Things and Flame*. I think it's safe to say that picking titles was never Elsie's strong suit. Seriously, both are bad. So bad. But it's the contents that apparently drove off at least twenty agents and a solid handful of editors. Tsk, tsk, Elsie McAllister. What kind of kink did you have to weed out to make *Tongues* publishable?

I've been up here an hour and have managed two boxes. I'm not sure Elsie thought I'd examine everything with quite this level of focus. I'm about to close the flaps on the box when I see a clean, unsealed envelope. I turn it over. Written on the front in that perfect penmanship:

Laughter like the ocean.

The envelope is empty. She must've needed a scrap of paper and grabbed the nearest thing. Which is odd for a treasure hunt; making them as kids always required planning. Then again, a woman who uses an old phone to hide her keys may be exactly the kind to store a treasure hunt in her attic disguised as random notes.

I've now found two random lines with zero connection to the contents of their boxes. Treasure hunt or not, I'm curious. I toss the envelope into the box with the sombreros, stash it under the eaves, and slap a new label on the box that reads *Misc: Mysteries*.

I go for another *Misc: Correspondence* box. This one is more cards, some with long letters inserted. The dates and the topics are all over the place.

Dear Miss McAllister: I had to write because your beloved father in the book reminds me so much of mine.

Dear Miss McAllister: I went to Maine specifically to see the places you described in your book. It was a journey that moved me so.

Dear Ms. McAllister: Have you thought about how your book

contributes to the industrial war machine by not confronting the militaristic structures warping the young men, as well as by the utter lack of feminist principles in your women?

Dear Miss McAllister: My brother died in Vietnam six months ago and I don't know how to be in the same house as his empty bedroom.

Dear Elsie: What happened to you?

That's it, that's the whole card. One line. I look at the envelope. There's no return address. It was sent to her agent's office. The writing swirls, a tempest on paper. I hold it up to my nose, smell nothing but dust.

Closer examination of the postmark dates the card to the year her book was published and shows that it passed through the Augusta, Maine, post office. Once Elsie left Maine, according to both Mr. Cooper and the internet, she *left* Maine. Her family, her town—she said nothing about them in interviews or speeches, they said even less about her when approached by journalists and biographers. But someone in Maine wasn't content to let her go.

I add the card to the box of mysteries.

Because now I want to know the answer too.

Elsie, what happened to you?

It takes me until lunch to check every letter in the box. I'm now very familiar with royalty statements and rejection letters and weird fan mail—I mean, holy crap, people have no sense of boundaries—but not with what acceptance looks like.

I learned in school about Elsie having a hard time getting her book published. She's one of those "real writers just persevere" success stories. But only now does it sink in: agents and editors did not like the original manuscript. Like, at all. I think I would've given up long before she did. *I'm afraid your youth shows*, said one agent. That's one of the kinder ones. The worst has what looks like stains from a coffee cup on it, though I couldn't blame Elsie if it was blood. *I find your writing, while possessing some rudimentary grace and verve, to be utterly without redeeming quality when it comes to subject matter. I would recommend that you consider seeking psychiatric help.*

Joke's on you, bud. I almost fold it up and stick it in my back pocket to show to everyone. Not just Robin and Maya... I mean *everyone*. It should be online, where the world can see just how badly these guys messed up. I settle for snapping a shot before returning the paper to the bottom of the box.

I mistake the voice calling me for the squeaks of the plywood floor until I hear several sharp raps on the ladder. I speed-crawl over and look down. Elsie is there, even paler than before. I can hear her breathing now, like wind rushing past the windows during a blizzard.

"Do you drive?" she says, only it comes out as a whisper.

"I do. I can. I don't have my license with me." Because I don't ever drive.

"I need a bit of help." Again, that wheezy whisper. "I need a ride to my doctor's, I think."

"Let me come down." I expect her to move, but she keeps leaning on the third step up the ladder. Suddenly fear hits me right about lung height.

"Can I call my mom?" I have my phone in my hand in no time.

"No, no. There's no need to be alarmed."

I book it down the steps, dropping past her. Up close, her eyes look like someone's rubbed charcoal around them. Her pulse shows in her neck.

"I just need a ride. I'd rather drive than deal with an ambulance." Just like that I realize that she really is in her nineties, with the end of her life traveling at lightspeed toward us. Not today, not today, not today, please.

I open the key box. "Which one?" She sucks another breath in and points to a plain metal ring. I take it.

"Let me get the car out of the garage and then I can come back for you." Or is that wrong? Can I even leave her alone?

"That sounds fine," she says.

I rush into the garage, open the car door and turn the key. Just as quickly, I remember that that is a very bad thing to do. I fumble for a garage door opener, finally finding it on the console between the seats. Backing a car is just as terrible as I remember, but I keep both mirrors from rubbing off on the walls, which is success enough.

Back inside, Elsie is in the same spot. She reaches toward me, and for a moment I think she needs me to carry her. Instead she takes my arm, and I hold steady as she stands. We walk together. Her little O2 canister dangles from my hand between us.

Every step takes three or four wheezes. Why didn't she call an ambulance? Why haven't I called one?

We make it to the car. I close her door behind her and head to the driver's side. From across the road a neighbor waves, as if I'm just taking Elsie out for a ride. I want to call for help—what was my mother thinking sending me to work here?—but I don't. I get in the car and drive.

She closes her eyes and rests her head back. While we're waiting at a light, it slips to the side.

This can't be it. I picture the headlines: *America's Treasure Dies in Car Driven by Slow-Moving Teen.*

I touch her shoulder. She opens her eyes. "What is it?"

She sounds annoyed. I blush, try to think of some cover, give up. "Just wanted to be sure you're alive."

"I have no plans to die just yet, Holiday. We still have matters to attend to at my house." She says it all in that raspy tired voice, but she also sounds pretty damn serious. She might as well be standing on a hill and shouting *No treasures will die today!*

I sit patiently in the waiting room. It's a family practice office; in one corner is the world's tiniest table, surrounded by four blue and yellow chairs. The little person there has turned one of them on its side, and they're banging on the leg with a block, their tangled hair swinging over their face. *Clunk, clunk, clunk*, no one moving to stop them.

I'm about ready to bang the block myself. I try texting Maya but get no answer. Try Robin too, but he's in therapy. Finally, I try Mom.

What's up baby?

I had to drive Elsie to the doctor. She was having trouble breathing.

I can sense her struggle, a dog trying not to chase a rabbit.

Did she need an ambulance?

No. She asked me to bring her and I drove her. That's all. I'm just stuck here.

How long has she been in there?

I don't know. Like half an hour?

The nurse calls the little person and their mother back. The silence is heaven.

Why don't I come meet you?

She said she didn't need anyone else. She'll be okay.

There's a long pause. Less a pause and more a silent tirade that I can sense, thanks to the high-frequency connection between us. All sorts of things are in there, much bigger and harder and scarier things than either of us wants to say, very little of it about Elsie.

Call me and let me know how things are, okay, sweetie?

K mom

The door to the exam room hall clicks open and a woman in a white coat comes out. She isn't wearing a mask—almost no one but me is—and even though I know Elsie's protected by layers of vaccinations, her own and everyone else's, it still doesn't sit right with me. This is, after all, where sick people come.

"Are you Holiday?" she asks. I nod. She smiles at me, and sure, it's part *I-can-relate-to-the-teens*, but it's also the kind of smile you give someone who is waiting for a really sick woman—a life preserver tossed to flailing arms. "Such a fun name."

That's me. All fun, all the time.

"We're giving Ms. McAllister a nebulizer treatment. She wanted me to let you know. She asked if you could wait for her as she'd rather not have to call for a ride. Will that be okay?"

"She's not dying?" I mean for that to come out in a different way than it does. Less like I'm going to cry and more like I'm making plans for my afternoon that don't include body bags.

The doctor puts her hand on my shoulder, clearly trained for such moments. "She'll be fine."

As fine as anyone who has to carry their own air with them can be.

"The nebulizer," she continues, "should make her breathing easier. This is part of her situation, Holiday. People can live with chronic illness for a long time." She pauses, smiles at me. "But let's use this as a teaching moment. Don't start smoking."

She squeezes my shoulder and leaves. I sit back down to wait.

Elsie does look better when she comes out. I still carry the O2 for her, and she doesn't stop me. The silence seeps into us.

We're almost home by the time she speaks. "It's what happens."

I assume that we're talking about trouble breathing. Until she continues.

"It's what happens when you're caught up in it. That's what I didn't say this morning. You become . . . blind. You lose sight of everything else. In that space . . . there aren't lies anymore. Nothing but truth."

Now I am lost. We're not talking about breathing at all. We're not even talking about writing, at least not any of the questions that I've asked or even thought about asking. "Yeah," I say. She goes silent.

It's 3:30 by the time we're back, which is close enough to five for a downright bad Friday. Mom's rearranged her hospice schedule to fit in an emergency visit with Elsie. When she arrives, I go into the attic and collect my stuff, guilt free. On the way back down, I snag a copy of *Tongues as of Fire*. She'll never notice, and I kinda think I need to reread it.

I stop on the Common on the way home. To clear my head, but also because I do this sometimes—sit for a while on one of the benches beneath the old maples, in this place that knows everything about me, and feel a part of things. What things? Life, I suppose: the dogs, the people, the thud of bass from a passing car, the squirrel racing across the path. We all share something here, even if it's just existing in this particular blip of space-time.

Today I sit cross-legged in the grass, watching some people toss a Frisbee around. I never played ultimate, but Alex and Hedy would join pickup games here occasionally and I'd watch. Alex ran like someone with much longer legs, quick and smooth. She was fearless too, going up against guys twice her weight. And getting knocked down, and losing the disc, and still laughing.

Why Alex? Why, Alex?

"Holi?" Either Noa's stealth or the depth of my mental haze has allowed her to walk up in broad daylight and crouch beside me without me noticing. The squeak I give is my penance for being—let's face it—a flake.

Her hair is loose today and hangs straight, with only a wisp of bangs to break it up. She's wearing a blue shirt with *Yosemite* across the front of it. She has double hoops in her ears, delicate ones, and a stud up higher in the cartilage of the left.

"That's correct, yes? Not Holiday?"

"Yes—Holi. Only everyone thinks it means *Holly*, like the shrub. I mean, I'm prickly and all—"

"Really? You don't seem prickly," she says in that slight and precise accent.

I feel something in a little space just to the side of my sternum. Not a flutter. Just a question.

She narrows her eyes, thinking. "I've seen cactus when I was traveling in Arizona. They're beautiful. Maybe you *are* like them." We're both silent for a moment, her looking deep in thought, me wondering if I misunderstood. "What are you thinking about?"

The quick and easy answer is *whether you just told me I'm beautiful*. But that's not really the truth, not the one she's asking for. And that truth staggers into sticky territory, like how much to say about your brother's life to his coworker.

Only it's my life too. I compromise. "About a friend of Robin's and mine. Alex. She died in an accident, the spring before last."

She'd probably be in her final year of college now if she'd lived. Robin probably would too. Life can go all kinds of ways and we careen on through it like driverless bumper cars and sometimes we careen right out of it.

Noa leans forward, hesitates, touches her hand to my wrist. "I'm sorry. You don't have to say more unless you want to."

Of course. Of course, I want to say more. I want to say that Alex was gorgeous, that magic bubbled up through her and out, that she and Robin were twins under the skin, meeting in all those secret rooms that exist in each of us. Except she had one room he didn't, and her room led to a door that she went through alone, leaving everyone else behind.

I want to say that before Alex died, Robin was solid: flesh, blood, skin and bones. And after he was cloud, then nothingness.

I shrug, pull out my pocket watch for the time. "Robin and I are watching Buster Keaton movies tonight. You should come. There'll be popcorn."

Keaton Night is a long-standing monthly tradition with Robin and me. Mom used to join us, but not often anymore. Any time that isn't eaten up by work goes to classes and studying. Occasionally, Robin's friend Betts stops in. He played bass in the Horse Caves and they've stayed close and I always feel better when he's around. More often these days, though, it's just the two of us.

Tonight there's a knock at the door as Robin's pouring butter on the popcorn. I didn't actually think Noa would come, even though she typed our address into her phone after I invited her.

"I hope I have the right time," she says when I open the door.

"Totally. Come on in."

Maya insists that I'm oblivious to my surroundings, and maybe I am. When strangers show up, though, I see everything through their eyes. The dust on the ficus tree. The Indian print spread on the couch and how threadbare it is. The stacks of books on the floor, next to the bookshelves, next to the chairs—everywhere.

Noa walks along the edge of the room, examining the cluster of framed photographs hanging by the bookcase full of Dad's books.

"Your father?"

Robin moves to lean over her shoulder. "It is. That's Hols with him. He died that year."

"So young," she says. "An accident?"

"He had a congenital heart condition," Robin said. "They fixed it the best they could when he was little—"

"But he died from the flu," I say. Someone crossed paths with him while sick with an illness they considered minor and it killed him. Took away what our lives might've been if he'd lived, who he might've become.

"I'm so sorry. And your mother?"

"She started nursing school as soon as he finished his PhD," says Robin. "She wanted to have something that would make it easy to find a job. He died in January; she finished school in May."

"So she's a nurse, and you, Robin, are a cook—"

"And Holi works for a famous author," Robin says.

"Not for long," I say quickly, in case he tries to namedrop. "This is just to make enough money to get to New Zealand to work on an organic farm."

Noa has these funny eyes: blue turning almost purple around the edges of the iris. She's watching me closely. "That'll be wonderful, I think, unless you dislike farming."

"I don't." I enjoy feeling productive and being outside. I do not *love* farming, though, the way Maya does.

"Shall we?" Robin's already on one end of the couch, remote in hand. Noa sits on the other side. I freeze. I'm supposed to sit next to Robin, I always sit next to Robin, only that means I'd sit between them. It's hard for me to do that these days, to bump up against other people. Even harmless, gentle people.

Before I make a move, the outside door opens and closes. I turn to find Mouse. "Hey, new and old people," she says.

Some people have sports friends and school friends and family friends and cousins—friends stretching out in all directions. I have Robin and Maya and Mouse. One is blood. One is complicated. One is the kind of person whose odd recognizes your own, makes it normal and creates an island that you both can return to on the days you need safe harbor from the world.

That's Mouse. I've known her since I was two. She's hardcore into science and cake decorating and her friend Hannah, who's hung up on her narcissist ex-girlfriend. Mouse can think her way through almost any problem, just not that one.

"You dressed up for us," Robin says.

Mouse eyes him, slowly, deliberately, until every spot and hole in his ratty old Bat Conservation International shirt has been cataloged. "Yes, I see now that I should've worn something more appropriate."

Mouse's wardrobe palette is minimalist. Standard outfit: black jeans, black tee. Dress outfit: black jeans, flowy black shirt. She mixes it up with earrings and the occasional choker. Her hair is brown, currently with a faint red sheen. She doesn't believe in bleaching, so it's always just a hint of red, or purple, or green. After the first time I dyed mine, she looked over my green hands and green forehead and the green tips of my ears and said, "Let's assume I'll handle this for you from now on."

Now, she glances at Noa and says, "This is Keaton Night, is it not?"

Mouse was raised on an eclectic diet when it came to entertainment; silent movies fit right in. Her mother, Juliet, writes scholarly tomes and teaches subversive feminist texts to her students while also maintaining a thriving career as a romance author; her father is a librarian who quit to become a homeschool dad. *Try everything and see what works for you* should be her family's motto.

Robin pats the couch beside him. "You're in the right place, Miss Mouse. Join us."

Mouse takes the seat and Robin introduces her to Noa. The Valley is like a web made by a massive mutant spider, strings connecting us all, with everyone fewer than six degrees of separation from a stranger who knows everything about them. That makes newcomers a very welcome curiosity.

I pull the marshmallow of a chair closer and settle into its depths with relief. This feels, if not like the past, then at least like a present in which no place has been held for ghosts, and that's good enough for me.

How do you talk with someone you thought might die in your car at a red light three days ago? Okay, *her* car, but the question remains. As I walk up the driveway with my bike on Monday, I'm trying to imagine what to say to Elsie.

The door opens before I reach it, and I'm expecting the housekeeper again but instead I'm face-to-face with a middle-aged man: a little short, a little stout, with a button-down shirt and a dark blue tie streaked by waves of stars.

Did they call in an astronomer?

Did she die?

"Holiday, right?" the man asks. He's holding a mask in one hand. "Would you prefer . . . ?"

COVID manners for the win, but it's not COVID I'm worried about right now. I wave him off. "Don't worry about it for me. Is Elsie . . ." Alive?

"I'm Dr. Harkness—sorry, Paul. Ms. McAllister's son." He finally catches the look on my face. "She's fine for now. Her doctor called me on Friday and I thought it best to spend the weekend here. Anyway, thank you so much for giving her a ride."

Processing, processing, processing. "No prob. I'm glad she's doing okay." But—"Harkness?"

"My father's name," he says. "My mother kept hers because of the book, of course."

Of course. No other possible reason, like not wanting to be absorbed into someone else's identity.

"I'm not sure if today—" he begins, only to be cut off by a thread of sound from within the house. Over his shoulder he calls, "Yes, Mom. But—yes, of course." He steps aside. "Come in."

Elsie sits in the glider rocker in the living room. She looks tired but better than she did on Friday. The dark circles remain under her eyes. It takes me a minute to realize the issue. She hasn't been able to do her makeup. I'd guess that Dr. Galaxy here would be no help with that.

Neither would I. The way Maya would paint me before we would go to Secret House is not what Elsie needs, and besides, I was only the canvas. The best I could do is a glittery star or two, which I doubt would do much for Elsie's self-esteem.

"Ms. McAllister, would you like my mom to come and help you a bit this morning? Just . . ." I give my best Fix-the-Face hand swirl, hoping some symbols are eternal. Also hoping Mom won't mind an interruption to her studying on her morning off.

Elsie studies me for a minute. "Yes." She sounds like she's got a load of soaked peat moss packed in around her vocal cords. "Yes, that would be a big help."

Her son holds up his hands. "I'm sorry. My mother's quite sick, you see, and I don't think she should have visitors . . ."

"My mom's her hospice nurse," I break in quickly. "It's how El—Ms. McAllister met me."

"Please call your mother," Elsie commands.

I go out on the front step to make the call. Mom's voice is full of fog and concern. "Holi?"

"Sorry, Mom. I didn't mean to wake you." For a moment

I consider saying never mind and telling Elsie I couldn't reach her. Instead, I launch into an explanation, speaking quickly so I can get through the request before she formulates a no. ". . . It's just that you're so good at these things, and her son is here and I think she's feeling . . . naked, I guess, and I can't help her, you know that."

"Hol—" she says, and I feel her desire for sleep and silence and a single solid hour without anyone needing anything from her. "Give me ten minutes to get dressed and snag a cup of coffee, baby. I'll be along."

We wait for her in silence, the wolf tree watching us patiently from within its frame.

Mom takes Elsie into her bedroom. When she reappears, she's alone. The act of being painted and dressed apparently exhausted Elsie, so now she's asleep. Mom gives Dr. Galaxy a private briefing and a business card, and by the time she leaves he looks utterly glum.

Now he sits on the bed in the guest room and sighs from time to time as I bring down the boxes I've already cataloged. Sometimes he peeks into them, as if doubting the labels. Maybe that's not it. Maybe he's looking for his childhood. Fragments of it, at least.

At some point I must trip a silent host alarm because he suddenly looks up and asks if I want a drink. "Water," he adds in a rush, like maybe I think he's gonna whip out the vodka and pour us each a mugful.

Drink water or go back into the attic that is slowly heating to roast-a-chicken temps? It's a harder decision than it might seem. Dr. Galaxy will likely want to talk, and I'd just as soon not, but my calculations still come out in his favor.

He tells me to have a seat on the deck. I head out, settling into one of the teak chairs surrounding the matching table, apparently bought with an optimistic belief in future deck parties, not just an old woman sneaking smokes alone. A blue jay yells from the crab apple just off the deck. I *pssst* at it. It weighs its options for a sec before flying off.

The clink of ice against glass draws me back. Dr. Galaxy carries a tray with a painted ceramic pitcher and two glasses and a plate of little wafer cookies. How did he end up more grandmotherly than his mother?

He talks like a grandmother as well, asking about school and graduation and my future plans. I tell him I'm done with school and I'm on my way to New Zealand, not college, all the while gauging the distance between his knee and mine, his fingers and my fist, until Elsie comes out to tell him they need to leave for her appointment.

Elsie lingers while he takes the dishes in. "Have you completed the list of what remains upstairs?"

I laugh. "Do you have any idea of how much is up there?"

She looks at me blankly. Of course, she has no idea because who knows when she was last up there and what her family has added since then.

"No, I'm not even close."

"Remember that I prefer you be finished by mid-October. Please balance speed with thoroughness. This task requires both."

"Doing my best. Maybe let me get back to it?"

She waves her hand in a royal dismissal.

Once they leave, I come back downstairs. The wolf tree calls to me. It's become a tiny piece of sandpaper rubbing in a slow circle on the back of my brain, and the rub will continue until I know who the photographer was.

There's no signature on the front. I glance around, as though there might be security cameras, but even if there are, I'm not taking anything. I'm just momentarily liberating the photo from the back of its frame.

There's a piece of paper tucked between the backing and the print. There's no signature on the back and I've come so far that it seems wrong to not unfold the note and read it. It's written in sharp zigzag penmanship.

Elsie,

I bicycled up and down the streets of your hometown one afternoon, curious to experience it as you saw it then. I suspect very little of that world remains. What I did find, though, is the field and the tree. The Kindly Oak. Mortality has caught up with it. There is a single limb on which the leaves still grow. Unlike the others, it reaches for the sky. On the other side it has suffered terribly. A lightning strike, I think, though I am no tree enthusiast. I sat beneath it and imagined you there as girls, flowers between your toes. I could almost hear your voices. In the end I came away with this for you.

—CKB

Holy crap! Never would've guessed this one. Charlie Kirk Brushmeier is a name all photography students learn, but not for artsy nature shots. He was mostly a war photographer, catching people in raw and horrifying moments in a way that made you want to weep for humanity, theirs and yours. He also had non-wartime work, but always of people.

He must've been a fan. I mean, yes, famous people can be fans of other famous people, but that relationship feels different when it's in your hands. Maybe they were friends. In *Tongues*, the Kindly Oak marks the line between woods and fields, between being a kid and whatever comes next. For Elsie, I'm guessing the reminder is of childhood. A pretty depressing one, though.

I return everything to its place. That's one mystery solved, at least. Score for Holi Burton, girl detective.

Robin calls while I'm eeny-meeny-ing which box will be my last for the day. All my internal sirens go off, but he sounds fine. A little excited, even.

"You have plans tonight?"

"None. Zero. Zip. Nil."

"Do you . . ." He pauses.

I wait. Just when I start to think I'll grow old and die waiting—

"Do you want to hit Secret House with me and Noa?"

A video plays in my head, a retrospective of sorts, beautiful and terrible. How do you separate them, the beautiful and the terrible things?

Founded by relics from the nineties rave scene, Secret House is a nomadic party, a pulsing heart circulating college kids and gig workers, anarchists and nonprofit grant writers, little kids carried in backpacks or front packs and dancing just outside the doors on their fathers' feet. It's a place where someone might OD against a wall and where fifteen other people would jump in, Narcan at the ready; where a table outside fills with canned goods and clean socks to be taken by anyone in need.

It is a pinprick of perfection in a terribly imperfect world, and it's more haunted than almost any spot I know, regardless of its location.

"Are you sure?" Three words that really mean *Should you, should I be helping you, is this the point where everything changes again, do you understand that it can't ever be the same, will you be looking for her the whole time? Will you disappear, this time for good?* I'm regretting the question, even though it has to be asked.

"Hols, it's not a big deal. I just miss it. I miss all of it."

Alex. He misses Alex. And he can't miss her without missing Hedy, who hasn't shown up since before Robin was in the hospital.

I miss it too, everything about it. "If you're going, I am." For a moment, I think about Elsie and her fragile lungs, but COVID manners say that's what home tests are for. "I'm gonna bring Maya, okay?"

"Totally. Tell her we need to leave before nine. It's out near Boston."

"Got it. See you soon."

I grab the nearest box. It's another *Misc: Correspondence*, but inside is chaos. The deeper I go, the more random it all becomes.

I snag a letter. It's like pulling the lever on a slot machine, never knowing what I might find.

This time, I get a payout.

Dear Elsie,

I think we're just about there. It's been a long haul but trust me that it has been worth it. Wait and see.

Please look over the proofs and return via messenger by the end of the week. You should make plans to come to the city by the 10th, let's say. We need to talk over details with Roy Andrews, head of Marketing.

This is going to make a splash.

Yours,
Joe Bell

The hairs on my arm prickle. This is what history feels like: two parts *Mad Men*, one part old woman, ten parts Pulitzer Prize.

I grab a copy of *Tongues* and open it to Elsie's picture again. She's barely older than Robin, not much older than me. She looks captured, like a trail-cam snap of a mountain lion in the night. In my mind she sits between the two men, martinis on the table, cigarette between her fingers, distant look in her eyes. What did it mean to her to be at that table, with those men, waiting for something unimaginable to begin?

I check my pocket watch. These are all good questions, but they'll have to wait. The letters have been here for decades. They can manage one more day.

Alex always laughed at my cutoffs. "You're like forty years too late, baby girl." She talked like that, like someone much more than three years older than me. She ran her fingers over everything, tugging at the fringe of threads that tickled my knee, tapping a nail against the birthmark on my shoulder. As I dress now, I can almost smell the citrus that always wafted from her, almost hear the unique rhythm of her speech. I never knew where that had come from—the long pauses between words that belonged together, the waterfall-quick flow of others. Alex just did it; we just listened, entranced.

The tank I'm wearing is one Maya and I made after Alex was gone. An eye centered in the black cotton, its lids opened wide to expose an iris as blue as the sky on a late winter's day. The surrounding lashes we painted with the teeth of a comb dipped in a swirl of colors. Embers fly outward: red, orange, blue curls and licks of flame.

I lie back on my bed. Above me hangs my poster of the Milky Way, clouds of white fire. Maya touches a paintbrush to her chin as she surveys the colors she's laid out beside me. Her lips purse in concentration, then relax when Robin enters, guitar in hand.

He folds himself into the butterfly chair in the corner and picks the guitar's strings as Maya touches the brush to my ankle. He's playing something he wrote with Betts during the Horse Caves era. The band played a mix of genres: blues, sea shanties, folk songs. One time they did half a set of hymns set to disco beats. Their following was understandably best described as cult. I loved the weird, between-the-cracks stuff that Robin dreamed up when no one else was around.

Hedy loved those songs too. Probably still does. I have no idea what she's doing now. Not being Robin's friend, that's the main thing. He needed her and she walked off and didn't look back. Fuck her.

I close my eyes, open myself to the lonesome road sounds of the guitar and the tickle of Maya's brush as it travels my shin. She smells of the paints, sure, but also skin and lemon and sandalwood soap her mother keeps in their bathrooms. Even before we moved past the stage of best friends, the smell of Maya, the touch of her, caused a shiver inside me like water under the touch of a dragonfly. Does that ever go away?

I don't know that I want to find out.

When she's finished, we admire her art. There's a vine of stars and flowers like the one on her shoulder, spiraling up my right leg and my left arm and along the front of my neck. It ends on my cheek with a crescent moon. Back when we could finally go along with Robin and the others, Maya did little things: a star here, a heart there, a spray of glitter across the cheeks. What she does now ignites a history of her fingerprints on me.

The Prius is a joke when we all cram into it. Robin barely fits behind the wheel. I get the passenger's seat because I'd have to fold up like a spider to fit in the back. I feel Maya's knees resting against the back of my seat, nudging over every bump.

We stop for Noa at an old farmhouse north of town where she's got a room through Airbnb. She has her hair pulled back and wears a white tank and black Lycra shorts. She could be a soccer mom, or a jock, or someone who just doesn't give a fuck about what other people think. I'm going with the last. If I'm being honest, I want to know what it's like, being that confident.

Secret House has touched down in an empty textile warehouse. Some of these old structures hang on to existence by the merest of threads; some house the foodie class in gentrified splendor. This one appears to be headed down that road, girders in the parking lot and scaffolding along one side. Tonight, though, it's ours. People duck through a chain-link fence to reach the back door, which opens into the vast space that once held machines and the women who ran them. The canned music feeds into the buzz rising from the crowd.

Robin escapes from me. I watch him move like a seal, bobbing and sinking in this human ocean, pausing to clasp hands, to bend for kisses from trilling women and stubble-cheeked guys. They'll have noticed that he's been gone, they'll be wondering why, and some of them will be asking him. I home in on him with the focus of a spotter in a fire tower.

"You're very close with him?" Noa hovers at my shoulder.

"Yes."

"My sister and I aren't as close as the two of you."

I feel like I owe her more. I'm not an obsessive kid following her big brother around. "It's just that he hasn't been to one of these since . . ." Now what? Is there any reason to be mysterious? "Since our friend died."

"Alex who had an accident?"

Score one for half-truths biting you in the butt. "Yes, Alex."

"She died at a rave?"

"No. It's more complicated." Not really. The facts are both common and predictable, but when it happens to you, you realize that odds and stats mean nothing.

Some conversations are limber, twirling snakelike past and around and over things, making new shapes, pausing to taste the air and then continuing. This is not one of those conversations. The thud of it dropping to the floor reverberates through my feet. Only, it doesn't feel broken either. Not completely.

The music cuts for a moment, drops back in stripped-down pulse. "Hello, my babies, my dear ones, my loves." Tonight's DJ, Cerulean, stands on a platform cobbled together from pallets and cinder blocks and milk crates. Six feet tall, dressed in what looks like an ocean, a blue wig electric against her rich dark skin. She runs her fingers over the turntables before her. "Sturdy hearts, do you hear me? You keep your great big ouchy beautiful hearts beating, you hear me? Keep showing up, babies, and I'll keep showing up for you."

With that the music ignites. Its flames surround me, rise through the balls of my feet and flow down through the crown of my head, expand into every empty space in my chest. There's so much more to hearing music than having working ears. It vibrates within me, changes me with each pulse.

Maya vanishes into the crowd. A girl with chocolate eyes peering out from a tanned face and a white wig in a Cleopatra cut moves in front of me, a boy with beestung lips slithers next to her. I close my eyes and breathe the music in. The vines glow on my skin.

I am here.

I am Holiday.

I am so, so alive.

❀ ❀ ❀

Robin's under the exit sign when I look for him. I have no sense of time; it might be an hour or ten since the music started. Cerulean glows on the platform, one perfect finger tracing circles in the air as she spins her old-school beats.

He's leaning against the wall. A sun-bronzed woman leans shoulder-first next to him, her hand twirling a strand of her long black hair. I take his other side, put my hand over his, feel his pulse steady against my palm. When I look into his face, I see no sign that he's rolling.

The woman, on the other hand—it's in her eyes, in the way she keeps touching things: the wall, her own face, Robin. I can almost smell it in the sweat that greases her skin.

"You need some water," I say to her. I'm shouting to be heard.

She looks at me with the same breathless expectation that she's been aiming at Robin. For her the dance floor is a network of nerves, all tuned to pleasure. I've been where she is. Robin has too.

"Seriously. Get some water, stick your head out the door. You gotta take care of yourself."

"She's right." Robin's voice travels like the tide, inexorable. It's not that he's louder, he just knows more about projecting than I do.

The woman turns to look along the wall, toward the bins filled with ice and water bottles. "Come with," she says and puts her hand on his arm.

"No thanks. Gonna hang with my little sister."

She melts away, sliding between bodies like silk over a long leg.

"I need fresh air too," I say.

One of the back doors is propped open. Outside, people gather in small clusters. I can still feel the music through the soles of my feet, my heart drawn to the rhythm.

A couple of guys join us. One clasps Robin's hand, the other holds out a joint to me. I shake my head. I don't want weed. I also don't want him closer. Not even with Robin by my side.

"How you been, man?" The first guy has stepped away from Robin, though he still holds his hand. "I been thinking about you."

I'm not really there, not really listening. I'm thinking about the way the city glow dampens the stars, leaves them to shine through a haze that drapes like a piece of gauzy fabric over a light.

Robin bumps against me. The other guys are gone, the two of us alone.

"You okay?" I ask.

"It feels good."

I hold my breath. I want it to be this simple—a magical musical pill that saves him.

"And hard. I needed to do this, but I'm not sure I will again. Maybe. Who knows?"

Hope and despair, hope and despair. I'm not even sure what recovery means. Is it a thing? A motion? Evolution or toxic mutation?

More people are coming outside. The DJ's bringing the fire lower and lower, down to embers. From inside, the sweet sound of Marvin Gaye tells us what's going on. A Black woman across the yard sings along in a strong voice as she heads toward the fence exit.

Noa joins us, her shoulders still moving sinuously to the music. Maya appears too, one hand on the door frame as she pauses, looks for us, purses her lips like an old-time vamp and heads over.

The music lowers still more. The pulse slows, our heartbeats with it. Cerulean's voice reaches across space to us all.

"Babies, be well. Put your hands on your hearts and know that as long as they still beat, you still have a chance to change the world. Carry the love with you." The blessing sinks into our skin, our blood, the spaces within our bones. In this moment, this blink of time, we are sacred.

I believe that. I believe that we build ourselves, atom by atom, word by word; that these things, these memories are more than simple electrical signals stored in some data depot in our brains. Alex exists in Robin's fingertips and the outer edge of his smile, his crooked big toe and the long muscle of his calf.

Me? I'm built of Robin and Mom, and Maya, and now probably even Elsie. I'm built of this night, of the way the music moved me, of the most terrible days and the mediocre ones, of my bike and the hill. Future me will have blood with flecks of New Zealand, muscle fibers from a hobbited hilltop somewhere.

There are bits of Dad in me whether I remember him or not. The myocardium of my heart, beating on no matter what pain I feel.

It's what I want to believe, anyway.

I run to the bus at the last minute this morning. We didn't get home until three and then the sun never really came up, or it did but the clouds sat on it. I hit the snooze five times before I realized what it meant, and I'd only left myself enough time to shower and go when I'd set it.

The rain tests the air with sprinkles as I sprint to the stop, pours as soon as I'm onboard. The driver, a college student with their hair in two frizzy braids and big owl glasses, gives me hardly a glance.

My grad student bus accomplice has abandoned me today. The women ahead of me speak far too fluently for me to eavesdrop with my mediocre Spanish. A trio of elderly Chinese women, clear plastic hoods on to keep the rain off, sit to the side and whisper to one another. A few grad students puddle together to my left: a white guy with pirate hoops in his ears and two white women dissecting some bit of departmental gossip. One has a scarf draped over her head to protect her pseudo-bedhead, every strand a dedicated effort of spritz and drying. The other wears a tight vintage tee with a faded logo for City Lights, her eyes so green that they have to be tinted contacts.

MFA students. I simultaneously pity and envy them.

John Allen will know them. I bet one or both of the women will be in his class this fall. He'll collect them like fan mail addressed to him and meant to be displayed in handfuls to casual acquaintances.

No harm, no foul.

Dr. Galaxy is waiting when I arrive, wearing what must be his version of casual: pale blue button-down, pressed pants, a devil-may-care gray cardigan with the top button undone. No tie.

"Holiday, I wasn't sure you'd be coming today." He adds, "Because of the rain."

I look at his round face and his earnest hair in its combed ordinariness. "Nah. I'll always show up." I'm very aware of the water running off my head.

So is he, apparently. "Let me get you a towel, Holiday."

"Holi," I call down the hall after him.

I'm staring at the wolf tree photo again when he returns. He says my name, and I jump. He's closer than I expected—not actually invading my space, but even so, I jerk away.

"I'm so sorry," he says. He looks like Maya's dog, Baby, when she knows she's done something wrong but has no idea what, much less how to make amends.

I take the towel from his hands. Spotless white, likely bleached to within an inch of its life just so it can dry my hair while the good doctor watches. A few quick rubs and I hand it back to him in a damp ball. "Thanks. I should . . ." I point toward the trapdoor.

"Yes, of course. Have you . . ." He studies me for a moment. Not rudely, but even so, I'm uncomfortable. It doesn't take much. "Have you come across anything of interest?"

I try to imagine what might interest him. Tinsel? Every card ever sent to the occupants of this house? "Not really. She likes to keep everything, huh?"

He grimaces. "That's my mother, through and through. She'd be considered a hoarder if she weren't so tidy about it all."

I shrug. My flinch is still on my mind, my nervous system still sounding the alarm. It should be simple; people touch each other all the time. In crowds, with handshakes, with knees bumping under the table when sharing a meal. So why do I avoid it like a bee sting?

It's embarrassing. It makes me seem like I'm helpless. I don't want to be helpless.

"I need to go up." I tilt my chin toward the attic. "So much not-hoarding to get through up there."

I spend the morning engrossed in yet another round of *Misc: Correspondence,* full of decades of student letters to the author from classrooms run by sadists.

Dear Mrs. McAllister: Tongues As Like Fire was pretty good. I liked the stuff about the fires. Did that really happen? Like the fires burning all the way out to the ocean? Anyway, the descriptions were pretty cool even if I didn't totally get the point.

Riveting stuff. I take out my own notebook.

1. Don't force children to write to authors after forcing them to read the author's book.

2. Don't force authors to read forced letters.

3. Don't force anyone to read said letters for hours on end.

4. No one is forcing me to read any of these.

5. In fact, it's snooping.

I text Robin, ask what he's up to.

He doesn't text back. I return to browsing letters. Look at me, not panicking.

The next envelope I pick up bears, in place of an address, a single typed line.

Smiling with the monk amidst the roses as gulls circle overhead.

A clue, a prompt, a sign of insanity? It should be thrilling. The only thing I can think about, though, is the silence of my phone. I toss the envelope into the sombrero box and text Robin again. Still no response. I check the time. Mom's at class, her phone silenced. Somewhere in the back of my mind a tinny siren starts.

Downstairs, no one's waiting in the living room. My pulse sounds in my ears, pushes my veins outward as adrenaline hits my bloodstream and my heart pounds out *GO*.

I find Dr. Galaxy puttering around the sink. "I'm sorry, I have to run," I say, pretending it's no big deal. "I forgot I have an appointment. I'm late, so just gonna—" I motion toward the door as I back out of the kitchen.

"Of course. The non-hoarding isn't going anywhere." He grins, and while I have no time for it, I still note that he, like his mother, has a sense of humor.

Robin isn't at home. I check his room, my room, Mom's room, the landing of the outside staircase where he and Alex and Hedy would cluster, sometimes passing a joint around. I hit the bathroom last, open the door with my chest pulled so tight that I'm not sure breathing is an option.

Nothing. No Robin. No clues, good or bad.

I'm back out the front door, off the porch in one jump. One of the UMass students who rent the apartment is on the phone on the second-floor deck. "I'm like 'what the hell,'" she says as she checks her reflection in the window. "I mean, we all know what he's like."

"Hey," I call and she peers down at me. "Have you seen Robin? Seen him leave, I guess?"

She shakes her head and returns to her phone. I'm back on my bike again and out onto the road.

I coast the short stretch of downtown, one eye on the sidewalk the whole way. Outside the pizza slice place I pause. Two regulars have staked out the sidewalk there as their daytime space.

"Hey, you seen Robin?" I ask the white woman crouched on the pavement, petting her dog. I can't remember her name, but Robin would. He hooks people up with food if they come by the diner. I extend my arm up over my head and wiggle my fingers. "Tall guy, skinny, wicked pale like me?"

The woman squints a bit against the sun. "I know who you're talking about, sweetie. Nope, haven't seen him around today. You seen Robin?" she calls to a white guy on a bench farther down.

He pauses, pizza slice in hand. Next to him is a sign that says *Homeless Veteran, Anything Helps, God Bless You.* "Nah. He hasn't been around. Not today." With that he's back to his pizza.

Not here, not at home. I text Kendra, the manager at the diner. She's out of town and all she can say is that she didn't schedule him for today.

Now the panic is gaining force, like a hurricane hitting warm water. I have no idea where Robin is, and I should, I should, because if I don't know where he is how can I know he's safe?

I bike down to the Cafeteraria and lock my bike outside. Inside, the whole Turkish coffeehouse vibe—velvet curtains, velvet cushions, chicks with long hair draped against dicks with long pseudointellectual thoughts—recedes as I head to the counter. The tanned woman there leans on one hand while pretending to wipe the glass clean.

"Mouse in back?" I ask, but it's not so much a question as shorthand for *I know she's back there so I'm going to go see her.*

"Nice," she says as I pass behind the counter. "This isn't a house, you know. It's a place of business."

I keep going, through the cheap calico curtain that separates the storeroom from the front. In the back I find Mouse, a box of coffee filters in hand. "Hey." She glances at the clock on the wall. "What's up?"

And I'm ready to throw up from the memory of holding the phone as the voice on the other end said *911 what's your emergency.* "Robin. Have you seen him?"

She gets it instantly. "Where have you looked? When did you see him last?"

"He slept in this morning. I've texted a couple of times but he's not responding. He's not home or at work."

She gives me a look. I'm too desperate to parse it beyond the fact that she doesn't think I'm foolish no matter what comes out of her mouth next.

What comes out is the sensible stuff. "Have you tried anyone? Betts? Hedy?"

"No." She's right. I've gone from point A to point 134,000. Rein it in, Ophelia. "Um, Betts will be at work, but I can text. Hedy—no way. And I don't know where else to look . . ."

"There's no one else, really?" The air contains the slightest hint of smoke, like the wisp of worry Mouse emits now has a smell and a taste.

"Noa, maybe? I don't know a last name, or a number, or anything else, just that she's Dutch and we picked her up at a farmhouse last night."

Mouse puts down the box of filters. "Just so I understand: you're saying we need to find one Dutch woman named Noa in a general population of transient students, many of whom are of international origin?"

"Yes?"

"Well, mission accepted." She looks at the clock again. "You're totally in luck because my shift ends just . . . about . . . now."

Once we're out on the street, Mouse says, "Have you checked at the diner to see if they have Noa's number?"

I groan. Mouse groans.

"You are the worst detective ever."

"I texted Kendra and she said he wasn't scheduled so I—"

"What about Meggie? She'll be there now."

Meggie, yes. She's been dayshift at the diner since the dawn of time, mothering countless college students and lost souls.

Only once I unlock my phone, my fingers don't seem to work. Mouse motions for it. I hand it to her; she scrolls through the contacts until she finds the one she's looking for and calls. She walks away for a moment, turns back. "Got it," she says and hands the phone back to me. I hold it to my ear. "—Hi?"

"Hiya, lovie. You're looking for Robin?" Meggie's voice is like the voice of God, if God were real and someone you'd want to hear from. "He took my car, doll. Noa needed a lift to Springfield and I told them to take it. He's fine. I'll chew him out a bit for you, though. He should know better than to not tell anyone."

"Thanks so much, Meggie."

I should be happy. Instead, I'm pissed.

The therapist I used to see told me that anger's a response designed to jumpstart us when something's wrong, but that we mess up and assume it's action, not just an alarm. That it's not an emotion to dwell in 'cause it burns away everything inside us.

I don't care. I left my job, where I'm making money to do what I want, because he decided to . . .

Because he decided to do something without telling me.

Mouse gives me a look that tells me my thoughts are rising in *read me* bubbles from my head. "All's good, huh?"

"He's a shit." Hearts are supposed to do their work in silence and unobserved, like earthworms. Mine bangs in my chest, Godzilla doing jump rope. Double Dutch, I think.

Mouse takes my hand. "Let's sit down," she says. "Right here. Like it's a picnic. Urban picnic," she adds as she sinks to her knees on the sidewalk.

I follow. "You're a freak. You know that, right?" But I'm dripping with sweat and the world's spinning.

Once down, I lean my head on her shoulder and try to ignore the helpless, queasy, weightless sensation that precedes passing out. Mouse squeezes my knee.

Down here, we're fragile. I can see that now, how every step bringing people close to us is a step that could end up on us. Same with the skateboard scooting by. Or a car jumping the curb. That happened a year or two ago, just one block down. A man was standing at a bus stop and then a car went over the curb and killed him.

These are the things you don't learn when you should. School teaches you how to stand in line and how to take a test that tells you if you deserve to graduate, but there are no classes called Shit That Really Happens. No teacher ever says *Kids, there are places in life where the air runs out, where your lungs keep working even though there's nothing for them to breathe, where you can't die and you can't live. And sometimes you'll see someone you love trapped like that and you won't be able to blow your air into them and make the struggle stop.*

The human river that eddies around us disturbs Mouse not at all. "Hey, it's sunny and we're young. We should totally go somewhere."

Not far away stands a pair of white legs, the feet in sandals. On the second toe on the left foot is a ring. The skin around it has turned that unmistakable green you get from copper. Maya wears a copper bangle sometimes, only on her skin it looks half alive, more than metal.

"So, yeah, I'm just hanging out on the sidewalk, you know, having my urban picnic with no food and talking to myself, apparently." Mouse has leaned back, her hands braced on the ground, face squinting up at the sky. "But it's okay 'cause that's my thing. That's me, just a free spirit, totally cool with whatever. It's not like I deserve attention or anything."

I groan. "I'm here now. Where should we go?"

"The Galápagos," she says, as if we've been waffling between two places. "That's where we should go."

My phone dings. Text. Robin. He's back at the diner and he's not a shit. He's my brother and I would stick both hands in the deep fryer there before I'd let anything happen to him again.

Hey. Sorry I didn't get back to you earlier. Left phone on silent. Will be back around dinner. When do you leave work?

Left already.

Something wrong?

Yeah, this whole thing. Me being the grown-up, him being the . . . what is he being? **Just hanging with Mouse. Gonna go.**

K, Holi Doli. Catch you later.

Mouse puts her chin on my shoulder. "For real, are we going to do something? I mean, I could go home and sort the spices in order of color but I'd rather hang out with you."

"Hey. You're lucky I even pay attention to you." I let her pull me up by the hands.

"Because you're a Kermit-haired hottie. I know."

I shove her. She knocks into me. That's also a thing about life. Sometimes it feels like the air is leaving, only it turns out you just didn't take a deep enough breath, and when you do, everything is suddenly okay again.

We wander for a while, talking about Mouse and Hannah and the mess that happens when you fall in love with friends. "It's like you're in a Netflix series and at some point there'll be a torrential downpour and you'll look at each other—"

"—and she'll say, 'but Ari says rain isn't wet' and I'll dissolve into a vengeful water spirit." She sighs.

"Netflix is getting more creative, I guess."

We pause at a crosswalk for a fire truck returning to the station. Mouse squints up at the sky. "Don't look at the sun," I say.

"You spoil everything," she says. "How's the job?"

"The one I ran out on this morning?" I give her a brief rundown of the thrills of the McAllister attic.

"Do you think there are skeletons up there? Real ones?"

"I'd know in advance. Its box would be labeled. Everything is."

"It could be the reason she quit writing, you know. She took killing her darlings seriously."

America's Treasure by day, serial killer by night. "I don't think that's the answer. Maybe she just didn't have anything else to say, like my teacher suggested in ninth grade."

"Really? Just like that, her head emptied out and she decided to do nothing? Brains don't work that way."

"Okay. So she took care of her kids. Your dad stayed home with you."

"Yes, but my dad was a librarian and he's gone back to being a librarian. And he sings in a barbershop quartet and volunteers on the conservation committee. It's not like you only get to do one thing at a time, or *be* one thing at a time."

Fair point. Mom is a shit-ton of things, ranging from my parent to Elsie's hospice nurse to a master's degree student. Mouse's mom is a writer and a professor and a parent. Robin's a musician and a cook and an incredibly complicated and sometimes annoying human being.

"Okay, but if the cumulative mass of seven decades of McAllister scholarship hasn't figured out Elsie's deal, I think my chances of solving it are small."

"But maybe one of *your* things in life is figuring out this puzzle. Something literally no one else has been able to do."

Elsie, what happened to you?

When we get back to the center of town, Mouse shakes my hand. She has a shirt at home with stick figures hugging and a red slash through them. No one crosses into the Mouse zone unless she invites them.

"Hey, thanks," I say.

"No problem. You can give me your firstborn, or more likely, someone else's." She starts to walk away, then turns back. "You're a tougher person than you think." She doesn't wait for me to respond, just keeps walking, leaving me with suspiciously blurred vision.

No one's home. I head up to my room and pull out my laptop. I need to write.

Only . . .

John Allen was right. That's what fills my mind every time I open a new document or turn to a clean page.

"You have some talent, Holi. This, though, this isn't even worth the time it takes to read it." He motioned toward the screen of his laptop. All I saw from my vantage point was the sticker on the cover: *Real Men Aren't Afraid of Feminism*. "I'm telling you this because I think you could be a decent writer if you try. If I didn't care, I'd leave you to struggle along and hit this wall much harder with someone else's criticism."

He came around and rested his hand on my shoulder, dug his fingertips in a bit to massage the spot.

"No one wants a story about a girl living all alone who evolves into a dragon. Where are your three acts? Your hero's journey? This is more of a narcissist's diary. Let me make a list of writers you should read and appreciate if you ever want to write anything of value."

I close my laptop and turn music on. This narcissist has learned her lesson.

13

Dr. Galaxy is fidgeting by the door when I arrive. A suitcase waits next to the couch. Battered light-brown leather, darker along the bottom, brass latches. Details, details. If writing were nothing more than a master list of tiny moles and toe rings and latches, I'd have my own Pulitzer.

Speaking of which, Elsie's waiting too. She's dressed in a pale blue sweater with a tidy white collar emerging precisely from the neck. Even her tan slacks look as though they've been ironed within an inch of their lives.

"I'm leaving, at least for now," Dr. Galaxy tells me. "But we've made some adjustments. Mom's been relying on the housekeeper and her neighbors looking in on her for too long. From this point forward, she's agreed to have an aide come every evening to prepare dinner and stay through the night. I'll plan on returning by the end of the month, but in the meantime, I thought perhaps you'd be willing to work a bit more? Overtime pay to come on weekends?"

His mother looks less than enthusiastic about that. Or maybe she had a lemon for breakfast. Either way, it's clear this is all his idea. Lucky for him, a clock with dollar sign hands ticks in the back of my head all the time now.

"Yeah, that sounds good. I'm sorry about leaving early yesterday."

"It's fine, no problem at all. We appreciate all this so much."

We stand there awkwardly for a moment. I can hear Elsie breathing, a soft rasp in and out. Finally he says, "Well, it's been an adventure, hasn't it? Oh, Mom, you need to wear your fall alert. All the time and not just when someone's watching."

Elsie shakes her finger at him. "It's not half as bad as you've made it out to be. I don't need a hen clucking at me at all times." She looks less sour now, more like she's gently suggesting he ate too much cake.

He briefly looks crushed but rebounds with a smile. "Holiday, do you mind helping me bring my luggage out to wait for the car?"

All two pieces of it? I pick up the larger suitcase and walk out the door. Outside, the air holds that faint smell that warns me summer's coming to a close. *Tick, tock, tick, tock.*

"I really do appreciate your help." Dr. Galaxy presses his hands together. "It means a lot to me to know that my mother has what she needs. It's hard to be away. My siblings are . . ." He studies the ground, as if the pavement ants trekking back and forth might be sending signals. They probably are. "They're less available for this . . ." Another pause, this time to wave his hand toward the house. "We're all very . . . individual. You may not know how it goes in families."

Not in this family. Maybe America's Treasure liked to break bottles and brawl barroom-style in the living room, and her kids had to paint over the bloodstained walls every Monday. Maybe under that pressed and perfect sweater swirls an inked dragon climbing her torso. *Elsie, what happened to you?* Something did, even if it's just a terminal case of writer's block.

Dr. Galaxy presses on, oblivious to the contents of my brain. "I wanted you to come out here so that I could ask that you keep an eye on her. She's determined to stay in control—she refuses to schedule daytime care beyond your mother's weekly visit—but she's frail, as you've seen. If you think she starts to look unwell—more unwell—I'd appreciate a call." He gives me a business card: *Dr. Paul Harkness, Pediatrics.*

"To be clear, I'd like to pay you an extra flat fee weekly to keep an eye on her while you're here. To ensure that she's safe."

Spy on her. Say it straight out, dude. If Elsie wanted him knowing how she looked and whether she coughed at noon and four, she would've asked him to stay longer. But . . . not my business to argue. Especially when he hands me a check for $250.

"First week in advance," he says. "This is so helpful."

He reaches out, and it suddenly occurs to me that he's about to hug me. Something animal happens in me, a quick step to the side and back. He blinks, holds out his hand instead. "I'm sorry, my error. COVID still exists, doesn't it?" He smiles kindly.

I smile back. I can let him believe I'm afraid of his germs. What I can't do is escape the slightly sick feel in my stomach.

His rideshare turns into the driveway. "Thanks again, Holi." He lifts both cases as the driver pops the trunk and I go back inside.

This afternoon Elsie begins the great adventure of reviewing the contents of each box I've cataloged so far. She sits in a wheelchair that's been stored in the corner of the guest room, a tired queen surveying a diminished realm.

She stares me down effortlessly though. "Remember that I'm the one paying you. You're here because *I* chose you."

Though not from a sea of candidates unless Mom brought others in before me.

"You did. You also told me not to snoop, but here I am looking through all of these for a second time. So that's a bit confusing."

She gives me a look that's nine parts I Will Take You Down and one part . . . I'm pretty sure it's amusement. It's quickly gone. "I need to see what can be donated and where. My memory is good, but not seventy-years-of-trinkets good."

"Why did you keep it all if it's only trinkets?" The reality that you can tuck away only so many picture frames and baby blankets before you cross a line into *Storage Wars* territory appears to have only just occurred to her.

She scowls. "It's all about words with you, isn't it?"

It shouldn't be. I could get through life with a couple hundred words. *Yes, no, please, thanks, I love you, screw that, fuck off, leave me alone, don't leave. Please, never leave.*

"Isn't it for you?" I ask. She doesn't respond.

The first box I open contains children's books, my alphabetized list of contents on the top. I pass the sheet to her.

She examines it, her lips pursed. "No."

The fridge down the hall kicks on and it's loud as a freight train in the silence. "Sorry?"

"No. It's not all about the words. Words are just the contents of a dictionary."

She beckons me over. I bring the box. It's too low for her to reach comfortably, so I grab a footstool from the living room and return. With the books at a comfortable height, she paws at them.

Somehow this is much worse than seeing her struggle to breathe. I could hold that whole box all day long. She can't even pick up some of the volumes.

"Real writers hear something else in the words. It's . . . it's . . ." She draws breath and coughs.

"An echo," I say. Because when I was writing the novel that's now gone, it was like the words were different, like they bounced to me off the rocks on a hillside too barren for flame.

"Foolishness," she says, looking at one book she's managed to pry from the rest. "I expect a number of these have inscriptions. I would like you to examine each and provide me with a more detailed inventory, noting title, inscription, date, and edition number. Do you understand how to find the edition?" Her eyes could cut glass as she waits for my answer.

I nod.

"I will arrange for those books likely to be of value to be appraised. I suspect my name will aid in their sales." Does she really need more money? "All proceeds will be donated," she adds as if reading my mind.

"Got it." I stash the box in the corner, write on it in Sharpie, and move to the next. The briefest of writing lessons appears to be done for the day.

I eat my lunch at the table out back. Elsie's down for a nap. A phoebe jumps from limb to limb in the crab apple tree. It'll be gone soon, hopefully to return next year, though the journey is long and there are so many ways to die along it.

I'm flicking a crumb off my shorts when the glass door slides open behind me. I look over my shoulder. Elsie isn't that good at opening the door.

An older version of Chris Evans stands in the gap. I make an entirely un-badass startled noise.

"I didn't mean to surprise you." He approaches, one hand out. "I'm Chris."

Of course he is. All clean-cut blond men found attractive by straight women and gay men are named Chris. I say nothing while giving him an obvious once-over. If he's murdered Elsie on the way through, I'd like to know before he gets any nearer.

"Chris Harkness. I'm Elsie's son," he clarifies.

Ah. Another one. My impression from Dr. Galaxy was that neither of his siblings would be showing up, and yet here one is, mere hours after he left.

Also, this one refers to her as Elsie. Not Ms. McAllister, not Mom.

"Holi, right? I've heard what a huge help you've been." He's put his hand away. Apparently the offered handshake had a shelf life. He takes another few steps closer. Rarely has anyone smelled as clean as Captain America here. Stick him in a tub and he'd provide the bubbles himself. Prep-school boys, even graying ones, all look kind of the same. He could be Logan, Maya's ex, fully grown and still hung up on himself.

"Does she know you're here?" I ask.

"She's asleep. May I?" He gestures to the other chair. I shrug. He sits. "Paul mentioned that you helped get her to the doctor. I—we—really appreciate that. We should've stepped in long ago, but she's stubborn and no one wanted to pick that battle."

He shoots me a look that suggests we both know how that is. Stubborn old women and their ridiculous ways. Dude, my mom is probably younger than you. Try again.

"I know you're already doing so much, but I have another request."

Somehow everyone imagines I'm doing so much more than

sorting boxes here. I'm not monitoring her O2 usage. I'm not keeping her from lighting up in the bathroom with the window open. I'm writing notes and moving things from one room to the next and unpacking them in front of her in an antiques strip show. And now I'm spying on her, but only in case she stops breathing.

"She's easily confused—I'm fairly certain that she's had significant mental decline. It can be hard to see it, but it's there. The confusion, the flashes of paranoia. It's a brutal thing, dementia. She masks it so well. Paul only sees what he wants. But a smart kid like you—you've likely picked up on it."

I say nothing, letting this play out.

"She has this idea that someone is trying to steal her writing. Of course, no one is. All we want is to preserve her papers. For posterity."

Posterity, yes. I'm all about posterity.

"We're afraid that she might do something . . . ill-advised with them. Because she's not of sound mind."

We? Either he's a hivemind creation, or he's doing this with . . . Dr. Galaxy? The one who told me to watch her more closely but never mentioned her papers? Actually, I can see Dr. G being too chicken to say what I know is coming.

"We're willing to pay you for anything you find and save. Let's say ten thousand dollars."

A mob of crows has set up somewhere down the road. They've found a predator—an owl, a hawk?—and now they're trying to drive it away from their territory. If I were alone, I'd go see what the danger was. I'm not alone, though, and I'm thinking about what ten thousand dollars will buy me. Enough that I won't be Maya's broke tag-along, surviving on crackers and water whenever we're between farm stays.

That's a lot of money to make for simply not destroying anything.

"*Tongues as of Fire* didn't emerge fully formed, you know." He flashes white teeth in a smile that has to make someone somewhere feel something. "She's been fairly stingy with it. Any additional drafts could strengthen her legacy."

He smiles. I bet he was a cute kid who became a cute boy who thought he got what he wanted because he was charming and not because everyone knew he had a famous mother.

I can see clear through you, bud. You're a frigging windowpane.

"Do you write?" Because if you did, you'd know that some writers don't want everyone to see all the ugly bits.

He laughs ruefully. "No, I deal in antiquities."

"Like artwork stolen from Indigenous cultures?"

He laughs again. "I'd forgotten what it's like around here. No, I broker deals for museums." Which doesn't mean he's *not* trading in artwork stolen from Indigenous cultures.

The crows are louder now, calling in reinforcements. A hawk lands on a branch nearby and swivels her head as the crows regroup to attack. I'm of no interest to her, neither food nor foe. Nothing as wild as a hawk has friends.

"If you come across parts of the manuscript, save them. Set them aside somewhere she can't access and let me know. That's all."

Cap has a scar on his hand so small that it's hard to see unless you follow the line between his thumb and forefinger. He's also offering me a lot of money to essentially steal from Elsie. Both are equally important to me at this moment.

He pats my hand. I don't move, but inside me everything shifts away in a slosh like the contents of a boat in a storm.

"And if I find nothing, I get nothing?"

"Correct. Otherwise, it might be tempting to humor her destructive impulses and collect the money anyway."

A tap on the glass makes us both look. Elsie's leaning on her cane, one hand to her chest. Not *that* way, not as though her heart is giving out. More *I'm so glad you're home* with a touch of *I know why you're here and it sucks*—her mouth tight, her eyes grateful.

Cap smiles again. "Think it over. I'll check in before you leave today."

Frigging rich boys.

Cap escapes on "personal errands" in the afternoon, leaving a recharged Elsie to oversee more content shuffling. We manage two more boxes of books signed by their authors. Another of advanced review copies, most containing personal letters asking her to provide a blurb—a line or two of praise that would've been printed on the back of the book. Those she says to recycle, which feels a little gross but right on the cover they all say *for promotional use only, not for resale*. No reason to cheat the authors by selling copies given out for free.

Still: "You really don't want any of these?" I'm holding a hardcover copy of a book called *Daughters of a Darker Past*, written by a woman I've never heard of. The famous books will always be famous; someone will always want a signed copy. This one, though—someone sweated to create three hundred and fifty-two pages of story and signed her name to it, and how many copies even still exist?

Elsie gives me another of those glares. "Do you imagine I'll be better soon, that I'll suddenly have the time and inclination to read them all?" She dismisses them with a flick of her wrist. "Writing is lying, and at some point you lose your appetite for lies."

She can't be serious. Ingrained sexism can explain a belief that women shouldn't be writers, but this is something else completely. Fiction isn't true in the way journalism is, but that doesn't make it *un*true. Right? Everything I've read in my life, every book I've loved . . .

"Was your book lies?" How cynical would you have to be to write something you don't believe in and then live off the money you make from it?

She narrows her eyes. "That one there, in your hand, you could burn it and not make a difference in the world for better or worse."

This is next-level contempt, and it sure sounds genuine. Has she always felt this way? Even about her own book?

Now she's staring out the window. She's picked up one of the Sharpies, holding it between middle and pointer finger and tapping it against her knee. Is this all just a nicotine withdrawal temper tantrum?

I replace the book in the box and write in obvious black letters on the cardboard top: *Misc: Inscribed Books to Be Sold or BURNED*. She glances at it, turns away. She doesn't tell me to cross it out.

R obin's feet dangle over the arm of the couch. He grins at me.

"You stink." I bat his feet before I notice Noa sitting across from him in the chair. "I didn't know you'd be here." Embarrassment wiggles in my gut for no good reason.

"I didn't either. Robin said we could go swimming, but to stop for you first."

When we used to go to Puffer's Pond as a group, we'd always go to the far side, away from the beach that the families used. Sometimes Alex would bring weed and we'd lie on blankets in the tall grass and blow smoke at each other while Hedy wove tiny grass baskets that Robin would wear like dainty fairy bowlers.

Is this good or bad, Robin's returning to the scenes of the old crimes? Is he saying *I'm back* or *goodbye* to these places? Or *goodbye* to everything? All I can do is to stick close and watch for danger.

"Let me grab a suit."

Noa's got a road bike she rented for the month. I like that she appreciates my bike when I bring it out. I like that she rides as though she and the bike and the road are one. She has tall-woman legs—long muscle instead of bunched—even though she's not a tall woman. If I had a list of things I like about Noa, I'm worried about how long it might be.

No one else is at the pond. I sit on the retaining wall on the bank for a few minutes, watching Robin and Noa kick their shoes off, shed their extra clothes, wade out to their waists. Eventually I follow.

Once we're clear of the fishing line snarls and hooks embedded in submerged logs and overhead branches, we slow. A heron wades along the shore where the brook comes in, ignoring us completely. We tread water, free of the day's heat and the clutter of the shore and the stress of boxes and diner grills and tables of grumpy people.

"Do you like it here? In Amherst, not the pond." It's easier to talk to Noa when we're merely heads on the surface of the water.

She studies my face. "I do, mostly. I'm ready to go, though."

I can't explain quite what it is about Noa. It's not like she's beautiful. Not the way Maya is, at least. She's just . . . she's an island, and as much as I tell myself not to, I want to swim to her shore.

"Do you miss Amsterdam?"

She's closed her eyes as she floats, her hands fluttering like gills. "My parents no longer live there. And there are so many tourists, because it's beautiful, because of the coffeeshops, because it feels safe and festive. It's treated like an amusement park."

She *is* a kind of beautiful. All the bits of her face that seemed common when I first met her—they're more complicated. Her voice, the motion of her hands as she speaks, how her eyes widen. I absorb them like my skin is permeable to her.

"But yes, I miss it. The cyclists, the safe roads. You'd love it." She opens her eyes and smiles. "The bridges—it sounds funny, doesn't it, to miss bridges?—but I miss walking over the canals on them. Once I found a collection of birds—is collection the right word? They stood at the foot of a bridge, all together, a heron watching over them. I miss them and the ducks in the canals. I miss my sister's houseboat terribly."

"Houseboat? She actually lives on a houseboat?" *On* or *in*? Does it really matter? I know, in theory, that people do these things, but in much the same way that I know that people have traveled to the moon. My life is such a tiny sliver of what's possible in this world.

"Yes. It's very small by American standards. It's outside of the city center, on a river in a green area. It's maybe not what you think of—more of a floating platform with a house on it. It rocks gently when a large boat passes, just enough that you can see the chain on the overhead lamp swing." She swirls her finger above her head. "Outside are swans and they harass the ducks that float by. Each houseboat has its own little garden between it and the sidewalk, all of them different. There are magpies everywhere—their wings flash when they fly. You can ride or walk all over the city from there, but when you're home it's quiet, and when it's time to sleep, the water holds you."

She speaks like a poet and I'm seeing it all. I can imagine it in a way that I don't imagine New Zealand, because when I think of New Zealand, I think of Maya, and all I see is her standing there, not the world around her.

"She's in Canada," Noa says. "My sister. I thought about returning now and staying at her place. She lets it out when she's away. But the truth is that I'm not ready to go home yet. I left because things ended badly with my girlfriend and I needed to be away."

I nod, dipping my chin into the water. Robin's floating on his back, ears submerged, feet moving just enough to keep him from sinking. The lines of his ribs still show through so clearly. "How will you know when it's time to go back?"

"I think there's a compass. Do you know what I mean?" She presses her palm to the hollow between her breasts for a moment. "And it will tell me when is right."

Do I have a compass? I've never been far enough from home to not know when or whether to return. I'm not sure I'd recognize what it felt like to be pulled away by something other than a person.

Have I been following other people's compasses this whole time?

Cap hadn't checked in with me by the time I left yesterday. He's not here this morning either. Elsie is, but I only know that because of a note on the kitchen counter telling me she's resting. I would probably have to rest frequently too if I'd had to spend the whole week with one or the other of her children.

Today my excavation hits a thick layer of kitsch. One whole box of coffee table books, none of them signed. *Maine: Land of Earth and Ocean. The Atlantic Coast Through the Years. Montana: Big Sky Forever.* Did she rotate through them, or at some point did she have a coffee table that doubled as a library stack? Whatever the answer, they appear to be in mint condition.

Clipped to the front of a book about clocks (yes, clocks) is a sheet of stationery with six words written where you'd expect a greeting: *Milkweed silk flutters in your hair.* These notes have become almost routine at this point. I slide the paper from its paperclip. It joins the others in *Misc: Mysteries*, those written on envelopes and stationery and in one case on the back of a recipe card for Meatball Surprise.

Later I add another card, one with an Andy Warhol-esque toaster on the front; inside it just says *If I had bought you this, would it have made a difference?* The zigzagging letters are familiar. This handwriting belongs to CKB, the war and wolf tree photographer. Was he a fan, a friend, a stalker? Are these the papers Cap dreams of?

The next box catches on a nail when I try to lift it, the side tearing free. Inside are old-school photo slides, hundreds stored in plastic containers of fifteen to twenty each. I pick one at random, hold it up to the glow of the light bulb. Children on a beach poking at something with sticks. The girl is taller than the two boys, her hair pulled tight by a bandana tied around her head. The littlest boy holds his hands to his heart in a middle-aged-man way. Dr. Galaxy was born old, I guess.

I pick out a different box, a different slide. This one's a baby on the lap of a little kid in a snowsuit, gender unidentifiable. I want it to be exciting, these glimpses of the home life of America's Treasure, but the fact is that family pictures are only ever interesting to family members, and often not even them.

Below the slides, in several manila envelopes, are black-and-white prints. The first one I pull out shows two teenage girls. One sits on a swing. The other pulls it back from behind. Both are laughing. Behind them is a small white farmhouse, a catalpa tree with long drooping pods.

I squint a bit and move toward the light to get a better look. Young Elsie on the swing is unmistakable to me, thanks to her author photo. The other girl is blonde, her curly hair pinned away from her distinctively heart-shaped face and pointy chin.

Another picture, of the blonde and a different girl, this one dressed in men's overalls that hang too loose on her bony shoulders. Her hair is much longer than the other girls' and is in a braid. She reminds me of a fox caught by the lens at twilight while trying to cross an open field.

Another photo, the three girls together, the blonde's arms

draped over the shoulders of the other two. Elsie looks at her indulgently. The long-haired one ducks slightly, as though about to spring away. This time she wears a dress like the others, trimmed with neat embroidery. I turn it over. *June 1947* is written there in a billowy script. No names, though.

One final picture. This shows a murder scene: the skeletons of trees twisted and hollowed by fire. In the center is a blackened circle. I pull the image closer, trying to make out the shape in the center. A charred collection of straight lines and arcs. A deer, turned to charcoal by the flames.

I drop it back into the envelope and close it up. Thanks to climate change, I've seen plenty of pictures of the aftermath of fires. Somehow, though, this one deer seen through Elsie's lens feels more real than any recent news footage.

The box is too damaged to move, so I assemble one of the new boxes and transfer the contents. After adding it to the list I'm keeping for Elsie, I make my own list in my notebook.

1. Who is in the picture with her?
2. Why did Elsie quit writing?
3. Elsie, what happened to you?

Mom arrives for her weekly hospice visit; it should've been yesterday, but shifting her schedule for Friday's emergency visit has meant bumping her Wednesday visit to today.

While she's with Elsie, I take off for lunch. I forgot to pack food anyway, so I head for the only logical destination.

Maya's working the CSA register today, selling the extras, like honey and canned tomatoes, that pull in members and nonmembers alike. She holds one finger up when she sees me.

I lean against the back wall and wait until the traffic jam at the register breaks and she's suddenly alone.

"Hey." Which can mean *I miss you* or *I love you* or *what the fuck* but in this case just means *I'm here and so are you.*

"Hey you. You on lunch?" she asks.

"Yeah. I thought I could pick up a yogurt." I walk over to the cold case and study the options.

She's close behind me. I can smell her there, feel the energy around her like she's lightning and I'm the girl standing on the bare hilltop, my hair on end. "You can have half of my food."

"Please tell me you have something better than lentils."

"I have lentils." The laughter just under her words warms me like a wood furnace in my chest. This is happiness. This is what I know of safety, the one thing that's stayed the same in whatever my life has become.

"Come on," she teases. "You know you want some."

Actually, her lentils are red ones, with curry and a smidge of coconut cream and a green salad beneath, and anyone would be a fool to say no. I follow her around the back after she signs out for a break. We sit on the cement loading dock, feet dangling off the edge. The red barn wall behind us heated up early in the day; by now it's a solar oven.

We share her fork, taking turns. "What were you thinking about inside?" she says. She catches me with my mouth full and waits patiently.

"Just stuff. Elsie."

"What about her?"

I tell her about the pictures, the writing on the back, the card, the things she's said. "I keep thinking all of it adds up in some way, but I don't know if it does."

"Adds up to what?"

"I'm not sure. I guess I just want to understand her better. Understand why she seems to hate being an author."

But I'm not even sure she *does* hate it. I picture the look on Elsie's face, the sound of her voice, as she said that when writing takes hold of you there is nothing else. I've felt that. I know that.

"Maybe it's just her age. Maybe she has dementia," says Maya. "My grandmother's personality is different now than before it developed."

"Yeah, could be." But Maya's grandmother became angry and started to treat Maya's dad like he was after her money. With Elsie, it's more like she's become a stranger to herself.

Maya pushes up against me. I lean back against her, the smell of the skin of her neck drawing me like nectar calls a bee. "How's Robin?"

That is an excellent question. I get out my notebook and write.

1. Worked at the diner for as many hours as he could get.

2. Made friends with a Dutch woman.

3. Hung out in his room.

I hand my notebook to her. She holds out her hand. I give her the pen.

4. Asked for a tattoo design.

5. Went to Secret House.

6. Stayed away from drugs.

Except drugs were never his problem. Alex died because she was in a bad relationship with a substance that didn't give a fuck about her. Robin was just the friend who went to straighten out the abusive ex and misjudged its strength.

Well, no: Robin went to the abusive ex and handed it a gun and said, "Me too." He was resurrected because we were lucky.

"Sometimes I can't imagine being away from him, you know? It's not like New Zealand isn't going to be great," I add when I see the worry in her eyes. "I just . . . I don't know if I can stop worrying about him and trust that he'll be okay."

Because people often aren't okay. So many people who put on a good show while dying on the inside. Including me, probably.

Definitely.

"You can't always stay here and watch him. You need to do your own thing."

People you love can be unbearably clueless. Maya's older sister is getting a PhD in linguistics and whatever else you do when you don't owe anyone anything. Maya's little brother is at Simon's Rock. The worst thing that happened to any of them in the entire time I've known Maya was their old dog dying, which is terrible but not quite the same ballpark.

Well, that isn't quite fair. The sudden shocking rip in the world that Alex caused tore through us all. Maya cried; she drew a maple tree on the plain wooden casket with the paints and markers Alex's parents laid out for everyone to use. She wasn't fully in the blast zone, though. Robin and Hedy were Ground Zero, and I'm walking through the debris every day.

If Alex were here . . . if they all were here, Robin would be on his back, soaking in the sun. Hedy would be watching everyone, drinking out of her water bottle with the mandala on it, the ends of her dark hair sunburned a copper color. And Alex . . . Alex would look at Maya, at me, and she'd say, "Babies, you're wicked cute." She'd lean in, pinch my cheek or Maya's. "Stay cute. Let us be the advance guard. We'll try it all out and report back to you. Just because we love you." And then she'd laugh like life was telling jokes only she could hear.

Hedy would be the one to pull her back. Hedy was always the grown-up, the one to steer us from danger, her husky voice sounding in the key of safety. Right up until she bailed on Robin.

I hope she's suffering every day.

Maya puts her hands over my ears, cooler than the air around us. "Start thinking more about mountains and sheep and less about the rest."

"You're not really selling it."

She pushes me, and I lie back on the loading dock. She does too. Above, the clouds make a thin film over a corner of the sky, threads blowing outward from them. She leans her head against my shoulder and sighs. I let go of Alex, of Hedy, and exist entirely here instead.

If this could last forever, if this could be all of life, it would be enough for me.

Elsie and I are back in the guest room. Sharpie in hand, packing tape at the ready, I open the first box. As promised by the label, it contains loads of tinsel garlands wound round and round like a nest for a Styrofoam bird.

"Nothing else?" she asks. She looks as though her rest rejuvenated approximately ten percent of her.

One hand in, I grope my way around. She can't possibly think—

"Can you lift it out, please?"

I obey. Once the box is empty except for a few stray glittery hairs, I move it close enough for her to verify there's nothing else in there.

"That can go to the hospice store if they'll have it. Christmas decorations never grow old."

I plop the garlands back in, minus the strands they've shed on the floor. "Seasonal decorations."

I wait for something along the lines of *young lady, in my day*, but it doesn't come. "We always had a fresh-cut tree when I was a child. When we were finished with it, we'd drag it to the edge of the woods and leave it there to dry. During the fire that summer, that deadwood burned hot and fast. I couldn't stomach fresh Christmas trees much after that. Somewhere up there"—I assume she means the attic and not Heaven—"should be the fake one."

I pick up the floor tinsel one strand at a time. "I'll keep an eye open for it. You do know you can't dispose of it the same way as the real ones, right? I'm not going to drag it out to the edge of your lawn and leave it. Plastic's forever."

"You're full of piss and vinegar, aren't you? Next box, please." She's amused, though. I've come to recognize the twitch of her lips, no matter how she tries to hide it.

"Your wish is my command."

16

No one's home. I can tell as soon as I lock my bike to the porch rail. Mom's left a note on the table.

I'm studying at the library tonight. Robin's working late too. If you need anything, text. Leftovers in fridge if you want them. Love you, baby. I wish she was here. I want to talk to her about Elsie. Not her medical info, but the rest—what Mom thought of Cap, what I thought of him and Dr. Galaxy both.

I hop in the shower. Once out, I sit at my desk in a towel. I used to do it all the time when I was writing *Dragon Girl*. Shedding everything of the world, just me and the story left. It worked best at night, when everything went quiet except the story in my head.

Now it doesn't work at all.

"Sometimes writers get blocked. You ever have that problem?" John Allen had been sitting at the desk in his home office, passing me old papers to file. Administrative things, student writing. "It happens to the best of us. I know it happened to your dad." He was like an artifact in a museum for me. Not the actual Alexander the Great, but a bit of pottery from a jar he'd drunk from, the imprint of the man's lips on its rim if you looked hard enough. I studied him endlessly for evidence of who my dad had been.

The stack he handed me next was a workshopped copy of a first chapter. The name at the top was Bear Newcomb. The book, finished while he was at UMass, was the critics' darling the year it came out. It didn't win *all* the awards, but do you really need a clean sweep? This, in my hand, had become that, the book in the bookstore window, and the man handing it to me had helped guide it into the world.

"I guess." I dragged my mind back to the question of writer's block. "Sometimes." Not really. I sat down every night and wrote until my mind ran empty. By the time I returned the following night, it would be full again.

"It can be a tough thing. The writers I know—hell, me too—find that it's best to change things up. Smoke a little pot, get drunk under the stars. Write in the nude. You ever do that?"

I wasn't entirely sure what to answer. *No*, and I'm uptight. *Yes*, and I'm the girl typing naked in her room. He looked like nothing could surprise him, though, like he was asking if I used Times New Roman or not. "Kind of? I write in a towel after I take a shower at night."

"See? You have the right idea already. Closer to the primal, that's where writers need to be."

Now, I jump up from my desk and dress quickly in shorts and a tee, add a ratty sweater for good measure. Real writers like Bear Newcomb and John Allen might write in the nude, but not me. Not in this skin, not in this life, not again.

I spend an hour looking at pictures of people's dogs and flowers and babies on Instagram before I'm ready to try. It hurts in the center of my chest, right beneath my sternum. Writing eats channels in there, a ravenous worm searching for sustenance. All I have to do is feed it, but what? Nothing seems to work.

New document. New formatting. I light the stub of a candle at the corner of my desk and imagine.

The trouble is that I could feel everything Dragon Girl did. I could smell the fires and touch the stones and hear that very specific sound of scales slipping against each other as dragons moved. That first moment, the one where everything ached like her bones were shifting inside her, as the coils of loneliness tightened around her neck and she longed to change—I felt that loneliness, that longing. I was there with her. Now I'm trying to feel things I just can't.

This town is full of writers with writing careers. People who probably never just sit at their desks watching words and characters wither in front of them. When they do struggle, it's over brilliant work and not just pages of meaningless text. I'm not a writer on a fast track to anywhere, not an MFA student, not even a talented youngster with a big-name mentor. I'm just a girl who didn't finish high school, working for a woman who only wrote one book.

I stare at the screen some more. I'm sweating in my sweater, and the candle wick is drowning in a sea of molten wax.

There were nights when the wind blew so hot that it was impossible to sleep. Dragon's breath, the elders called it, as though the beasts crouched just outside the light of the lanterns and blew at the huts in an attempt to tear them from the land and send them drifting across the plains.

On those nights, she would lie against a stone outside and search for patterns in the sky. Which direction was right, which would take her to the home she'd never had?

AND THEN THE DRAGON COMES AND THERE IS NO GRAND MEANING IN ANY OF IT, NO SUDDEN REALIZATION LIKE AT THE END OF THAT STORY

IN DUBLINERS AND CRAP THIS SHOULDN'T BE WRITTEN.

I erase it all again. I know there's no shame in writing things that don't win prizes, don't make faculty members weep with pride and envy. Deeper, though, I know something else.

John Allen told me that I needed to study more and much better work if I wanted to even think about writing well. *Well*, not brilliantly but *well*, as though good punctuation should be my goal. "Read some Updike," he said. "Read some David Foster Wallace, hell, some Kerouac. Real writers study the best."

Real writers. Real writers smoke pot and write in the nude. They take on every experience that comes their way. There is nothing they won't try.

I am not a real writer.

You want to know why else I'm not a real writer?

Because real writers don't delete their novels.

One entire novel, the only good thing I built for myself after my world collapsed, deleted completely from existence in a single afternoon. Gone forever, except for the bits I try to write again and again.

I close the laptop and blow out the candle.

Friday morning, Cap takes Elsie out for breakfast before he leaves for home. I sit in the guest room in peace and work on the annotated list of signed books. Most of the inscriptions fall in one of two categories: holiday business pleasant or gushy fan overkill. People will pay money for them—that's a fact—but only because people will pay money for anything. Collectors and fetishists come from the same family. Survivalists are their demented cousins, whose fetish is destruction and whose collections come with expiration dates. And I . . . am someone with a brain that needs to chill out.

It's funny to me how some of the books have only a signature. Male authors mostly, as though certain that their mark on paper will be plenty for her.

"What it means, bud, is that your book never gets read and is eventually written up as *one hardcover copy with author signature* by me, to be sold to someone only interested in the fact that Elsie McAllister once owned it. Good work, Arnold Snobbler." I double-check his name. Poor guy.

The second-to-last book, *The Roses of Penobscot Bay*, published 1894, shows obvious signs of age and use. Inside, it's signed—but not by the author, Father Joseph Barrett. The inscription is written with graceful loops and swirls.

Dear Elsie,

Do you remember the smell of the roses along the shore, the taste of the rosehips? That day with the three of us and the boat—how magical it was. I like to think that we're on the waves still, all of us, always.

P.

I recognize the writing, no need to compare it to the card upstairs. P and I both want to know what happened to Elsie. And now I want to know what happened to the three of them. Because one of the girls in the picture has to be P, and one is Elsie, and the third one is . . . ?

I put the book on Elsie's wheelchair. She'll want to keep it.

Cap catches me in the guest room, busy with my annotation. He pauses at the door before entering and closing it behind him. Such a simple thing, a closed door, but the sound of it clicking into place makes me feel like all the air has been sucked from the room. Fuck this, fuck the crawling sensation along my spine and the sinking sensation everywhere else and the deer-in-the-headlights look I must have.

"Have you given some thought to my request? I'd really love to know what you think. So I can make other plans if needed." He keeps on smiling, as if that makes the fact that he's threatening my job okay.

As it so happens, I have given it some thought. I've thought about what ten thousand dollars might buy, and how Elsie doesn't strike me as confused, and how I hadn't believed she'd actually destroy anything but now a box of books in the corner of the room begs to differ. Mostly, I keep thinking about how this is a situation where yes means nothing more than keeping the possibility alive. My promise is just to watch for her writing. Not to give it to him.

"Sure," I say.

"Wonderful." Cap glances around the room, opens the nearest box, the one with the children's books. "I have friends in antiquarian book circles. I should check in with them about these."

A hotheaded hornet circles in my brain. "Elsie already has someone." Whether she does or not, I'm not letting Cap have this win.

"I'm sure she does, but that doesn't mean they'll give her a fair price. You wouldn't want someone taking advantage of *your* mother, would you?" He gives me another of those earnest looks.

"All the money's being donated anyway."

"She's donating it?" He glances down at the box again, but I still catch the flash of annoyance. "Do me a favor—she has some valuable pieces in storage. If you think she's being foolish about any, text me a picture?"

He takes a business card from his wallet and hands it to me. *Chris Harkness, Dealer in Antiquities*, tasteful cream cardstock, tasteful bronze font. His mother raised him well.

"I'm not sure I'm a good judge." I pull out the tinsel box and open it. "This, for example. Not valuable?"

He grimaces. "No, absolutely not. Sometimes I question what she's done with her life, aside from the book."

The brain hornet buzzes more loudly. "Other than raise

you?" I shouldn't hate him quite this much. This isn't my house, my stuff, my mom's life.

He suddenly looks . . . different. Not mad, not sad, not fake. Just different. Real. "I'm sure you see her as a brilliant writer and imagine she was the same at everything she did. That's not the case with brilliant people in general, or with her in particular." He seals his realness away again. "Thanks again for keeping an eye on the contents of the attic. I truly don't know what you might find up there."

He gives me a tip of his imaginary hat and leaves. A few minutes later I hear the front door as well. The house feels emptier and I feel lighter and this work feels so much more complicated.

I eat my PB&J on the deck while standing at the railing. By the time I return to the guest room, Elsie's seated and holding the book I left for her. She looks exhausted again. "We need to start a new box."

I go get one, set it up, and wait, Sharpie in hand.

She hands me the book. "Please label the box *To Go*."

I keep thinking there's more to it than that, so I wait.

Finally, she speaks again. "We'll need a burn permit and a barrel to use for things like this."

You've got to be kidding me. America's Treasure really has hired me to burn books. "If you don't want people to see the inscription, you could always take that page out. It's a pretty book."

"Do what I ask. You agreed to it before I offered you the job."

"But . . ." But what? But that was when I thought we'd be dumping musty old holiday decorations?

Shock silences me. She takes the list from me and examines it. "All the rest of these, they can go to Frederick. There's an address book in the utility drawer in the kitchen. If you look in there you can find an entry for . . ." She pauses, fingers pressed to her forehead. I can almost see the gears inside, desperate for a thorough oiling. "Forsythe's Fine Books. Call and ask to speak directly to Frederick. Mr. Forsythe. Explain that you work for me and detail what we have. He'll know what to do."

She's crumpling as I watch. I don't have words for what I see happening to her. It's kind of like frost spreading over a window, faster and faster.

"Ms. McAllister? Should you lie down?"

She looks at me. *No*—that's what her mind is saying. Her body's telling it to quit the heroics and rest. "I think I might." She tries to stand and wavers, halfway up.

I stand up too. She grips my hand, clings with a porcelain claw. Together we walk from the room, down the hall, to the dim light of her bedroom. I pause at the doorway. She keeps moving, shuffling tiny steps until I continue too, inhaling still air and a faint powdery smell. The blinds are cracked to let a little light in, and it stretches across the yellow chenille bedspread in perfect parallel lines.

She leans against the bed when we reach it. I don't move as she holds tight to me and sits down. She waits. I'm not sure for what, until I notice the slippers on her feet. I kneel and take them off. Her right foot twists a little, the toes gripping a nonexistent pencil.

"Does that hurt?"

She doesn't answer, just tries to swing her legs up. She doesn't make it more than halfway. I lift them as gently as I can. They're so thin, so light. I set the O2 tank on the nightstand. She's drifting between asleep and awake, so I pull the bedspread up to cover her legs.

Do I walk away, or sit on a chair in the hall, or sit in her room? Call Mom for help? No, Mom's in class and this is my job. Call 911? No, I can't call 911 because an old woman is tired and needs a nap. But I also don't feel right going far away.

In the end, I move a chair next to her door and sit there, reading about the roses of Penobscot Bay.

Elsie's back up by the time I leave for the day. I exit after a neighbor arrives to have dinner with her. Once home, I shower and dress in a worn tank and ancient PJ bottoms before returning to my desk.

Outside someone yells—a welcoming call to a friend, not anger. Farther into town an ambulance siren sounds, heading north, away from us. The girls in the apartment are drinking on the postcard-sized deck. I can hear the clink of ice mixed in a glass pitcher and fragments of conversation. Something about chemistry, something about working late.

I ache. This is life. I know *Dragon Girl* wasn't about any of this, but it also was. She saw her world the way I do mine—how all the tiny things, like pale green ferns shimmying in a breeze, can feel like everything of importance. Only at certain moments, though, only when you hold still and see.

I love it all. I hate so much—dying songbirds, dying forests, dying hopes for anything like justice or a future—but I love it too. And somehow at the point where the writing took over, it was as though the story came from all of this, this big messy world funneled through me, its magic distilled into words.

What made it all go away? Maybe Elsie was right and it was just a lie. Maybe cold, flat reality is the only thing left to write.

I pick up the copy of *Tongues* I took from Elsie's and open it. It's hard to imagine that there are answers here that haven't already been found by the academics who've studied the crap out of it for decades. Still, I turn to a fresh page in my notebook and begin my excavation.

The three acts of the book are simple:

1. Frannie, the protagonist, is twelve and lives in rural Maine in 1947. Frannie's brother Luke and his best friend Harry come home from World War II changed. Luke is no longer the warm, loving brother Frannie remembers. Harry, who wants to be a minister, spends all his time with Luke offering spiritual guidance. A girl from a local German family is found strangled. It's Luke, right? Because he's come home all weird and everyone hates Germans, and soldiers hate them most of all. Harry tells Frannie that war's rules run contrary to God's and it's hard to find a way home.

2. Basically all of Maine catches fire. This part is true. Mr. Cooper showed us reprints of 1947 newspapers that described the scorched places, the inferno that devoured much of Mount Desert Island and all of Millionaire's Row and required a rescue of islanders via bulldozer. But the fires happened everywhere in Maine, not just the island, because a drought had turned the entire state into tinder. In the book, a fire starts near Frannie's town and continues through their farm and on out to the ocean. Luke joins the men fighting the fire, even though no one trusts him anymore, and they're overrun. Frannie and the women of the town gather on the beach, with the rising tide on one side and the flames on the other and only one another to depend on.

3. When everything burns out, Luke and Harry have died in the fire. A written confession is discovered in Harry's things. Luke knew it was him all along but wouldn't give him up to the cops because they were soldiers together. Frannie comes

to terms with Luke dying, and war, and fires, and how to be a person in a fucked-up world, and everything is poignant.

That doesn't really do it justice, but I've read it before and these notes are for me, not for a grade.

The following are all confirmed facts about Elsie McAllister's life:

1. She was a girl living in rural coastal Maine during the summer of 1947.

2. Her father was the town doctor and her mother was a housewife.

3. Her town did burn during that terrible October.

4. She did have a brother who went to war and returned home injured.

5. No German girls were murdered in Maine that year.

6. Elsie left home at eighteen and never looked back. Like outta there, gone and done. No secrets shared to tabloids either; whatever the reasons for her leaving, her family and the other locals carried them to their graves.

In the book, Frannie has a best friend named Ruthie. Total tomboy, totally coded queer, and I may have had a wicked crush on her when I read *Tongues* for the first time. While there's no proof—Elsie's hold on her privacy is pretty extreme—everyone assumes Ruthie was based on Elsie's real-life best friend, Martha Bower.

Let's assume Ruthie is Martha, and she's totally into girls. Which could mean requited or unrequited love existed. I'm not the only person to have wondered about LGBTQ subtext in *Tongues*, but I may be the only one with potential evidence that it wasn't subtext in Elsie's life.

After an hour of online research, I've learned surprisingly little about Martha Bower. She left for Portland after graduation and vanished. Even Elsie's biographers found nothing about her beyond a year of secretarial school after high school. No news items, no social media accounts, no Reddit leads, no obituaries for someone of the right age with that name. Rather than go down an expensive rabbit hole of post-1950s census data and PIs, I'm going to trust that Martha Bower is simply not to be found.

I already knew Elsie had married and had three kids; the internet informs me that she met Roger Harkness in the '60s and they were together until his death about fifteen years ago. That doesn't cancel out a potential romance between her and Martha when they were young. Maybe meetups when Elsie traveled.

And maybe Martha is P. Romantic books about roses, cards suggesting Elsie's changed—sounds like an unhappy breakup to me.

Or is P the other girl from the photos? There were three of them, after all, and Elsie is my only positive ID.

Existing *Tongues* scholarship isn't going to be much help with this. The history of Martha/Ruthie and Elsie/Frannie is a sliver of the overall academic interest around Elsie and her book. Their friendship isn't that complicated or even that important to the plot. It's the older brother and his friend, the murder, the family and community that matter.

Which is not to say that all scholarly interest lies in those pieces of the story. Multiple generations of readers have lost their minds over a single scene so out of place that it seems to have come from another book entirely. It's as though Elsie's editor just tuned out for a page and a half.

In a nutshell, Frannie's out biking on a road by the ocean. She sees a strange girl standing by the side of the road. She decides, out of the blue, to stop and talk with her. The girl has a monologue about the milkweed along the hillside down to the ocean. She describes watching a caterpillar every day, for whole days, until finally it disappears into a chrysalis. After that, she continues to wait and watch, *as patient as the earth waiting for rain*, until, on *a day the sun loved dearly*, the butterfly struggles free of the chrysalis, dries its wings, and flies away.

That's Butterfly Girl, as she's come to be known. There's at least one band named after her and weird-ass fanfic where she's from another dimension or is a time traveler. A whole little fan culture grown out of a character whose single scene doesn't advance the plot in any way. She never appears again. The hillside never burns. People assume she's metaphor, but for what? There's no theme of emergence and transformation to be found elsewhere in the book, other than the whole coming-of-age thing, and the metaphor is so cliché that it feels beneath Elsie. Modern critique—at least what I skim—is best summed up with this catchy line: "She is the ethereal trapped in the modern world, the fae heart that beats out of time with the industrial age."

Of course she is.

If Martha isn't P, is Butterfly Girl? Even if she is, I still have no idea how to identify her or verify their friendship.

So I'm back where I started. All I have is one romantic book, one concerned message on a card, photos of three girls. A series of random sentences sprinkled throughout the attic. One old woman who hates her book and her awards and fiction itself— maybe. So many questions. I'd like some answers, please.

The phone rings at 8:04 a.m. How do I know it's 8:04? Because I've been sound asleep, and in the process of dragging the phone to my ear I come face to face with the time. Awfully frigging early for a Saturday morning, that's what I think as I try to figure out who Paul Harkness is and why I should want to talk with him.

I croak out a hello as my heart goes from zero to sprint. She's dead, already, and so are my chances of New Zealand, and it's also sad, right?

"Holi? This is Paul Harkness."

Is he contacting me using the guts scraped from his mother's black rotary phone? Because otherwise he should know that I know who's calling. "Yeah. Is something wrong?"

On the phone he sounds less like a fussy old man and more like a doctor. Parents probably expect confidence when they're calling with a kid who's swallowed a cup full of pennies to see if it will make a magnet stick to their belly.

"Wrong? No, not at all. I was just calling to see when you'll be stopping in at my mother's today." Meaningful pause. "Is this too early to call? I'm so sorry."

You're a pediatrician and it didn't occur to you that I, a teen, might be sleeping late on a Saturday? I sit up. "No, it's fine. Um, I hadn't been planning on being there today. I—"

"Oh. My mother's under the impression that you are. Remember, we talked about you doing extra time? If you haven't yet arranged hours with her, perhaps you could at her house today?"

"I guess. I won't be there before . . ." I look at the time again, in case I read it wrong the first time. Nope. "Not until ten."

"Good, I'm so glad. She'll be relieved. And you can stay for the day?"

I think about boundaries and the importance of fresh air and exes and plane tickets. "Sure, I can do that." Screw it, I'm a capitalist whore.

I ride to Elsie's instead of busing, hoping to clear my head. The farmers' market crowd fills the Common with their mesh bags and graying hair—either neatly ponytailed or free-range—and toddlers in Swedish clothing. Car doors and unsignaled pullaways from the curb are the hazards du jour. I buzz out of the center like a mustang hitting the range. Joggers pushing baby strollers, weekend bikers stretching their legs, students sneaking out of houses and regretting the things they did last night, a gaggle of kids headed for the park—I simultaneously love and hate this place. I speed on by.

I'm making lists as I go. The two old white men stopped on the sidewalk, one of them raising his hand in the air, then bringing it down with a slap on his thigh, both of them laughing. The short Black woman at the bus stop, nose in a paperback copy of a book whose title I can't see. The scent of wild grapes drifting from a thicket of scrub along a field by the river. Breath, breath, breath, the air damp and still, the whispers of coming afternoon storms in my ears. Just a road that, if I don't look too far ahead, lasts forever.

There's no sign of Elsie when I enter through the slider. I cough, loudly, set my helmet on the counter with a sharp crack. Zip. Down the hall I go, flat-footed to make the most noise possible. Her door is slightly ajar, so I peer in. She's curled on her side, eyes closed, under the chenille. The wheeze of her breath reassures me that she's alive.

So, yes, clearly relieved that I'm here. I take out her notebook and scrawl a quick message to let her know that I'll be in the attic. After leaving the torn-out page on her dresser, I trudge upstairs.

So much stuff. Every single box needs to be sorted through before it goes downstairs.

No, it doesn't *have* to be. I could simply glance in and correct labels as needed. But I'll admit that the whole burn-the-book issue has me thinking that maybe Cap's right. What I see of Elsie may be a costume designed to hide her mind's decay.

I open the first box of the day. The outside says *Figurines*. The inside says what the fuck.

It does contain figurines, of a sort. I expected those ceramic ones—little kittens and red-cheeked girls in bonnets and boys carrying ice skates. What we have is an entire army. Little metal soldiers, carefully painted by hand. They're wrapped in tissue paper—I don't bother to unwrap every single one, just enough to feel confident that there aren't any kittens mixed in. Beneath them is a folded piece of what feels like a putting green. I remove enough soldiers to pull it out and discover it's a replica of the Gettysburg battlefield. Not that I recognize it; there's a handy name tag pinned to the bottom with a dollhouse-size safety pin.

I put everything back as I found it. A few passes of the Sharpie add *Civil War* to the figurines label, and I push it to the space for boxes to go downstairs. It could belong to one of the kids, but I'm laying money on Roger Harkness, the Treasure's consort. I envision him as a cardboard cutout to be set up at events. In the pictures I've come across online he's just Joe Guy in age- and era-appropriate clothes.

More random collections await me. Packing peanuts, an entire box of them. Hand-knit baby clothes—tiny sweaters with matching hats and booties—all tastefully done in pink and blue. Here and there a defiant lemon outfit makes a lonely stand against gender conformity. Pinned to one is a page of flowered stationery with a single line as cryptic as the others.

The sky is bluer through the limbs of a tree.

The writer has a point. What it has to do with baby clothes, I have no idea. I add it to *Misc: Mysteries.*

When I carry the baby clothes box downstairs, Elsie's standing in the entryway to the living room. Her mint-green track suit makes her look like a little marzipan decoration, or the type of figurine I didn't find in the box of soldiers. She even has a bit of color to her face.

"I didn't expect you today." Subtext: she doesn't want me here.

"Paul called and told me that you were. This morning," I add, as if the time makes a difference.

"No, that's incorrect. I didn't expect you."

An impasse—that's the correct term for this. We may as well lay out the Gettysburg rug and prepare the infantry.

She takes a few steps forward and gives a faint but unmistakable royal wave toward the box in my hands. "What is that?"

A frigging box. I smile sweetly. "Baby clothes. Handmade. They're really cute."

"Really cute? Is that what you'd write about them?" Another wave, an imperial *screw that*. I can't help wanting to impress her, wanting her to see me as more than a waster of words.

I try again. "I'd say they were made with delicate, perfect stitches. That someone had loved the children they were made for, or . . . or had needed money so much that they would put love they should've given elsewhere into things made for a stranger's child. I'd say they were boxed away like memories that had lost their meaning." I'd say anything if it would mean she'd look at me as if she were impressed. Or if she'd even just smile.

And she won't. "Yes, I suppose you would say those things. Overstatement, of course, and too much sentimentality. They can go in the collection to be given away. There should be a shelter that needs such things."

When I bring the next box down, Elsie's vanished. She doesn't want me here. I don't want to be here. They're paying me far more than a home health aide gets paid and I know far less. As much as I want to call Mom to come, Elsie doesn't need a daily nurse. Just someone who knows when a nurse is necessary, and that's not me.

I decide to tell her I'm leaving. I locate her in the study. She's asleep in the desk chair. In her hands rests an open paperback. I creep closer and get a glimpse of the cover.

Hers and Hers: A Lucky Ladies Romance. There are two women on the cover, one cupping the chin of the other and leaning in for a kiss.

I crouch to read the back.

Laura is a woman with a mission: to make the best cupcakes in her hometown of Elliotville, Maine. All she needs is an assistant. Enter Brenda, a woman with a hidden past and a deft hand at mixing batter. Together they may just manage to bring true cupcake delight to the town, but what they bring each other could be so much more—if they can let go of their pasts and find their way into the present.

If the creased cover is any indication, this isn't Elsie's first go-round with Laura, Brenda, and the cupcakes. What the hell, Elsie McAllister? You tell me that *I'm* sentimental?

And just like that, the answer's clear to me. All she ever wanted was to write chaste gay romance, only she was trapped by her frigging fame. Writing feels like a lie because she hasn't been true to herself.

Wait, no, there's another possibility. She did keep writing, only she did it under the name of—I tilt my head—Monica Meyers. The secret of America's Treasure is that she's anonymously devoted herself to her true love: two women, one happily ever after.

Elsie sucks in a breath. I jump back. She opens her eyes and looks at me, looks at the book, looks at the motionless clock on the wall.

"Good book?" I can't help but ask.

She gives me a wide-eyed, confused look, like she's not even quite sure who I am. Screw it. I'll have to stick around until the aide Paul hired gets here. Maybe Chris has been right about her mental state.

"I'm sorry. I didn't mean to startle you. Do you want me to help you move to your room? Or to the couch? I can work downstairs for now, so you can reach me." I hold out my arm to her.

She shakes her head. "Let me stay here for a few minutes. Just until my head clears."

"Of course, whatever you want." I move to leave the room. But when I drop my eyes to the book, I see that she's holding it closed and close, one hand splayed over the back jacket copy.

I get it now. "Or do you want me out of here so that you can hide this wherever it goes?"

"It's none of your business." That royal look again: I Am America's Treasure, Look Upon Me and Despair.

"You really think that's gonna shock me?" The book totally shocks me, but only because it's her. "I'm eighteen. I have a girl-friend." Had. "I know at least as much as you do."

"You are very much mistaken."

My phone buzzes. I ignore it. "Okay, whatever. You know more about hot sapphic action than I do. You win." I hold out my hand again. "Let me put it away for you. Or help you up."

Her breathing comes harder. She does need help. She needs help all the time, just not from me. Still, she shakes her head.

"I'm not going to read your book," I promise. "You can stay all the way in the back of that closet and keep the light off. It doesn't bother me. I just don't want you to die right in front of me because you're too afraid to let me help."

She looks so tiny, tied to her tank, not even allowed to keep her secrets anymore.

"I get it. It's private. Let me help, though. I can put it on your bed, under the mattress even. Then I'll come back to help you."

Her grip on the book tightens, the knife-points of her knuckle bones sharp under the drape of pale skin. "Give me the encyclopedia volume on the table."

Please tell me that she has a book-sized hole carved out in the middle of the encyclopedia. Please, please, please. I hand her the surprisingly light book, and . . . holy crap, she has a book-sized hole carved out in the middle.

She casually tucks the paperback in. Has she checked out life outside of her house lately? Noticed Pride parades in the paper? This isn't really necessary.

She hands it back. I replace it on the shelf—*M* for My Secret Hiding Place, I guess—and resist an overpowering urge to examine everything in the house for more secret compartments. Instead I dip my arm toward Elsie, and she grasps it with the strength of someone who really, really doesn't want to fall.

Once she's rested for a bit, we return to the Westminster Box Show. This afternoon I'm handler for children's skates, and notebooks full of schoolwork and report cards, and women's summer clothes from what looks like the eighties. The soldier box is the last I open for her. I watch her closely, curious. Slowly, her face takes on one of those complicated expressions out of a closeup in an art house film.

"Oh, Roger." She lifts a single figure and unwraps it. A tiny drummer continues his silent drumming, one stick up, one touching down. "You foolish, funny man."

Whatever the reality of *Hers and Hers* is, there's also this: deep and genuine affection for a dead man who loved him some Civil War paraphernalia.

Sharpie in hand, I wait for direction. "Lucy," she says. "Lucy will want these."

First time anything has been set aside for any person other than a book dealer. First I've heard of Lucy.

"It's time to stop. I think I'll have a glass of water and then I'll return to my room."

She waits. I get the hint.

The glasses in the kitchen have blue stripes around the rim. They're designed for fairies, I think, or children who don't drink more than two thimblefuls of water at a time. I fill one and bring it to her.

Her hand trembles as she lifts the glass to her mouth and back again. I study the boxes, listening to rather than watching her. One sip, two, three. She leaves the glass half full. Or is it half empty? Does it even make a difference to anyone other than cheerful pessimists and pedants?

I stay until the aide arrives. She's a small woman with a walk that says *don't mess with me* and black hair with purple tips. We introduce ourselves, adding a Portuguese accent to the facts I have about her, and she asks how the day shift went. I explain that I'm only here to pack and unpack and pack again. She purses her lips.

"She really shouldn't be left alone. I assumed she had daytime coverage."

I want to say it's not my fault, but maybe it kind of is? If I just said I wouldn't work they'd have to make other plans. "I don't know why they don't have round-the-clock help. It's not my call. I'm just here for . . ." I wave my hand at the ceiling, as if I'm the second coming of Michelangelo.

She looks me over. I focus on the two rings on her left hand. Plain gold circle on the second finger—wedding band, I assume—and a broad silver band inlaid with what looks like amethyst on her thumb. My notebook calls to me; common sense tells me the details can wait.

Whatever she's looking for, she's realized I don't have it. "I'll talk to her son again. This is foolish. All it takes is one bad fall."

Robin's bike leans against the wall in the living room, but his room is empty when I get home. Mom's left a note on the table: *At library, then study group, home late.*

I text Robin: **Where is u**

Picked up a shift. Home 10:30ish.

K luv you

Saturday, dinnertime, a hot late-summer day. I head back into the thick, lazy light in search of takeout.

By the edge of town I pass the two rocks topped by metal silhouettes of Emily Dickinson and Robert Frost. Would they even have anything to say to each other? Poetry isn't a common language any more than novels are; poets argue all the time. On the other side of town is Emily's actual grave, her headstone behind a waist-high wrought iron fence, dotted with change and flowers and odder offerings. I have no idea where Robert is buried or what people might leave him there.

I'm halfway up the street when I see Noa. She's alone too, wearing loose overall shorts and a green tank, her hair damp. I hold up my hand to wave but hesitate. I'd hate to be that person—the one waving to someone who'd hoped to avoid them by ducking down an alley.

Only now she's waving back. When she reaches me, she leans forward into a polite hug and a kiss on the cheek. She smells of almond and clean damp skin, exactly like a girl outside on a humid day as a thunderstorm builds over the hills *should* smell. I'm seeing all the details—the pale moustache above her lip, the little amethyst stud in the second hole in her right ear, how sweat makes her skin shimmer—and I want to stay exactly this close to her.

"Hey." I sound funny to myself. A recorded voice, probably not mine.

"Hi." She waits. I wait. It feels like everyone's waiting to see if we might be able to make conversation, but of course no one is. We're alone on a tiny island in the sidewalk river.

"What are you up to?" This level of awkward is ridiculous. I point toward the white bubbles of clouds. "It's probably gonna rain."

She smiles at me like she can see all the thoughts playing tag in my head. "I saw that. On my weather app." She tucks her thumbs in the sides of her overalls.

Mostly strangers—that's us. We're not falling in love. Nothing magical happens between us in the next scene. That's generally not the way things work in life.

Remembering that takes the pressure off. "If you're not doing anything, you want to grab something to eat with me? I'm getting takeout."

She looks up at the clouds again. When she looks back at me, I see the tiny color lines that fan outward from her pupils like daisy petals. Details, details, all tucked away in the strange lockbox of my mind.

"And maybe we could watch a movie? At home. Like a date night." A supernova of embarrassment sears my skin.

"Are you wandering the streets looking for a woman to ask on a date?" She has a Mona Lisa smile that makes me think she's laughing at me, but it could be *with* me.

"Not really. I mean, no, not at all. Or maybe I was. Sometimes I don't know what I'm doing."

Is it my imagination or is she blushing a little? "So this isn't a date?"

And suddenly I like this, this opening the curtains and being honest. "I don't think so. Nah, it's just dinner and a movie."

We both laugh. She links her arm through mine and tugs a little. "Then, friend, shall we begin?"

It is enchanted, though, all of this. The thunderheads building over the Holyoke Range, still in the pale puffy stage. The little kid with their long hair over their face as they crouch down to look at a beetle on the sidewalk; the clean-cut white dad waiting, watching, a sleeping baby in his arms. The colored tile with a line from Emily Dickinson splashing brightness amidst the red brick of the building. The Black man with his long locs pulled back in a ponytail, browsing the rolling shelves of used books outside the bookstore. The sound of lo-fi coming from the tea shop as the door opens and a couple of high school students exit, the white boy with bangs drifting over his eyes, the brown girl with long straight hair and glasses and an electric look in her eyes, like she's completed an experiment that will change everything and only she knows it.

And us, arm in arm, walking up the street through air that is seventy-eight percent water, just like we are. I don't pull away. This closeness is honest too. Magic passes through us all, every day, all the time, and there are moments when it shows itself, when you can feel it like power, like joy, like everything in a single bolt of being alive.

That moment is now.

✸✸✸

This is us: two girls sitting on the couch, eating noodles with chopsticks and watching a movie about a French DJ in the nineties, a fan blowing sticky air across our faces. It's a good movie. Melancholy, full of Daft Punk and French house. When it's over, it's dark outside, the incoming thunderstorm spreading its molasses fingers across everything. The rumbles run through me, and my animal brain tells me to take cover.

But I'm not that kind of animal tonight. Running away isn't what I want to do.

We've shifted, each of us on an end of the couch. Noa's cross-legged; I've got my legs sprawled over more than my fair share of the space. The only light on is in the kitchen, and it makes a yellow trail into the living room, over the scratched-up wood floor and onto the ficus tree.

"Tell me about your work," Noa says. She's tucked her hair behind her ears. Only tiny wisps escape, blown by the fan.

"My work? It's—" I almost say *boring*, but I realize that's not true. "Basically I get paid not to snoop, but also to kinda snoop."

"Snoop?" She wrinkles her nose. She does that a lot. It's not about disgust, I've figured out. It's when she doesn't know something, and when she thinks something is kind of funny but not quite to the point that she laughs.

"Yeah." I wipe my forehead, the sweat that collects along my hair. "I sit in an attic alone and look through boxes and boxes of old stuff. Elsie's. Elsie McAllister, the author? You probably don't know her work."

"Of course I do." Now she looks like she wants to wrinkle her nose in disgust. "Do you know any Dutch writers? Besides Anne Frank," she adds before I can speak.

"I don't think so." It's embarrassing. Aside from some basic World War II history, I know very little about the Netherlands. Or, if we're honest, anywhere else in the world.

She doesn't follow up, instead touching my big toe with the tip of one finger. "A famous author's attic must be full of secrets."

I want to tell her about everything. The book Elsie wants me to burn. The romance novel that she stashes in a hollowed-out encyclopedia. Only, if she's gone far enough to hide books inside other books . . . it's not my place to out someone, or even to speculate on their orientation with other people.

"It's mostly ordinary stuff." I tell her about the soldiers and the baby clothes. "Things that anyone's grandmother might keep in an attic, except they're hers, so they're famous by association."

She's taken an ice cube from her empty water glass, and she touches it to the tip of each of my toes. I thought I understood what tonight was, but the feel of the ice and the shiver of my skin confuse me again. I'm not even sure if she's doing this on purpose, much less how I should respond. "And you? Are you famous by association?"

"No, of course not." I hold my glass to my face, the condensation and sweat transferring back and forth between me and it. I'm not in a teen romance; I'm in a noir, trapped between a sultry dame and an approaching storm, trouble thick between us.

"Have you read her book?" It's the only thing I can think of to say. I've never actually made a pass at someone. On the one hand, I want nothing to change in my life, but on the other hand, my body argues that it's time to move forward. I haven't even been able to touch myself for a really long time and not being able to write *or* to get off is a unique kind of hell.

It's not as simple as plain old sex, though. What I want is

that, but also this: sitting on the couch and laughing about random things or talking about Elsie, or anything, really, as long as we're doing it together.

"Yes, it's a very American take on World War II. Only the returning soldiers to think about, the German family as a prop. The writing is . . ." She pauses, sniffing the air for the word she wants. "Devastating. The story, though—it's as if the center lacks balance."

Noa's right, the writing is devastating. It's what makes the book special. Elsie captured a single tree burning in a way that burned my heart too. A writer is so much more than their plot.

Why did she never write again?

"It's the writing that I think of, I guess," I say. "More than the plot or the point of the story—the center, like you said. Isn't the center her relationship with her brother, how she tries to hold on to him even though she doesn't know how?" Or do we all just find the story we're looking for in what we read?

Noa frowns. "There's . . . an edge missing. As if she settles on sentimentality."

I know how Elsie feels about being sentimental. Also, I know how it feels to be haunted by all the things you hate in your own writing. That could be enough to dry up her ink well, I guess.

The urge to be touched vanishes. I pull my foot away and stand. "I should get the candles out in case we lose power."

"Let me help," Noa says. She doesn't look hurt. More like she's simply surfing whatever waves arrive in this ocean.

I open a kitchen drawer and pull out a fresh pair of tapers. She helps drip wax into the holders we take from the top of the fridge. Sealed into place, the candles sit contentedly in the center of the table.

"What if we light them now? Pretend the power has already gone out?" I want to make up for breaking away.

"It'll bring more heat."

No, I think the heat is done for now. "There's always more ice water."

She lights the candles. I turn off the light. By candlelight everything is more beautiful, including her.

She points to a piece of paper on the fridge, next Friday's date in Robin's handwriting followed by *Devil's in the Details—DON'T SCHEDULE WORK.* "What does that mean?"

"We're going to see them—Robin and me and some friends—and he's reminding himself not to . . . well, schedule work." I grin the way you do when you feel ridiculous.

"Who are they? More EDM?"

"It's kinda indie pop? The whole singer-songwriter vibe?" I fill her in on Blue Riley's backstory, her coast-to-coast hunt for her sister via hitchhiking and freight hopping and the kindness of strangers.

"Cool. Sounds fun. And why the reminder here?" She points at the note.

What has Robin told her? "He just has some trouble with memory sometimes and paper lasts longer than phone alerts, so it's better for long-term reminders."

"Memory trouble because he had an overdose."

If she knows, he told her. If he told her, it means he's talking to people about it. That's good, right? But also, how did he explain it? "Yes, that's why."

"Because of his friend Alex?"

I nod. My chest has been wrapped with iron bands. To draw a deep breath is impossible.

If Robin's told her this much, he's probably said it all,

except the bits he never saw. I start talking.

Alex first stepped on the gas pedal that was opioids after she had her wisdom teeth out. A year later she sped all the way to a dead end on a hilltop when the apple trees were just leafing out. It wasn't something she chose, even though people always act like it's a choice. Part of it was genetics, probably. Part was chance and timing.

Robin and Hedy walked up to meet her, just a little late, and found her cooling in the quiet evening chill. Robin broke Alex's ribs with frantic CPR while Hedy sprinted to the nearest house to call 911 because their phones had no reception.

Then, after, Robin was the one who needed help. That wasn't a choice either. I think he broke along lines that had already been cracked by loss long before he'd ever met Alex.

What matters to me now, the story I'm telling constantly whether I mean to or not, is that late one afternoon months later, Robin took what remained of Alex's stash into the bathroom with him and ended his life. Mom brought him back by breathing for him. One of our tenants brought him back with the Narcan she carried. The EMTs brought him back when all that wasn't enough. The ER doc brought him back and forced him to stay. Me?

I did nothing.

So now it's up to me to do everything. Does he eat? Sleep? Take his meds? How about his balance, his memory, the little bits of him death refused to return? That job is mine and I can't ever fail.

Noa touches a finger to the pool of melted wax and lets it flow free. The fading flame brightens. "From the outside, it seems to me like he's trying to bring himself back now. But you've also had a journey."

"Yeah." I force a smile to hide the sudden feeling that I'm one step away from falling. "And honestly, I'm not sure how to find home."

"For me, it's come from in here." She touches one hand to her chest, the other to mine. For a moment I can feel something there—a shift, a flutter, the motion of a needle swinging back and forth to find north.

Mostly I feel her hand on me. The color rises in my face.

She looks at the clock that ticks slowly over the sink. "I should go. I'm working early tomorrow."

Someone has thrown the world in a blender and pulsed it once or twice, leaving nothing whole, nothing defined. Just swirling scraps and a sense that I should understand what it all is. I don't, though. I'm just a girl with a whole lot of feelings and a busted compass.

I walk her to the porch. The storm flashes over the hills, but no rain falls. This time, it's passing us by.

"Thank you for the not-date." She smiles. Nothing special, no hidden meaning. None that I can tell, at least.

"Yeah. Thank you too. How much longer are you in Amherst?" She'll tell me that she's suddenly decided to stay a year. She'll be staying here while I leave and until I come back.

"Only a week. Then I go to Barcelona. I've a job as an au pair for six months. Maybe longer, depending."

"Oh. Cool." Not cool.

It shouldn't matter.

She leans forward and so do I. Her shoulders flex as she hugs me, her body sturdier than Maya's. She kisses my cheek, but I don't return it. Lips confuse everything.

She leaves. I sit in the hanging chair on the porch. It's a good night to wait outside for Robin.

❀ ❀ ❀

This is what I do later, long after Robin's in bed. I take out my notebook, lay it open on my desk. Take out my favorite pen, the one where the ink flows at just the right thickness with just the right amount of pressure from my fingers. I think about talking to Noa: how it felt, how I feel now, whether it made a difference in her life or mine. I think about the stories I haven't been writing, the ones stoppered up inside me, the silence I keep.

What has that silence meant?

1. I make lists.

2. My laptop and I stare at each other every night, wishing something would happen.

3. I hate myself for not writing.

4. I hate myself when I do write.

5. My writing is more like a battlefield than a story, all characters and ideas and lines dying as soon as I type them.

6. It hurts.

7. Other things hurt too. The things I don't say.

8. I can't believe I destroyed my novel, purged it completely.

9. Why did I ever think that was the right thing to do?

10. Why do I keep choosing silence?

I'm ready to call Dr. Galaxy as soon as I wake up. In this life of general chaos and uncertainty, I deserve to get answers to the questions that have them.

"Hello?" He sounds confused more than sleepy. He's probably been up since six, having oatmeal and coffee for breakfast and reading the *Sunday Times*.

"It's Holi." Screw formality. I'm the girl who knows his mom's secrets. Some of them, at least.

"Is something wrong?" The fear in his voice reminds me that she *is* his mother, fragile as fuck and under my uneducated care.

"No, everything's fine." We both recalibrate for a moment. "I'm just trying to figure out"—go big or go home, Holiday—"how much you're wanting me to work. And what you really want me to do. She still doesn't have anyone there during the day except my mom once a week for like an hour—and I obviously can't provide medical care."

"The problem is that she won't accept any help. Not the kind she needs," he says. "For several years it made sense; fewer people in and out of the house meant less chance of contracting COVID. Only now . . . my siblings and I can't force her unless she's legally deemed unfit to make her own decisions."

Perfect.

"It's not so much that you need to care for her physically. I'm thinking . . . well, like you did when you took her to the doctor. If you're there and she has trouble, you can find someone to help. Her doctor, an ambulance, if necessary. Just that."

My stomach knots up. "She sometimes needs me to help her walk. I'm really not—"

"You're what she needs right now, Holi. I have faith in you."

It's not his frigging faith I need.

"Of course, if she starts to act confused, out of touch with things, then it becomes a different matter."

"Your brother, Cap—Chris, insists she *is* confused."

"Holi, I'm a doctor. She's my mother. Do you really think I'd leave her in a dangerous state alone?"

We left Robin in a dangerous state alone because we didn't believe he was in one. I try again. "The other day she got so upset about something we unpacked that she had to go lie down. I didn't know whether to be worried or not."

He pauses again, longer this time. I can hear a muffled voice in the background. I picture him sitting at the kitchen table with . . . someone.

"It's a question of her wishes. I could give her an ultimatum, if your sense is that she's failing and needs to be placed in a care facility."

Motherfucker. So it's *my* call whether Elsie gets to live in her own home or not? Me—the one who can't decide her own future, let alone someone else's.

"I don't think she's confused. I just can't be there all day, every day. And I'm only supposed to be there for sorting." Plus some light book burning, let's not forget that.

"Money isn't an issue. We can say thirty-five dollars an hour for the sorting and the availability?"

Money doesn't change what I can safely do. Do I care enough about Elsie to accept his offer—or enough that I insist she needs better help than me?

But he's offering a lot of money. The one thing in my life that I can plan for requires a plane ticket and spending money and emergency money and I don't know how else to make it if I quit now.

A bad caretaker is better than none, right?

"I can't be there every day. I need days off."

"Of course you do. Let me think about how best to make that work. In the meantime—"

"I'll go today, but I'm serious about days off."

"Wonderful," he says, and I realize that he truly is happy. I hear voices again, but now I wonder if he's actually eating with someone, or if he's at a coffee shop or a diner. Maybe he's sitting there with his soft hands, getting egg yolk on the belly of his polo shirt while reading. Alone. Like his mother.

Elsie is waiting in the living room. The radio is tuned to a Red Sox pregame ramble. Really? Elsie McAllister, proud member of Red Sox Nation?

Really. She has a Sox cap resting on her knee. She lifts it to her head when she sees me looking.

"Gonna be a good one?" I watch exactly no baseball—or football, or basketball, or any of the teams that Massachusetts loves and hates.

She shakes her head a bit. "It's no fun these days. Too much winning."

"You want them to lose?"

"I want to root for them. Too much winning steals that away and you have to root for someone else."

"Okay." Not exactly how I think sports fandom works, but you do you, ma'am. "Well, I'm going to . . ." I gesture toward the ceiling. She dismisses me with a wave of her hand.

Instead, I pause. "Um, were you expecting me?"

She gives me an impossible-to-decipher look. "Of course."

Up in the attic, I pull a box to me—*Silver: Place Settings*—and open it with a *Working: Sunday* lack of enthusiasm. Inside I find, unsurprisingly, a wooden box of silverware for ten and plenty of tablecloths, placemats, and linen napkins. Everything looks as though it was ironed before its exile.

She knows. That's the look she gave me. She knows full well that I'm here to babysit as much as to box and carry. We're just not going to discuss it, because to do that would mean acknowledging that we both know she needs help.

With that, my annoyance rises again. "I could be doing something else," I say to the linens as I return them to their perfect layers. "I could be riding somewhere fun. I could be helping Mouse with an experiment. I could be . . ."

Maya's away with her sister for the weekend. Robin's working. Mom's working. Mouse's likely working. I've got no one around. Except . . . No, Noa is working too, and even if she weren't, last night messed with my head.

"Between you and me," I say to a tarnished spoon, "I'm reconsidering whether I'm a loner. I may just be a loser."

According to John Allen, no sane person ever called Hemingway a loser. I'm sure sane people have called him that and worse. I'm sure I could find at least one book that devotes four-hundred-plus pages to how the word *loser* inspired Papa to greater artistic heights. Dudes and their fragile selves, am I right?

I've never cared about Hemingway. Not when John Allen told me I should study *A Farewell to Arms*, not when I was trying to be a real writer instead of a maker of lists.

I know what he said was shit. I know it.

I think I do.

No harm. No foul.

Right?

I put the spoon back in the box. A slip of paper has fallen to the floor. On it, in that beautiful script: *Anklet socks under farm boots, covering your callused feet.*

Elsie McAllister, you are one weird chick.

On the way home I stop at the library to pick up a book on hold for Mom. I'm unlocking my bike when I hear my name. A moment later, a hand touches my shoulder.

"Hey there, Holiday love."

I take a deep breath, turn, and look into the eyes of Hedy.

If Alex hit you like a golden retriever, Hedy is a deer stepping from the forest. She watches with these big dark eyes, and even when she's being silly, you have the sense that she's studying the equations governing your atoms.

She's cut her hair, and it curls around the curves of her ears and dampens by her forehead. Some of her hoops and studs have vanished, but the owl charm on a gold chain around her neck has been joined by another. I instinctively lean in to see it, only to move back when the lines connect into a recognizable shape. A tree.

"Hey. How's it going?" How's it been since you deserted my brother? Sleeping well?

"Good." She pulls her hair back and fully exposes the red birthmark over the side of her face. She used to hide it, keeping her hair long, but stopped when I was fifteen. When I mentioned the change to Robin, he laughed and said she'd opened herself to the mysteries of the universe. It took another year for me to understand he meant they'd been tripping.

Everyone gets their own room in my heart. Alex and Hedy—their rooms wait, doors open, walls still covered with snapshots of all the things I saw from my little-sister perch. I wish I could find a new use for them. I'm not sure that's possible, though. Love makes the spaces—all we get to do is to furnish them.

"It's really good to see you. It's been a long time. I miss you." That focus, the sense that she wants nothing more than to be here with me, right now. I miss that, I miss it so frigging much.

But why the fuck has she never even texted to say hi? "Yeah, it has. I gotta get going. I have to meet someone."

The look on her face tells me that she's seen all the way through me, that my stupid little lie shows like a dirty handprint on a window. Isn't that what I want, though, to tell her I'm angry without wasting the words?

"Okay." She touches two fingers to her lips and holds them out to me. I want, so much, to bend and touch my forehead to her blessing. Instead, I flash her a peace sign and head off.

I think the people who don't believe in ghosts are the ones who have never lost someone unexpectedly. I can feel Alex like wind blowing across my skin; I can hear her laughter in the hall. I don't know if it's forever or not, whether she's confined to this place or will travel with people. I do know Robin needs her to let go.

At the same time, I don't want her to leave. I want her here. Her finger in the brownie batter I was about to dump into a pan, chocolate on her teeth as she grinned. Her golden retriever energy everywhere as she planted a kiss on me, grabbed a carrot out of the fridge and bit into with a loud crack.

"What's happening, hot stuff?" she'd ask.

"Hey," I'd say, or "same old," or "fuck off," depending on the day. She'd never pause, though, already breezing past me, one hand behind her, fingers wiggling.

Hedy always stopped. She'd slide her fingers over the back of my hand and wait as long as it took for me to say something honest to her. Sometimes it would make me feel real; sometimes it annoyed me, like she was a hug that went on too long. It's not that Alex wasn't loving, not that Hedy wasn't fun. It's just that if I were to write a story about them, that's how they'd enter it.

And I know how they'd leave it as well. Alex planted like a time capsule in a pine casket decorated with paint and ink; Hedy like the true ghost, her footsteps the ones we should've been hearing on our porch, in our halls, in Robin's room.

That's not the story I want to write, though. Living it is hard enough.

Dr. Galaxy calls back at 9:30 p.m. Long after the end of my thrilling day of cataloging croquet sets, plastic floral arrangements, and report cards—who could've guessed that young Paul had been "a quiet and thoughtful child"?

He says that his sister, the elusive Lucy, will possibly commit to being with Elsie two days a week. Which two? We have no idea. But he assures me there will be days.

Downstairs, Mom's singing along with the *Camelot* soundtrack. She's no Julie Andrews, or Richard Burton for that matter, but her enthusiasm is what counts. I could fuck that up by asking to talk with her about Elsie. She'd quit her singing and listen, and I'd tell her everything, and it would change nothing because her job is hospice nurse, not support staff for her over-paid, undertrained daughter. Elsie is alone because Elsie wants to be alone. I can refuse to work overtime and she'll have no one, or I can earn the extra cash and be there to call 911 if needed.

And if I tell Mom everything, she might tell me that I shouldn't be there at all. That this isn't the job I accepted, the one she recommended me for.

I choose to zero in on my research instead. There's a scrap of *Tongues* that's been haunting me.

We weren't allowed to see what remained of Luke because "it'd only be a darkness, and one you do not need." Instead, I imagined his face nestled amongst the coiled limbs of every forest creature that had met its end alone and afraid.

Entire stands of trees had survived, the fire leaping past them. In other places, though, the forest was populated by those yet to learn of their own deaths. The water had boiled away inside these unlucky ones. Upright still, they waited for spring, as though the rains would soothe their charred flesh and fill their thirsty roots. No spring existed, though, that could call them back into life.

At the very edge of our forty acres waited a stand of these igno-rant dead. Among them, breathing in air heavy with ash and soot, I rubbed their charcoal on my face and took my rightful place. In that terrible stillness, where no bird dared to make a sound, I would end. Stop breath. Stop heart. I would be the grandfather clock by the door, the motion of my pendulum ceased with the touch of a hand.

And yet I lived on.

I understand now what I didn't in ninth grade. Sometimes tragedy is huge and obvious—think earthquakes and mudslides and islands disappearing under rapidly rising oceans—but more often it's hidden from the view of all but a few. And when you're among those few, that's when you want to stop time and stop your heart and don't understand why you can't.

I leave my room and tiptoe to Robin's door, push it just enough to fit my head in.

"Still alive," he says.

"I knew that." I slip all the way in. He's propped up on his bed, one earbud in, one pulled out to listen to me. The fan in his window makes a slight click as it spins. "Don't ever not be alive, okay?"

"Doing my best, Hols."

It's not blood that binds families together—real families of people who love each other and choose each other—it's this. Words we say a certain way. Fingertips that hold the memory of the hair on a head, and noses the scent of skin, and ears the sounds of footsteps or even a cough. Somehow, they become trust and love. Somehow, we survive.

"Think I'm gonna go bug Mouse. Don't stay up."

He shakes his head at me. "Call when you're leaving and I'll meet you."

Amherst is as safe as college towns ever are. There may be rapists lurking in the bushes here and there, sure, but more stand in plain sight at frat parties or departmental functions. "Whatever. If it makes you feel important to meet me on Main Street at midnight, be my guest."

"I've always got your back, wherever you go."

22

Mouse lives in genteel Amherst, in an ancient house with a porch in the front surrounded by antique climbing roses and a hidden garden designed for native pollinators out back. The front door sticks when I push it. As I bend to put my shoulder to it, Mouse pulls from the other side and drags me in.

"I'm pretty sure it's a fire hazard if your door doesn't open without a prybar."

"Keeps people out." Mouse's hair drips from a shower, and she shakes her head just enough to spray me.

"Is someone here?" Juliet's voice comes from the sumptuous mound of couches and cushions they call a living room.

"It's just me."

"Holi," she says, peering out at me. Juliet isn't particularly tall, or particularly loud, or even particularly unusual-looking, but she still controls any room she's in.

"Hiya," I say.

Juliet pulls her reading glasses off. She's got gray hair and white skin and a kind of blocky nose that calls your attention more than her eyes. "I can't figure out how people put their glasses on top of their heads." She pats her own. "I do that and can't get them out again."

She does have hair with the temperament of a puppy—good-natured but utterly unable to follow directions.

"Yours," she says. "You could set anything there and get it right back out. Are you happy with it?"

Am I? I cried, very quietly and alone, after paying the barber fifteen bucks to buzz my hair. The green I did myself over the bathroom sink when no one was home, and I looked like I'd been mauled by a swamp monster for a week afterward. At the time it felt like . . . like I needed to shed something, I guess. Now I think of the me before—the quiet girl with long hair who loved her bike and her girlfriend and didn't have a clue what was coming her way—and feel sad for her.

Which is totally not the question. "Yeah. It's easier like this."

She fluffs her own tangle. "I wonder if I could handle green?"

"Mom, go have your midlife crisis somewhere else." Mouse makes shooing motions with her fingers.

Juliet taps the stems of her glasses against her lip absent-mindedly. "I've been thinking about you, Holi. You should come by more. How's your writing going?"

Juliet is a famous writer and a good person and right here asking about my writing. Why do I torture myself with Elsie instead? "Haven't really had time. I've been working a lot."

Mouse shakes her head again, catching us both with water droplets. "You know how kids are these days, lady. They're all about eating Tide Pods and complaining about climate change. No time for literature."

Juliet rolls her eyes and sinks out of view again. I head to the kitchen and start opening cupboards. Mouse pushes me away from them.

"I assume you're looking for these. Which is rude, since it's ten at night and you weren't invited." She pulls a plate of unfrosted cupcakes from where she's hidden them in the oven.

I reach for one. She slaps my hand. "They're naked. Show a little decency."

I sit on the counter and watch as she mixes butter and sugar and vanilla to the consistency she wants. She stuffs it in a pastry bag with a broad tip attached and swirls each top, deceptively casual. When she's finished, there are a dozen bakery-perfect cupcakes begging to be eaten.

"This is why you and Hannah are in love, isn't it? This whole kitchen thing." I take one and this time she doesn't stop me.

"First, Hannah doesn't know we're in love, and second, we have far more in common than mere pastry technique." Mouse takes a cupcake too.

Mouse has frosting on her nose. I grab a dishtowel and mop her with it. She takes it patiently, eyes closed. "Hannah does love you. She's just got this nasty infection known as an ex that she needs to have treated first. With arsenic, like they used to do for syphilis."

We take our cupcakes outside and sit on the broad porch swing. "Can I tell you something weird?" I ask.

"Always." She puts half a cupcake in her mouth and rests her head against my shoulder. I can feel her jaw click as she chews.

I tell her everything I've pieced together about Elsie in the past few days, from the roses to the romance novel, navigating a potential outing with the one person I know would never tell a soul. She listens quietly to the end, because when she wants to listen, she does so harder than anyone.

After I stop and she's wiped the edges of her mouth clean, she sits up. "Why is that weird?"

I feel like a fool, at least a little. "Because it's not—"

"Like the stereotypical white-bread old lady? Have you met the world at all?"

I flip her off. "Just . . . doesn't it make you curious? About her?"

"Not really."

"But you agree it's a weird-ass way of hiding a book."

"Maybe she hides the book because she thinks people might assume something about her if they see it." She gives me a pointed look.

"Okay, but why just that book? You know how many romance novels there are in the world—I bet that isn't even the only two-women-make-cupcakes one. I think the author's the reason."

"You could just ask her."

"She's not like that. She gets pissed at questions."

"Perfect. You must get along really well."

"You think I ask too many questions?"

"No. I think you hate people asking *you* questions." She taps my chin, scrapes at something there with her fingernail. "Have you Googled the author?"

"I don't want to look up things online. I want to look at things I can touch with my hands." I want the texture of Maya's skin under my hand, the smell of approaching snow, the taste of these cupcakes. To be a person and not an amalgam of pixels and likes and data.

"So do it your way. Read the book, look for clues."

"Maybe." More likely I'll find chapter upon chapter of cupcake competitions and longing glances, culminating with a few pecks on the cheek and some handholding against the backdrop of a pretty sunset. "Do you think your mom might know her? Monica Meyers?"

She sighs. "Did you come here for me or my mom?"

"Your mom."

⁂

If Elsie is royalty when it comes to American novelists, Juliet is the revolutionary at the walls. As Rosemary Quill—I adore her pen name—Juliet's created a feminist utopia where women love and help each other heal from trauma, find their happy endings in fulfilling and respectful relationships, and have loads of great consensual sex. Academics may love Elsie, but people who need a reason to get up each morning turn to Juliet.

John Allen says the only woman authors of real note in the last century are Virginia Woolf and Toni Morrison, and that both are overrated. Juliet says that books by women about women's lives or hopes or pleasures or anything else that doesn't center men's experiences will always be treated as lesser in a misogynistic culture. I'd like to know what kind of conversation she and Elsie would have if they were stuck examining boxes together.

When I explain who and what I'm looking for, Juliet purses her lips. "I don't know Monica Meyers, though she could have more than one pen name." She opens her laptop on the counter and puts her glasses on. After a minute: "Some of her backlist was reissued within the last few years, so you won't have a hard time finding copies. If it's Monica herself you want, she lists her literary agent as a contact. I could ask my agent to reach out to hers if you'd like. She may have better luck than you."

"Curious," says Mouse. "It's kinda like all the information you wanted was available online. If only someone had pointed that out to you sooner."

I groan. "Thanks, Juliet. You're the best, even if your daughter's evil."

I text Robin, cupcake booty call completed. Mouse stands on the front step with me for a minute.

"Buy the book, okay?"

"I thought you didn't care about human mysteries, just owls and fungus and baking powder." I nudge her. She leans against me in return.

"I care about interesting things. That's all." She pushes herself away from me. "It interests you, so it interests me. I want you to have the things you need. You know?"

Hearing that she cares about me shouldn't make me want to cry. But here we are. I change the subject. "Ready for Devil's in the Details?"

"The best band in the entire galaxy? Would. Not. Miss. It. You sure you don't want to go with us? Hannah, Coe, Hedy . . ."

Well, fuck. I should've known Hedy'd be there, but it's still a splinter under my fingernail.

"Gonna stick with Maya and Robin. Tell Hannah she's wicked dumb for a smart girl."

"Young woman, please." Mouse pats my butt. "Get going before Robin decides you've been kidnapped. I don't need the drama."

When I arrive at Elsie's in the morning, there's yet another car in the driveway. I head to the back deck a little more slowly, lift my bike onto it while watching through the window for a face.

No one waits at the door for me. She's dead. I know it. Or she's in the hospital. It's nothing good.

A woman comes around the corner from the kitchen as I click the door closed behind me. She looks surprised. I feel surprised. The room itself does not seem surprised in the least. The clock swings its pendulum in the corner. The photo of the wolf tree lurks on the mantel.

"You must be Holi," she says, holding out one manicured hand. "I'm Lucy. Elsie's daughter."

She's small and wears jeans with a white blouse that hangs like silk. Iron-gray hair, long and just a little wavy. Small gold hoops in her ears.

I give her hand a hearty shake. "Is Elsie okay?"

"Oh, she's fine. I thought I'd come for a few days now and work out a schedule for later. I didn't have your number to let you know."

And you didn't think to ask your brother? Or your mother? "It's okay. I can just go up—"

She's shaking her head. "Oh no, you should take a few days.

I'm sure you need a break, and I'm staying the week."

"I can work. I came prepared." I hold up my backpack, the full water bottle in the side pouch, my lunch inside.

Lucy gives me a look that's just a little too wide-eyed, a little too like her mother's when caught with *Hers and Hers*. The McAllister women know how to play the game.

"Let me pay you for the day anyway. Consider it a bonus for being so understanding. Go ahead and say hello while I grab my purse."

In other words, she's dismissing the peasant. She retreats down the hall. I follow her as far as the kitchen. Elsie sits at the table glowering like a grumpy, tired seven-year-old. She's eaten none of the breakfast in front of her. I wouldn't have either. Only sadists and the insufferably cheerful make eggs first thing in the morning.

"Hey," I say, "I guess I'm not working today. Or the rest of the week. I'll be back after that."

Elsie gives me that unwavering stare I've come to know so well. She either hates me or wants me to plan a jailbreak for her. "Have you been keeping track of the boxes upstairs?"

"I said I would."

"You promised you'd do whatever I asked. And no snooping."

For fuck's sake. "You hired me to look in all the boxes. I can't look in the boxes and not see what's in them. That's like the exact opposite of what you want. In fact—"

Lucy returns, twenties in hand, like I'm the babysitter. "I think this is right. Do you want to count it?"

No. I have absolutely no intention of counting it out in front of the two of them. I get it, lady. I'm the hired help.

"I'm good, thanks." I stick it in my back pocket. "You sure you don't need anything?"

"Of course not," Lucy says. "Oh, by the way, it would be best if you leave your bag downstairs when you work. Okay?"

Did she really just imply that I'm stealing? I mean, yes, I took one copy of *Tongues*, but there were so many and Elsie clearly had no use for them.

Lucy smiles sweetly at me. I could just quit, right now, and walk off with some pride.

Elsie shakes her spoon at me. "Holiday, before you leave, please go upstairs and take pictures for me."

"Of?" Maybe she is starting to lose it a bit.

"Pictures of the boxes there. All of them. I know you'll be thorough."

Wha . . . oh. I get it. Documentation of everything that's there now. She's telling Lucy off right here, in front of me, in a way Lucy is helpless to confront, because what she's implying is that Lucy's the one who can't be trusted. Elsie McAllister for the win.

"Got it. Give me a minute up there. You want me to text them to you?"

I swear that I see some genuine pleasure cross her face. "Yes, I would appreciate that. Everything, please. And I expect you to be here on time tomorrow."

"Mom," Lucy starts.

"I've hired her to do my work. You can do as you like. Holi will be here tomorrow as usual."

Lucy doesn't look at me as I leave.

After, I stop on the Common and take out my notebook. I keep thinking about Elsie treating her daughter like a thieving maid in order to knock her down for treating me the same. Who *is* Elsie? I've been neglecting that answer in pursuit of the others.

My pencil has a nice sharp point.

1. Elsie wrote one unbearably famous book.

2. She never wrote anything else.

3. She left Maine after high school and never went back.

4. She got married and had three kids.

5. She did nothing else.

The last one isn't fair. She gave talks and received medals, she recorded herself reading the book and went to a movie premiere. It's just that slowly, bit by bit, she stopped being important to the world as a real person.

5. She lived a quiet life (full of boxes).

6. She has a sapphic baker romance hidden in an actual carved-out encyclopedia in her living room, and she reads it from time to time.

7. She hates a book about roses so much that she wants it burned.

8. The girl who wrote in the rose book asked the question I now want answered too: Elsie, what happened to you?

9. She won't let anyone look after her. Except me? (WHY?)

10. Her kids all want to pay me more and more money to . . . do something. Stay there all the time. Keep her from throwing things away. Take days off.

11. She thinks women shouldn't write and writers are liars, even though she's both.

12. She is dying.

That's the biggest truth of all. Whether I box everything or not, whether her kids pay me for their weird needs or not, whether she's famous or not, she is dying. Her blue lips, the rasp of her breathing, the smell of cigarettes on her clothes.

Suddenly I feel very lonely. Not for myself—for her. What did writing *Tongues* do for her? There's a box of awards overhead and a picture of a dead tree on her mantel. Long hours when the kids napped or hit each other with sticks or whatever they did back then—what did she do with that time? Smoke in a lawn chair and think about meatloaf? Ten thousand dollars tells me Cap believes she did more.

And what about the decades since they've been grown? All that time spent in her bedroom, at her table, tugging her little wagon along, sneaking smokes when no one can see her?

She had everything: adoring editor, adoring fans, adoring husband, home and money and fame. I can't write because I write crap. She doesn't have the same excuse.

13. Why?

14. Was there another book?

15. Elsie, what happened to you?

24

The line at the Painted Lady stretches a long way down the street. It's Friday night, only an hour left till showtime for Devil's in the Details. I've spent most of my week completing tasks that kept me clear of Lucy. Which means I haven't seen much of Elsie either; Lucy seems intent on killing her mother with kindness. Or at least watchfulness. I, on the other hand, used Elsie's car to bring clothes to the Survival Center and distribute knickknacks across a range of thrift stores. When Mom came for her weekly hospice visit, I was busy with Mr. Forsythe, the bookseller, and discussions about signed first editions of minor classics.

And now I'm here. I've been waiting for this concert for months, and instead of enjoying this moment I'm stretched tighter than twine holding a hay bale together. I almost ask Robin to go home, now and without question, before the past arrives.

I see Hedy across the street, her long cotton gauze skirt blowing in the breeze of a passing car, just before Robin does. He hesitates a moment. She gives a little wave, then freezes. He ignores the car he brings to a halt as he strides over to her. I'm a satellite trained on a single target, but I can hear nothing of what they say—can't even see their faces, just Robin's back and Hedy's hand gesturing from behind him.

Maya links her pinkie around mine. I can smell the jasmine

rising from her scalp. The slender green vine tattooed across the length of her shoulders twists a bit as she shifts closer.

Hedy's hand rises to Robin's shoulder. Robin leans toward her enough that I can see her brown curls above his shoulder. They part, Robin walking toward Betts waiting at the end of the line, Hedy approaching the front where her brother and his friends have collected. Maya and I beeline toward the comforting bulk of Betts as well. There's nothing in Robin's face to tell me what happened, so I just stand close to him, my hand on his.

It's good to see Betts. He and Robin met at an open mic at UMass and bonded over a shared love of the Muppets. He's love packaged as a human tidal wave, and when he hugs my brother I can almost see him sucking out the pain and filling him with quiet peace. If old souls exist, he totally is one. I sit next to him for the whole show, feeling relaxed. Safe, I guess.

The concert's great, even though we end up seated in the second-floor loft. It's as far from the stage as you can be, but still close enough that I could probably count the sound guy's fillings when he opens his mouth to test the mic. I don't believe in Ouija boards or chakras or UFOs, but I do believe that lives have echoes, and that music always has a life of its own.

For two whole hours, I can't take my eyes off Blue. She's not showy, not pushy about being the center of things. She stands on the little stage and looks out at all of us and we all take one big breath together. And another, and another, until we merge into something much larger than our little bubbles of self. Her speaking voice sounds ordinary, the kind you only recognize if you love the person. Her singing voice, though, grabs your throat and pulls you to her, face to face. Her sister, Cass—beside her in a long clingy dress that contrasts sharply with the overalls Blue wears—pulls attention in a much more obvious way.

At the very end, Blue leans to one side, laughs at something the drummer says. Then, more serious, she says, "I want to leave you with something for everyone who's ever been haunted, who's longed for someone not with them."

It's like I've been wearing armor all this time, and tonight I've taken it off because it's been so heavy and I'm so tired and I'm safe. Now, though, Blue Riley sends an arrow my way and I cannot protect myself from that sudden sharp pain. Below us I can see Hedy's curls tremble between her brother's head and Mouse's. The same pain vibrates back at me from Robin.

In this moment, we are sewn together, heart to heart to heart, with the crude stitches of a child repairing her stuffed bear. I can tell Blue knows this too, as she launches into "The Ghost in You," played at lullaby speed and sung with voices made of empty rooms and echoes.

Maya grips my hand. This is the world, no matter what anyone tells you: breaking and building and breaking again, until you stop loving the solid and start loving the life.

After the concert, Maya and I wait by the now-closed bar while Robin and Betts talk with the manager in a corner. Maya tucks her hair around one ear, and I touch the tiny turquoise heart in the lowest piercing. "I didn't think you still wore these." We bought them together on a day when we wandered Northampton for hours before riding home at twilight. That night we stopped on the park and lay on the playing fields, our shoulders touching, until something changed. I don't know if it was her or me, if it was a decision or just some cosmic imp rolling the dice on their night off. All I know is that we kissed. The first time she'd kissed a girl. The first time I'd kissed anyone.

She tips her head against my hand like that's all the answer I need, and maybe it is.

"I have to go," she says. She'll be doing the 4 a.m. green market run to NYC tomorrow. Then she leaves on Monday to spend a few days with her nana in Boston. I don't want her to go. I want to stay up all night talking.

Instead, she kisses my cheek, quickly hugs Robin and Betts. I watch her leave, curving herself past two guys kissing against the wall.

Robin and Betts follow Sasha, the manager, to the bar. For a while the Horse Caves played here as an opener for local bands, then graduated to midweek shows of their own. When Robin was in the hospital, Sasha showed up. Once he was home, she stayed in touch. I can hear her asking about the band, about when they might be ready to play again. I'm holding my breath, waiting for an answer as Betts studies Robin's face.

I'm so busy watching that I don't notice a woman slide up next to me until she bumps against my elbow and murmurs *sorry*. She's dressed in a boxy sundress, her black hair in an intricate bun, a few long curls escaping. It's not her face that I recognize first; it's her dark plum, almost black, lipstick.

"Hey, Sasha," she says. "Can you recommend a good place for dinner? Cheap," she adds.

I study Cass Riley, a thousand details vying for my focus. The tiny pale line to the left of where her neck meets her shoulder. The makeup so artfully done that the only places you notice it are those she wants you to see.

Sasha frowns as she runs through a mental list. "Eleven is bedtime in Northampton, unless you want pizza or booze."

"Not really." If Cass were an animal, she would be a cat, and right now she looks like one shaking dew off its feet. "I think one more night of pizza might just end the tour for me."

"That sounds like a truly dire situation." If Robin were an animal, he'd be a lab suddenly discovering the back door left open.

Cass looks at him in the way women used to all the time. She moves closer to the three of them. A trail of soft cinnamon spiciness drifts past me in her wake.

"Absolutely dire. Do you have any recommendations?"

I suddenly have the sinking feeling that I'm babysitting toddlers, all of them about to start touching things they shouldn't. It's been a long time since that happened.

"Well," Robin starts. "We could—"

And, just as quick, someone else bumps my elbow, face inches from my arm as Blue Riley comes for her sister. She shakes her head slightly in the eternal sibling language for *you embarrass me everywhere we go but I love you just the same*. Robin and I have shared it more times than I can possibly remember.

"Hey, great show," Betts rumbles.

"Hey, thanks," Blue says. Her head comes to my shoulder. She keeps her voice quiet—not a whisper, just quiet. Her hair's a stubble field, either a recent shave or a regular date with a clipper. She's in denim overalls and a black tank, looking exactly like a Hampshire student on her way to work on a sculpture or a song or a paper on Wicca.

Inside, my nine-year-old self shrieks with disbelief, with joy.

Robin smiles a smile I thought was extinct. "Betts is right, that was pretty phenomenal. Thank you."

"I'm not eating pizza again," Cass tells Blue. She shapes her plum-colored lips into a stagey pout.

Robin shoots Betts a glance. "We could make you dinner at Betts's place."

Blue rubs her hand back and forth over her head. She too is dealing with an escaped sibling, I think. "We don't know these people, Cass."

Cass looks at Sasha. Suddenly we all do, like she's the ref about to make the pivotal call for a big game.

"Only thing I can say is that these guys and Holi over there are good people. You should go with your gut, but they have my stamp of approval. If I had kids, I'd be happy knowing these folks were looking after them."

Now everyone's looking at me. I give a half wave as my skin burns. Under the house lights I must look as red as one of the doomed roses in Elsie's book.

Cass links her arm through Blue's. "Come on, Blue. Live a little."

Blue sighs. "Do you even know their names?"

"Spencer Betts, friends just call me Betts." Betts points to Robin. "And Puck."

Puck died when Robin did; hearing the name brings the thrill of how we used to be and the fear of how things could end again.

"And his sister Holi, who'd love it if she's not the center of attention."

"Now we know them. And we know Sasha and she loves them, so . . ." Cass gives her sister a kiss on the cheek. "Just a quick dinner," she says, exactly like every lying sibling ever.

It's after one when Robin starts washing dishes, Cass and Betts helping. That leaves Blue and me sitting at the picnic table out back. The traffic on the highway hums. Cass's laughter spills out the kitchen window. Real laughter, not ha-ha-ha-let's-screw hookup stuff.

I'm more than a little tongue-tied, but our silence is too much for me. "How'd you start on the new record? You know, after the long break." Blue's a shapeshifter—one minute a small-scale celebrity, the next a normal woman. I'm not sure myself which version I'm speaking to.

"Everything felt so bleak, you know? So small and pointless. For a while I just felt like mush creatively." She rests a finger in the center of her forehead. "Only then—epiphany! I realized humans need to create, even in really dark times. Maybe the most during those times. I had to do something."

Inside there's a crash, the sound of glass against the hard floor. Robin and Cass laugh and Betts says something about needing new plates anyway.

No big deal. Just Robin acting human. Leaving me to worry about heartbreak. I think about the story of Blue and Cass. "Did you really just wake up one morning and decide you'd do anything to find her—your sister?" *Was it easier to travel hundreds of miles instead of blundering around in the room next door?*

She looks at her hands. "It seemed simple at the time. I didn't expect it to be as . . . huge? I don't know that I understand all of what happened yet, if I ever will. You know what I mean?" She's just a person, sitting here full of questions too.

I do know what she means. I know I want to write the book that gives us all happy endings—Robin, Maya, Mom, Noa, Blue and her sister, this whole constellation I'm part of. Right now, I want that book more than anything. To know that we will all live long, happy lives, that we'll all hold our spots in the cosmos and love will be the force that keeps us there. If I could write that one book, it would be enough.

"What about you? What's your thing?"

Destruction. Loss. Debris. Only, tonight feels enchanted and enchantment means I can say anything. "I write. A bit. Mostly I fail."

"Screw failure. What do you write?"

Immature stuff. Disposable things. Labels on boxes and words on lists.

I tell her about *Dragon Girl*. Everything I remember about what I deleted, what I would add if I still could. How real it made me feel to write it.

The one thing I don't tell her is that it no longer exists.

"So cool." She hasn't looked away from me once, like she's breathing it all in. "Do you love it?"

I don't mean to cry. I dip my head so she won't see, then raise it and look at the passing headlights.

She reaches out and touches my hand. "Hey."

"It was kind of immature. Just the main character by herself for most of it. No big three-act plot. Not even a romance." John Allen told me all this with a smile.

She backhands the air. "First, as a person who's spent a

176

lot of time alone, I can tell you those stories matter too. As for romance . . . that's like one of a zillion spices on the rack, right? The entire time I was on the road looking for Cass, I was focused on finding her, and on people like my best friend, Steve, and on what I saw. Not on falling in love."

Cass appears by the table. "Don't listen to her. What kind of story doesn't have romance?"

Blue flips her off over her shoulder.

Cass continues. "Romance is what gets everyone to the end of a book, even if it's tragic."

"But that's because you pick the stories that match what you want, right?" says Blue. "You want to read about how the girl gets the boy, and someone else wants to read about how the girl gets the girl. That's what makes a book good for them, at that time. Honestly, I'm kinda into the ones where sometimes the girl gets herself. Sometimes that's all I want on the final page."

"Because you're frigging weird," Cass says and we all laugh.

Which story is mine? Is it following Maya to New Zealand and getting her back? Is it keeping Robin safe? Is it solving Elsie's mysteries? Which way does my compass point, that's what I'd like to know.

Eventually Blue brings out her guitar. Robin grabs one of Betts's and the two of them noodle around until eventually a tune coalesces. Robin stops as Blue starts to sing, Cass chiming in. "Wish You Were Here," sweet and melancholy, trails out, the questions Cass and Blue ask going unanswered by the night. Betts holds my hand in his giant one. Robin's face is lit by the lights along the deck railing and the battery lantern Betts set out earlier. My brother's not here now; it's not hard to know where he's gone.

Somewhere beyond the edges of the light, Alex waits. She'll always be waiting there. It's up to him to stop looking for her.

He picks up the guitar again and starts strumming. I must've squeezed Betts's hand, because he presses his other over mine.

My book of happy endings is open in the dark, and for a moment I can see a page. It's not easy, and it doesn't look quite how I imagined. It's okay, though.

Maybe nothing looks the way I expect. Maybe *okay* looks like yarn tied in knots slowly being teased out into strands, day after day, night after night.

Betts drops us off at home as the sky turns into streams of pink and pearl. Blue and Cass left in their van at the same time we did, Blue groaning about hitting the road with zero hours of sleep. She hugged me, told me to find them the next time they come to Massachusetts.

Now, walking up the porch steps, I'm more tired than anything else. Robin looks tired too, though he'll be able to sleep for an hour or so and be ready for anything.

He bumps into me and we're giggling as we creep into the entryway, trying to be quiet. Only . . . Mom is not being quiet. And she's not alone.

"Oh shit," Robin whispers, and we tumble over ourselves to back out the door.

We stare at each other. Yes, there are things that you never want to know about your mother, but there are also things you do—like whether her life will always revolve around working and paying bills and checking to make sure Robin takes his meds and finding jobs for me, or if there's more. And whether *more* might include more of Martín.

"Fuck," I say.

"Yeah, no shit." Robin shakes his head. "Come on, walk me to the Cafeteraria and I'll buy us some coffee and we can try to drown our memories of that forever."

26

'm in the midst of a lack-of-sleep hangover when I come downstairs at noon. Mom and Martín were having coffee on the porch and talking about his trip when Robin and I got home for the second time. Neither of us said anything to them. It's not as though they needed our permission, or as if either of us felt like Mom needed to stay true to Dad's memory for the rest of her life, or even that we were shocked. So we stuck with *hi* and *concert was great* and I went upstairs to sleep.

My thoughts have been a mess, though: equal parts last night and Maya and Elsie's attic . . . everything, really. It's a relief when Mouse texts about going for a walk.

But leaving the house means walking *through* the house, which means thinking and speaking. Downstairs, Mom's sitting on the couch. Robin's eating cold leftover rice from his favorite blue ceramic bowl while standing by the window. He's working later. Mom's studying later. This is the only time we'll all be home together today. I catch his eye. He gives me a hint of a nod. Enough to tell me, through the mystical language of siblings, that he's leaving it all up to me.

"Hey," I say to Mom, not sure where to go from there. She looks up at me. I don't know what she sees in me, but I see a happy person in her. Just . . . content.

And Robin? I see him in the glow of the light last night, in the sooty dark after Secret House, in the sunlight streaming through the window now.

"We know about you and Martín. It's good. We're happy."

She starts to say *how* and then has a lightbulb moment and I say, "It's good," again, to save us all further embarrassment.

Robin says, "Hols is right."

I think a glacier swept through our house when Alex died. Probably even before, when Dad did. I think Mom and Robin have been trapped in ice, and lately something—a hair dryer, a heat lamp, the motherfucking celestial sun—has started to thaw them free.

I think that maybe I've been caught in ice too. And I'm pretty sure I know where my thaw needs to start.

I'm standing ankle deep in the Fort River with Mouse, and I'm bone tired. Mouse is not tired. She is busy kicking the water like she's three years old.

"How's Hannah?" I ask. "Is that why we're here?"

Mouse kicks at the current some more. "Hannah and I are not really speaking at the moment. I may have . . . said some things last night."

"You'll work it out. It's not like you said something unforgivable. Or did you?"

"Nooooo. Mostly, no. I may have said some things about Ari." She's silent for a moment. "I may have said some things about waiting around for a person like that too."

"She knows all that already. She's just mad at you for confirming it. Right?"

"Right. Everyone's cool with being accused of willful blindness to reality."

Mouse has always been good at knowing how to show up for someone without smothering them, and at knowing when to turn the conversation to the shark population of Cape Cod or how she's started yet another terrarium. This thing with Hannah—I wish I could Mouse her through it.

I hold out my hand to her. "Let's walk?"

The trail along the river is hard-packed dirt, thanks to a steady mix of joggers and dog walkers and rain. It's pretty, though, with open fields of corn and pumpkins to one side and water to the other. "Do you want to talk more about how things went?"

"Not really. It's just . . . it causes me actual physical pain to watch her whole Ari thing. Ari is never coming back from California to be with her. She's moved on, likely more than once by now. That's just me as her friend, without throwing the whole stupid love thing in."

"You *sure* you don't want to keep talking about it, because this is—"

"Totally done. Something else, please."

"What did you think of the concert, minus the fight with Hannah?"

"Well, what's not to love about two hot women singing songs written on a freight train somewhere? It should've been twice as long."

For a moment I consider not telling her, but that doesn't seem fair. "What would you say if I told you I got to hang out with Blue and Cass afterward?"

She grabs my arm and spins me to face her. "I would say where the fuck is this magical land you live in and why don't I live there too?"

182

"It was just me and Robin and Betts and them." I tell her about Robin inviting them at the club, how he played guitar with them, how Blue leaned against Cass at five in the morning when we all decided to go home. All the little details and most of the big—the things ready to be shared.

Mouse squeezes my arm again. I prepare for jealousy. Instead: "Hols, that's amazing. You deserve it."

We've come to a little box mounted on a post. Inside lives a family of three tiny stuffed bunnies. Mother, father, baby, in a room with a table and chairs and a rocker in the corner. On the wall hangs a minuscule portrait of a rabbit general. Every time I come here, I imagine myself as one of them. Settled in happily, everything in life orderly and calm and always the same.

"I can't even say you're lucky," Mouse continues. "It's like life stomped on you and then let you borrow a puppy."

Right there. There's my space, there's the warmth. All I have to do is speak. Why is this so damn hard?

Because my voice is part of what's been frozen.

"So, I . . . you know how I quit my job in the spring?"

"The one sorting John's crap? For someone who doesn't like being indoors, you spend a ton of time on other people's paperwork." She does that: calls the departmental faculty by their first names, calls out their bullshit the way her mother does.

My throat tightens. Mouse looks at me more closely and stops talking. She starts walking instead, to a stone bench down the trail. I touch my fingertips to the tiny woolen bunny heads in the tableau before joining her.

She waits. The bike trail crosses the river ahead of us. I want to be on it, listening to the changes in sound as I cross from pavement to wooden bridge and back to pavement.

"Yeah, so, I didn't quit because he was running out of work."

"He trashed your writing, right? I figured that one cut."

"Well, yeah, he did." That hurts more, I think. The rest feels just out of emotional reach, a home movie belonging to someone else. "It's more than that, though."

Mouse stares straight ahead, at the lone cyclist pedaling dutifully along with a kid wagon behind them. I could stop. Now, before I say things I'll regret.

I can't stop. "This other thing—it's not that big a deal. It just made me feel uncomfortable, so I guess it made it easier to quit."

Still nothing. She'll wait until I'm done, like I'm an otter she's watching through binoculars. That's exactly why I'm talking now, to her.

"It was just . . . we were in his office, I was sitting on his desk and he . . ." My thigh clenches with the feel of his hand, as though it's still happening right now. "He put his hand here—"

I motion to the place, high up, thumb on the inside of my leg.

"He stepped up close, you know, with his hand there and he said *shall we*, like we'd been talking about it."

It. We'd been talking about how the endless folders of student work were like geological strata. That's all.

"And he leaned in a bit."

A bit can be a nothing, a tiny motion, or it can be the rub of a goatee against your neck as uninvited lips blister your skin.

"I should've understood what was going on. I keep thinking that I should've noticed, that I should've understood." Some parts of those few minutes are so clear and some aren't. All of them have played in my head again and again. "Anyway, I said I liked girls, because I didn't know what else to say."

He'd tightened his hand then, just a bit, enough to let me know that he had hold of my leg, and something in me shrank so small. Not something *in* me—*all* of me. Small and still.

I should've moved, stood up, walked out of there. Instead I froze, with just my feeble *I like girls* as a shield.

"Anyway, he just said . . ." Again, why didn't I stand up, push him back with my hand flat against his chest? "He said that real writers try everything in life at least once. That they know experience is necessary for great art. That I'd enjoy it." What I don't say is that he whispered it into my ear. Like Maya whispering in my ear when no one was home and we lay naked in my bed. Like I wanted him.

Mouse still waits. I have no idea what she's thinking, and I'm not sure I want to know. But it's too late to take it back.

"I said that maybe I wasn't a real writer."

And I believed it, right then and there. Me—I told us both that I didn't have what it took, that my curiosity hung small and useless on a starved vine.

"And he said I'd seemed pretty sexually conflicted for a while. But then he moved away. So it's not really a big deal. It's not like he hurt me. It's just . . ."

It's just all of it. It's just the way he stepped away, shrugged and then said, "No harm, no foul," as if he'd offered to tutor me in Spanish and I'd said *Thanks, but I'm good.*

"Fucker." Mouse finally looks at me. "Of course it's a big deal. That's seriously fucked-up shit on his part."

Below, something moves along the stones of the retaining wall. A mink, not the least bit scared of us, lopes along and disappears into a crevice.

"Did you tell your mom?"

I shake my head. Not with everything else going on.

"Robin?"

God, no. I think that would've been even worse.

"Maya?"

No, I didn't tell Maya. Not then, not when I kept coming up with excuses every time she wanted to fool around. How exactly do you tell your girlfriend that your body's gone underground, that the only way to pack away the rest is to pack that away as well? The truth is that Maya may have broken up with me, but I left her first.

"You know it's not your fault, right?" Mouse bats a leaf on the musclewood tree beside her.

"It doesn't feel that way."

"Yeah, because this whole country's so fucked up that it's hard not to assume it's all normal and that we're the problem if it upsets us. But you know I tell the truth. I don't screw around. And I'm telling you that this isn't on you. You ask my mom, she'd tell you the same. And then she'd burn his life down." She pauses. "Do you want to do that? Tell her?"

I can imagine Juliet saying all the right things, offering all the right options, encouraging me to tell my mom and the department head. But I also feel like I've just run a marathon and hopping up to run another would sink me. "I love your mom, but no. Not now, at least. I just . . . I keep trying to think of what I did that—"

"Told him that he alone could free you from your inhibited girl-loving ways?"

It's possible to feel like crap and still laugh. I'm proof.

"Really, Hols, you can hear how that's all fantasy on his part. It's like the two of you were acting in two different movies. Yours was an Oscar contender about a chick *returning to life after tragedy* or something. And his was—probably always is—bad eighties porn."

I snicker again. It's like laughing with broken ribs—the amusement and the pain trying to share space. "You don't think I give off a conflicted vibe?"

Mouse glowers. "The only way anyone could think of you as conflicted is if they just didn't respect your autonomy. And also, what the fuck? You could be conflicted all you want. You could *tell* him you're conflicted and it still doesn't give your boss and mentor and family friend the right to say, 'Hey, I can take care of that, let's do it on the desk.' He was saying it because it fits his bad eighties porn narrative, with the bonus that it puts everything on you."

"Have you ever watched bad eighties porn?"

"Of course not. I have nine hundred and ten thousand better things to do with my time."

"Nine hundred and—"

"Ten thousand. Yes."

I'm shivering like I have a chill. It seems like I should cry, or feel powerful and free of it all, but I don't. Maybe later those things will happen. What I do feel is that a tiny window has opened in the smoky room I've been trapped inside and I know that fresh air's reaching me even if I can't yet smell it through the haze. Once I get enough air, then I can find the door and invite Mom and Robin in. But for now, this is what I've got.

I nudge Mouse's ankle with my toe. She pushes back.

"Love you, freak," she says.

"Right back atcha."

I eat my dinner alone. Robin's with Betts, Mom's either studying or with Martín. I'm glad Mom isn't here. I don't want to talk with her about my job. More and more, Elsie feels like my responsibility rather than my employer, which I know isn't what Mom intended. I can't justify the things I've said yes to, but I also can't bring myself to say no.

After dinner I get a text from Juliet. **Hey kiddo, here's the contact info for Monica Meyers. Remember, approaching as a fan gets you a lot further with authors than just asking questions. Maybe read a book or two before contacting her?**

I scribble down the email address, then begin my research. I don't usually do ebooks, but sometimes speed requires cutting corners. Within ten minutes I've got *Hers and Hers*, as well as *Hers and Hers and Theirs*—the sequel—and *The House on Blueberry Hill* on my ancient and sadly underused tablet. Someday I will be a middle-aged woman, I tell myself. I'm just getting a jump on my future reading list.

I start at the beginning. The very beginning. Title page. Publisher. I'm not sure what I think I might find. *Pen name of Elsie McAllister* wedged in between copyright and ISBN? Unless it's written in invisible ink, it's not here.

The dedication is *For Bridget.* That's it. Does Elsie have a double life as Bridget? I would say no, but I also would've said that people don't store secrets in carved-out books and keys in phones, and I would've been wrong.

The dedication at the beginning of *Tongues* is another of those tantalizing side notes that torment biographers, like Butterfly Girl. *For the wild things that perished unknown, but not unremembered.* On the question of who the wild things are, scholars' answers range from the plausible—the wildlife that died in the fire, whose bodies Elsie may have seen and grieved—to the way-way-out-there. I, for one, feel comfortable with my belief that Elsie was not making a cryptic reference to either women of the French Resistance or the environmental devastation wreaked by colonizing forces in New

England. I could be wrong, but I don't think I am.

I read a chapter of *Hers and Hers*. I'm not being a snob when I say it's not for me; I'm just not the target demographic for the story of a middle-aged baker and the middle-aged woman she hires and the bawdy jokes they share while getting serious in the kitchen. I open the sequel, examine the introductory pages again. Once again, *For Bridget*.

I open the third and go straight to the dedication. *For Bridget*. Okay, so at least there's a pattern.

Next stop: the publisher's website and Monica's bio. I breeze past the picture of an elderly woman and dive into the facts. *Monica attributes her collection of happily-ever-afters to a lifetime spent with Sarah, her one and only.*

Well, that must sting, huh, Sarah? Unless Bridget is a sister, or a daughter—does anyone dedicate romance novels to their kids? Not Juliet.

I scroll up to look at Monica's photo. It shows two women— one in a flowing dress, the other in a green pantsuit—who look to be . . . let's leave it at not young. The caption says: *Monica (rt) and Sarah at their long-awaited wedding in December 2015.* I look more closely at the woman on the right. Her hair is very white, but also thick and curly. She's grinning like she's wanted nothing in the history of the world more than this celebration. She has a pointy chin and a wide forehead—the ultimate heart-shaped face.

Um.

I know why Elsie's reading Monica Meyers's book.

I think.

I'm sure.

The rain's falling steadily when I leave for Elsie's this morning. *Plunk plunk plunk* go the droplets on my hood, the hoofbeats of tiny plodding horses echoing loud in my ears. *Plunk plunk plunk* goes me as well, as enthusiastic as the beat of a drum wrapped in a blanket and hit with a wilted carrot.

I keep returning to my conversation with Mouse, about how it felt and how I feel now. It's not peaceful but also not bad. The hard part is not wanting her to look at me differently. I'm not sure I could stand that.

The grad student waits at the bus stop. This time he's holding hands with a tiny child. The child wears a blue raincoat, with frog heads for the pockets, and green rainboots. They look at me with huge eyes. I look back. How old are they—three? I don't remember being that age, but my hand knows Dad's gentle grip even now. I let them get on the bus ahead of me.

Elsie already looks tired. Still, she settles herself in the guest room while I drag down boxes for us to go through.

I lift the lid of the first and hold up a vase as though I'm an auction assistant. She waves a hand at it. "Donation."

"It's all vases."

"All donations then." She pauses.

I can't tell if she's waiting for the next box or her next life, so I reach for more.

"What are you saving money for?" she asks abruptly.

I shouldn't have to share my life if she doesn't share hers. Mine, however, hasn't already been dissected by everyone everywhere. She may deserve a bit of her own prying. "Going to New Zealand with my girlfriend." Close enough.

"What does your mother think about that?"

"In what way? She's fine that I'll be with my *girlfriend*."

"Do you think you're shocking me? I've seen far more of life than you."

"Do you think you're shocking *me*, Elsie McAllister?"

Her mouth quivers in with that silent glee. "Piss and vinegar," she says.

I've come to think that means *you get me*. Which just might buy me a little leeway. "Do you know Monica Meyers?"

"Why would you ask that?"

Because I know you know her, that's why. I try another angle. "Ruthie is Frannie's best friend in the book. Who was the real Ruthie?"

Elsie says nothing at first. I've bumped something that she doesn't want bumped. "Martha Bower. You could find that if you looked. That's just laziness."

"You're right. It is lazy. Was she your girlfriend?"

"No. Why would you even care about these things? They're all long past."

She's daring me with her eyes, though. My heart beats like it's developed an interest in freeform jazz.

Elsie gives me a fuck-it glare. She knows I'm chicken and

it's up to her to do the work. "Ask it. It's the only thing anyone wants to know anymore."

Go big or go home, Holiday. "Why did you stop writing?"

She draws a bellows wheeze of a breath. "The real question is, why did I ever start? I told you from the beginning: a woman's stories have no place in the world."

"But that's not true. I know you know that. All you have to do is stand in a bookstore and see all the women's names on the spines to know it's not true."

I know I'm right, and I'm angry for every woman who's ever poured herself into her writing and has had to believe not just in her story, but in her very right to tell it.

I'm angry for me.

I keep going. "And if you really believed that, why did you work so hard to get *your* book published? I've seen the rejection letters. I know what you were up against. You had to have believed your work had a place. *When it takes hold of you, there is nothing else*—what happened to that?" *Elsie, what happened to you?*

Her makeup shows up on her pale skin like colors painted on a porcelain doll face. Her breathing sounds like a bellows. "Sometimes you don't know the truth until too late. That's what I've been trying to tell you if you'd bother to listen."

"You've been telling me not to write—"

"Do as you damn well please. It means nothing to me." Her voice is no more than a whisper. "What is in here"—she clutches her head—"does not belong to you. My life is mine, not yours." The long drag after the final *s* sounds like the hungry suck of smoke into lungs.

I see tears in her eyes. I see how she holds her secrets under her arms like chicks beneath a hen's wings, just as desperate and just as defenseless. Why? Are they secrets like mine, the hot office and the closed door and the thumbprint on the thigh? Like Alex's, the pills and the needle and not being able to walk away? Or like Rosebud from *Citizen Kane*—just something that means so much to her and so little to the rest of the world?

"I'm sorry. I'm really sorry. I was out of line."

She waves me away, tries to stand but can't without my help. I hold out my arm without meeting her eyes. She takes it without a word. When I deposit her at her bedside, I see what looks very much like the cord of her fall alert dangling from her nightstand drawer.

She sees I've seen as she sits on the edge of her bed. She says, as haughtily as is possible when you have oxygen streaming into your nose and still can't breathe fully, "I'll be taking my rest now. Please continue working upstairs."

I'm a shit. I have no right to her story. Her life is hers just as much as my life is mine. Her fame doesn't change that.

I check the volume on my phone. This is such familiar territory: checking and waiting and wondering if I'll miss that one time I should've looked. Did her kids know that when they hired me? I can imagine the family meeting: Dr. Galaxy with a plate of cookies, Cap breezing in with perfect hair, their sister's chair empty until the moment of the decision. *All in favor of the aimless girl with the suicidal brother? The one who'll do anything for money and who knows all about watching someone obsessively?*

I'm thinking about Elsie dying, about respecting her instead of poking at things I have no business with, as I pull a box labeled *Kindling* out from under the eaves. It's too light to be wood. What I find instead are giant pinecones, their resin crumbling off in amber crumbs. When I sniff one, the ghost of pine forests past fills my nose.

Another slip of paper waits here as well, Elsie's elegant penmanship on display: *The smell of seaweed and salt and my regret dried into your hair.*

It gives me pause, the regret. The others have all been descriptions without a narrator inserted. I'm full of my own regret, though; even if all of these add up to a treasure hunt, Elsie never meant it for me. I try to tuck the paper back in, but it sticks to resin on the side of the box.

"Pinecones. Because you want boxes of flammable material in your attic just in case you have a campfire in the yard? Elsie, are they right? Is your mind going?" That's the important question, isn't it? She's living here alone, with the ingredients for an inferno packed overhead and without the strength to escape. Why did no one do anything about it sooner?

I push the pinecones aside to see what else lurks in the bottom of the box. Some old bills, pages from what looks like many old address books—more fire-starting material. Farther down, a stack of paper. Not modern paper. This is yellowed, almost slippery, and when I hold a sheet up, the shape of the glowing light bulb hanging behind it shows through.

Old, old paper, in a box labeled *Kindling*, and Elsie's face and the book of roses and *burn it*, and I can see the smudge of typed words through the backs of the pages beneath my fingers, and my heart stops.

Oh shit.

I leave the attic. I have no clear idea of where I should go or what I should do. I just know that my heart will pound harder and faster and finally burst if I stay next to the manuscript. I go no farther than the living room, where I stop in front of the picture of the wolf tree.

I lean in to stare at it. The lightning strike may have killed it, but the leaf says the message to die hadn't reached all the branches yet. When Elsie said it was a reminder, what did she mean?

Does it matter? The only thing that matters is upstairs in that box. It's got to be one of two things. Even I don't need to write a list that short.

One, it's the original manuscript for *Tongues*. Which, by rights, belongs in a carefully curated collection of her documents, or in a frigging sealed display case where people only touch it with white gloves.

Two, it's an entirely different manuscript, in which case, HOLY CRAP. I mean, HOLY CRAP. She would've written enough material to use up a ream of paper and then . . . forgotten it? I find it hard to believe that someone like her, someone who could've probably published anything she wanted, would've typed the entire thing and then decided to toss it.

Right, 'cause no one would ever do something that stupid.

Cap must've known it was somewhere in the attic. That's why he offered me the money. Maybe she talked about it, or maybe he remembered her writing. I can picture it now: the Elsie from the author photo clattering away on a vintage Underwood, pausing occasionally to take a drag off her cigarette, while her kids played with tin-can phones in the backyard.

The clock starts to chime the hour. My phone blings with a text. Elsie. Like she knows where I'm standing and what I'm thinking.

I'm ready for more boxes. Please select several and bring them to my room.

I can't meet her eyes. My guilt—for simply doing my job—chews away inside me, crawls up to peer through my eyes and to grasp with my fingers. "You sure you're feeling okay?"

"It was just a spell," she says as I get the boxes situated. "They come and go. Nothing to fret over."

I swallow. She's trying to make me feel better about interrogating her earlier, but she's tiny and pale under her bedspread and I feel so much worse. The room smells faintly of Castile soap, and much less faintly of cigarette smoke. How her kids don't notice it is beyond me.

"This box has party goods." I tilt it toward her so she can see the label. I pull out the kinds of paper products I associate with New Year's festivities on *Mad Men*. Red plates, rolls of multicolored paper streamers, pointed hats with their thin elastics and noisemakers with paper fringes. I stick one in my mouth and blow lightly. It unfurls with an unmistakable snap.

She gives a twitch of her head. "Foolish, isn't it? At the time they seemed important to save."

I want to tell her that it *is* important. That these red plates, these silly hats, meant laughter at some point in the past, and that the laughter still lives in the paper and dust.

But she'd tell me I was being sentimental and overstating things. Instead, I take a hat and set it on her head. Her scalp shows pink through her white hair. She touches it briefly with one hand. Gives a bark of a chuckle.

"Still foolishness, on my head or not. The box, the lot of it, can go to Goodwill. Surely people still have parties." She leaves the hat on her head, though.

The next box is costumes. A clown to rival Pennywise, a deeply offensive sixties version of Native American dress, a tiny sailor suit. I try to hold up the box for her, but she shakes her head again.

"I trust you to show me anything misplaced." She continues about where it can go, but I'm thinking of the manuscript and the money and the mystery, and guilt gnaws inside me with yellowed rodent teeth.

When history knocks at your door, when money falls in your lap, when cliché punches you in the face—what do you actually do?

I leave the box as far back as I can push it before I head out for the day. Instead of home, I head to the Cafeteraria to meet Maya.

She's already chosen a purple-cushioned corner and set out two mugs. Hazelnut latte for her, chamomile rose tea for me.

"You're going to put me to sleep," I say.

She lies on her side and puts her head in my lap as soon as I sit, only to promptly sneeze.

"Silly. I'm rolling in dust, all day, every day."

She looks up at me. This is the thing about loving someone: you can make lists of details about them, but nothing you write can capture the reality of the person. It's not just that Maya has brown eyes, molasses dark and fringed with thick lashes that somehow are also not long. Or that she has delicate baby hairs along her hairline that are lighter than the almost-black waves she pulls back from her face. Or that she can smell like all sorts of soaps while also smelling of something that pulls me in like a beehive pulls a black bear. The wholeness of her makes me drunk.

I didn't mean to let go of her. It can happen like that; you don't realize the hand you're holding in the dark has slipped free until the sun rises on you walking alone. But here's a real and terrible truth: as much as I hate myself for letting go, as much as I've told myself I want to go back, I think I needed to let go.

It doesn't make sense. Together we were perfect. I wanted to talk with her, I wanted to listen to her, I wanted to hear her laugh and I wanted to let her cry sloppy snotty tears on my shoulder. I wanted all those things. I still want them.

But here we are. In the past day I've come clean about what happened with John Allen and driven an old woman to collapse by interrogating her about her private life and, just to round it out, may have discovered an unknown wonder of the literary world. Do I say any of this to Maya? Because that silence right there, some might call it a red flag.

"The concert was beyond brilliant," she says. "I would've followed them across the country. In a heartbeat."

"I . . ." What happened after the concert should've been the first thing I told her. Again, whose hand opened, whose held on? "We kinda of hung with them that night."

"Them? *Who* them?" Her eyes still have that contented cat look to them. She doesn't understand.

"The two of them. Blue and Cass."

A sudden wariness shows in her eyes. "You're screwing with me."

I shake my head.

She sits up, scoots back from me. "What the hell, Holi? You didn't call me?"

"You had to go home—"

"I could've found a way to come back out again! I can't believe you would do that."

"It wasn't like that. We just . . . Robin invited them to Betts's house—"

"You hung with them at Betts's house? Not even like you leaned up against a car in a parking lot for a bit?" She pulls her arms in against her waist.

It's not that I feel called out, it's how hurt she looks. "I thought they'd just grab a snack and leave. Nothing big. Then it turned out to be longer."

"How much longer?"

People lie all the time. This time, when it would hurt her less, could be one of them. It isn't, though. "All night."

The whites of her eyes have gone rosy, tears catching on her eyelashes. "Were you embarrassed of me? Is that—"

"No, never! Of course not!" I try to touch her knee but she pulls it away.

"So you didn't call me then, and you didn't tell me about it after. Did you hook up with one of them?"

No, never, of course not. Because in my head Maya and I are the leads in the *sometimes the girl gets the girl* storyline. That one starts with a middle school meeting and ends with a happily ever after and a kiss, where everything that hurts does so only briefly and then heals. "We just talked. They played a few songs with Robin."

"I wouldn't have done that to you. Not ever."

She wouldn't have. That's true. It doesn't mean she hasn't hurt me in other ways. She told me about Logan over the phone. Not text, at least, but still, not in person. I froze, I always freeze. I said *okay* and *bye*, and I put the phone down and curled up as small as I could, my teeth gritting together so hard that my jaw ached for days.

"I'm sorry." But I don't know that I am.

"I need to go." She stands up, arms crossed tightly. She bumps the table and her cup wobbles, sloshing coffee.

I'm up too, holding the table steady. "Please don't leave."

"Is this about punishing me?" Her voice gets quieter and higher, breaking on *me*.

"No. No, no, no."

Only it's too late now. It was too late fifteen minutes ago, and a month ago, and I don't even know when it wouldn't have been too late. Back in September of seventh grade, when I sat down next to her in my new math class and she stared at me as if I had no place sitting there, and I turned scalding red, and she abruptly said *Was I doing my stupid mean face, I'm really sorry, I'm just nervous and . . . do you know what that's like?* And I'd looked down at the cover of the sketch pad she held, at the swirl of leaves twisting over the brown, and the brilliant red flowers, and the single hummingbird poised above, and maybe we saw into each other right then.

What would we see if we met now?

"Text me later?" I call out. She's already halfway to the door. She doesn't turn back.

I want to punch something. I want to yell. I want to cry. I follow her out into the rain, but the bus she boards is gone before I've reached the road.

Silence when I walk in the door. Silence as I go from room to room. A note sits in the center of the table.

I picked up an extra shift till 11. Mom's working until eight and then "studying" at Martín's. Eat this note once you read it. ~R~

It's begun to rain again. It splatters from the leaky gutter at the back. The smell of damp earth rises, traveling across the room with the fine mist blowing in. I turn on the little speaker Mom bought last year and connect to it. The recording I choose is three years old, a bootleg from Secret House. From back when my world made sense.

I crank the sound up and turn off the light. As the music starts, Alex laughs and says *are you sure?* Robin says *always.* He laughs too, and the sound is briefly muffled, and then the music kicks in fully and for a moment there's nothing else.

I up the volume more.

There's magic in that energy, that time. Alone, though, I'm just a girl on an uneven wooden floor with rain tapping at the windows and a heart filled with all the broken things I've tried to box away.

I don't know how long I've been standing there before an itch starts between my shoulder blades and spreads outward. When I turn, Noa's there.

"I knocked. The door wasn't locked and I heard the

music . . ." She moves forward a step or two. She's beautiful in the way that bark is, or dense green velvet moss, or snow falling at night. "I was walking by and I thought I'd stop in."

I turn the music down. She doesn't move, not even as I walk over and reach past her for the light switch. Electricity runs along the wires. It runs through us as well.

"You're dancing?" Rain dribbles from her hair along the edges of her face, the lines of her neck. She wears a green rain poncho, the cheap kind that comes folded into a pocket-size package. Her legs are bare beneath it.

"Not really." I fill a glass from the kitchen tap. "Things are . . ." *Confusing as fuck. And you being here isn't helping.*

"Do you want to talk about it?"

I shrug. "Probably not." Not at all, because I feel like I'm drowning in words, in everything I've been saying and not saying, and I want to turn them off.

Noa watches while I drink the water as though I will save the world by consuming it. No glass has ever been more fully drunk than this one, now, here in this kitchen.

I'm the fool with the beautiful Dutch woman standing two feet away from me while I quietly catalog my mistakes. I should kiss her or tell her to go . . . anything other than holding this glass and waiting for life to solve itself.

She doesn't move—closer or away. The half circle between the curved lines of her collar bones flutters with her pulse, draws slightly in and out with her breath. She shivers a little.

"Oh, do you need dry clothes?" I ask.

"Perhaps a towel for my hair."

"Totally. Follow me." Bathroom? Perfect. Just me and her and the shower . . .

Once there, I take a towel from the shelf and hand it to her.

When she bends forward to tousle her hair, a hidden tattoo appears on the back of her neck, just below the hairline. Line art of a full moon with a bird—a goose I think—flying in front of it. She catches me looking as she lifts her head.

"I did it for love." She smiles as she squeezes the ends of her hair in the towel.

"Like matching ink for the two of you?"

"No. She was the artist."

Of course. She's probably beautiful and talented and utterly unlike me.

Noa blots her neck with the towel, looking at me. "It was meant to symbolize us always finding our way back to each other."

"Do you think you will?"

"No." She holds the towel out. I take it and scoot closer to her so I can swing the door closed and drop it in the string bag hung there. My arm brushes hers.

Neither of us speaks for a moment. I follow her gaze as it travels the room: the tight shower stall, the toilet with the iron stains, the faucet that drips at a snail's pace, the ceiling with brown stains from the upstairs plumbing leak last year.

"It's small," I say.

"My sister's houseboat is much smaller. You can touch your knees to every other thing in the room when sitting on the toilet." I must look surprised, because she adds, "How much is necessary?"

How much indeed. Maya's house has two and a half bathrooms, one with a Japanese soaking tub that I would happily live in. That bathroom is bigger than my bedroom.

Noa's poncho has left drips on the vinyl floor, and one on my toe. Too close, I think. "Can I get you something else? Like tea?"

"I should go. I have to work early tomorrow. Last shift before leaving for Spain."

I've been so silly. This isn't the start of something. It's just whatever exists between two people when one is drifting through the world and the other is drifting through time. People, relationships, even dogs at the shelter—all of them should come with little tags that explain their potential future with you. *Will eventually bite you, but out of fear and with great remorse.* Or *One kiss will definitely go further and you'll never regret it.* I don't know if I'm brave enough to risk *it* without a sign.

Still . . . "Can I take you for a walk in the woods before you go? I think you'll like the place I've got in mind."

"Yes, please. I'd like that very much."

I walk her to the front door. She kisses my cheeks, actual lip to skin contact. She stands here. I stand here. We breathe the air back and forth. A thread hangs from the exposed neck of her shirt. I could reach out and pull it free for her, but then my hand would be touching her neck.

I reach without looking until my hand connects with hers. For a moment our fingers just rest against one another—until her hand turns, both our hands turn, and they touch, palm to palm. I can feel it from my feet to my scalp and every single place between. Her hand and mine, transmitting everything— the essential and the ephemeral—as we hit pause on the world.

She steps away. "Don't forget about the walk."

"Never," I say as she leaves.

I wake up in the dark from a dream of skating around and around a pond—really, that boring—and panic at the thought of the manuscript waiting in Elsie's attic. Screw Stephen King's giant rats and killer clowns; the scariest thing I've ever known to haunt a place has pages, not teeth.

The rain's tapered off a bit. Enough that I don't care about it. I need my bike. I need to work the crap out of myself because something lurks behind my breastbone, hammering to get out.

I take the long way to Elsie's. Even though it's a beautiful ride, I don't usually go this way anymore. The reason why is fast approaching on my right. It's a mud-colored Cape with a Mini Cooper in the driveway.

Fucking Mini Cooper—that's the kind of guy John Allen is. *No big deal. Just riding by and everything is fine. This is my town too.* The fine mist slimes my face, and the smell of the horses stabled nearby hits me in a rolling wave of warm air, and whether I like it or not, I'm alive and in the midst of it all.

I hear a voice call out behind me and pedal faster. Was he waiting by the door in case I rode past? I don't have to talk with him, I don't have to turn back. Even after talking with Mouse, I keep thinking about whether I misinterpreted everything, like maybe it really *wasn't* a big deal. He put his hand on my leg and kissed my neck and said *shall we*—I mean, that was it.

Only it wasn't. I know that. I didn't misinterpret it and I didn't lead him on, and that might be the scarier thing, because if it was something I did, then I could learn not to do it. I could avoid doing that thing. I can't avoid being this person living in this body, though, and I can't try to control how people react to it without losing at least some of myself.

Mouse is right, it's all fucked-up shit.

I hear the car come up behind me. The muffler sounds like it's held on by exactly one thread and a bit of duct tape.

"Holi." He rolls down the passenger's side window and leans toward it as he shouts. "Holi, I thought you could come back for coffee. I'll run to Dunkin's and be back in a flash. You know the way in."

Yes I do. I know the way in, and where all the books are, and what bodies are buried in the files. I know everything I want to know.

He grins at me. That look might've worked on girls he went to high school with (probably not), or college girls when he reinvented himself (maybe), or students wowed by published writers (unfortunately), but it sure doesn't work on me.

I can feel the breeze on my neck, but also his lips, and they feel like betrayal and something more. Even if I wasn't twenty-plus years younger than him, even if he wasn't a professor and I his teenage assistant, if he'd truly thought touching me was reasonable, he could've asked first. I get it now. His fingers and lips were one giant assumption about me.

I flip him off and swing right onto a cutoff to the main road. I'll be gone long before he makes it there. If he even tries. Whether he's seeking Elsie's secrets or my promise to keep his, he's not getting what he wants. Not today or any other day.

I am Holiday Fucking Burton and this is my story, and no other person gets a single page in it unless I write them into the space.

Elsie is sitting on the couch. Macabre as it sounds, I think Death sits here as well. On the same couch, legs crossed, arm stretched out along the back. Not touching her, not talking, just listening to her breathe and keeping her company.

She beckons me closer, pats the couch beside her. It's not as though she's dangerous, but I still feel like I'm sitting down next to Dracula.

She's opened the box of slides and photos without me. I know because she's holding the envelope containing the pictures of her and Martha and the third girl. Up close, I can see that her eyes are red, as if she's been crying. "These go in the box for burning."

"You don't think your friends would like to have the pictures? Or their kids?"

She shakes her head. "They're gone. You live long enough and eventually everyone goes."

That's not true, but I don't want to admit I've been spying. "Your kids—"

"Please add the prints to the things to burn."

It feels a bit like murder to me. Burning the rose book, burning these pictures.

"You will do what I ask?"

I look to the wolf tree on the mantel for help. It offers none. "I mean, it's what you're paying me for, right? To do what you want."

Another of those not-taking-any-shit looks. "It is. I was foolish to leave it this long. I should've known . . ."

Should've known she'd get too old to climb the stairs and root out the things herself. Maybe I'll just burn my stuff as I go. No sentimentality for me. I can't imagine getting that old, but at some point, neither could she.

It's like the manuscript in the attic is alive. It taps back and forth up there, a malevolent mouse with its teeth on the ring of a grenade.

I do my best to pretend it isn't there and continue with my inventory. Ha. As if that's possible.

If Elsie is of sound mind, the manuscript should be hers, and I should tell her about it and not her kids. If she's not—if her hoarding and hiding and burning are signs of illness—then it would be like handing the car keys over to a tweaking tween.

Just before lunch I finally pull the box forward and open it. This time I examine the title page.

Of Wild Things and Flame
By Elsbeth McAllister
July 1949

This manuscript predates the publication of *Tongues* by years. I recognize the name from all her rejections—it must be the original draft.

This is what history feels like in your hands. Heavy, brittle, capable of sucking the air straight out of your lungs and smelling ever so faintly of evergreen.

I place the cover page on the floor beside me and scan the first paragraph.

The fall that the world burned to the ground, I did nothing but watch. When flames rise from the lies that surround you, what else is there to do?

The first chapter is a single page. In it, I learn that the narrator believed her town *deserved* to burn to the ground, without giving a reason why. Everyone always talks about writers starting in the wrong place when drafting their books. I'm beginning to think that I may be holding America's Example of that bad habit. *Tongues* finds its mark from line one, that game-show-answer iconic first line. Scary, but with Mom swooping in for the rescue. This . . . this is bleak. Jaded.

I skip a few pages, handling each as delicately as blown glass. Girls on bicycles, seagulls, five kids in their class at school. Welcome to rural Maine in the 1940s, where one-room schoolhouses still existed. Biking, biking, biking, just the narrator and her best friend—named Patsy in this draft, not Ruthie—riding along on a sunny day until, under a big old tree, the Kindly Oak, they meet up with another girl.

The back of my neck prickles. Not because of the text—bikes, sunshine, three teenage girls. No, it's because of the photo on the mantel downstairs.

Some run wild and that is the only life for them, my mother explained when I was young and didn't yet understand Bridget. Not that I ever really did, not any more than it's possible to understand the fox that cries out in the night, or the doe that passes in silence through a glen. For that is what Mother meant by wild: a creature not meant to live among humans.

Monica Meyers dedicated her books to a Bridget. This doesn't feel like a coincidence.

My phone buzzes. It's from Elsie, just one word: **come.**

I swear she knows what I'm up to. Nothing to do but pack *Wild Things* oh-so-gently into its pinecone sarcophagus and go in search of Elsie.

She's not in the guest room. Not in her bedroom either. No response to my text. I go back through the house, room by room. I'm about to circle through again when I notice that the sliding door to the deck isn't fully closed.

The prickles are everywhere, not just my neck. I rush to the door and slide it wider.

"Elsie? You out here?" Nothing to the right, but as I turn left I see a shape draped over the three stairs down to the yard.

I cover the distance in two leaps. Her O2 canister is on the ground, its tubing pulled away from her nose. Her skin's the color of one of her pressed white linen tablecloths, her eyes closed and her pale lips pursed. On the top stair a black smudge mars the wood. The culprit lies in plain sight.

Cigarettes will be the death of her, one way or another.

I touch her onionskin hand. "Can you talk?"

"Of course," she says. Her voice sounds more like *maybe*, though, and I keep my hand pressed to hers. Just to let her know I'm here, I guess.

"I'm going to get your oxygen sorted out, okay? Um, can you feel your toes?" This is totally not the order of things, or even the right things. Her "Yes" is still a relief.

I step over her legs to reach the canister. As I lift it toward her, I see blood on her lip, and on one hand. For a moment I pictured me getting her back on her feet and into the house, where I'd make her some tea and everything would be fine. That's not how this is going to go. I see that now.

"Elsie, I think you need a doctor." I tuck the tubing behind her ears and set the cannula to her nose.

"No doctor," she whispers. If she was white before, she's become a noncolor now.

"I think you have to go."

"Please." I see the tear dribbling along her cheek. So much crap, all of it, every single bit.

"Hold on." I hit Mom's number. She picks up on the first ring. "Elsie fell on the outside stairs—"

"You need to call an ambulance." The *no arguments* voice, the one she used with me when Robin was lying on the floor in the bathroom.

"She's awake—"

"Hang up and call an ambulance, Holi. The likelihood that she's broken something is so high that you shouldn't even try to shift her yourself. Call now."

She's hung up. I ignore Elsie's pleas and call. I explain what happened, and that Elsie's conscious and that she's bleeding, and they say help is coming. The whole time Elsie cries silently.

It's not until after the ambulance arrives, after I've responded to the paramedics' yells and led them around back, after they've poked and prodded and listened and interrogated until she agrees to go with them, after she's packed up like a milk-white burrito, that I have a chance to say the only thing that matters.

"I'm sorry. I'm so sorry," I whisper to her as they hoist the stretcher to waist height.

She doesn't look at me.

Dr. Galaxy doesn't answer his phone, so I leave a message for him to call me ASAP. I'm scrolling through to find the number for Lucy when he returns my call.

I explain that Elsie's in the hospital and why. He asks if I know how she fell. *Yes, I do. She fell because she will never be able to quit smoking, in case you haven't noticed.* Only I think of Elsie's tears and how it feels to have everyone watching over everything you do. So I tell him I'm not sure, and that she might've been trying to sit in the sun and her canister fell and she went after it.

He thanks me for looking after her and asks if I can lock up. He'll be in touch, he says, once he knows more.

All I have to do is go upstairs, get my stuff, lock the doors and ride away. So simple, but somehow nothing is working. Not my legs, not my arms, not my mind—especially not that.

I pick up my phone and call. "Mom." The words come awkwardly. "Mom, can you come get me?"

"Hold on, sweet pea. Just hold on. I'm on my way."

I can't leave without going upstairs again. I have to know what I've actually found before I make a final judgment. The tinder's coming home with me.

I spend the rest of the day in bed. Mom brings me tea and rubs my back and makes me a grilled cheese sandwich and calls in a favor to have someone else cover the house calls she had left. I don't want her to stay. I don't want her to leave either. Mostly I want to melt down, through the sheets, through the bed, through the floors and on into the ground itself. I want no one to depend on me, no decisions to be left to me to make, nothing but silence and stillness.

When Mom comes back up late in the afternoon, she has peppermint tea for us both. She's got her hair in one of those plastic clips that's like a mouth full of very long and dull teeth, and my head aches just from looking at it.

"Mom, do you think Elsie can be trusted with decisions?"

She puts her clinical face on. "Yes, I do. Her body's tired out, but her mind's sharp. Do you disagree?"

"No, but Lucy and Ca—Chris—they think she has dementia."

"Sometimes it's easier to believe someone is incapable of making their own choices than it is to accept that they'll make choices we don't like. Things like living alone at her age and with her health issues."

"She's going to die." I want Mom to tell me *no, not yet,* but she doesn't. "What do you think happens? You know, when you die." *Comfort me. Tell me that we never end.*

She sits on the bed, propped up by a pillow, and holds my hand. "It's just belief, Holi. At some point you choose the thing that makes the most sense out of life for you, and that belief may have nothing to do with mine. But, since you asked, I think we're like caddisfly larvae in the stream. We're just grabbing things that surround us and gluing them on to try to make a home. At some point, we no longer need that home and we shed it. Become something new, only that little shell left behind."

Except we leave ghosts here instead of shells. "Do you ever hate that you were left with all this . . . everything?"

"You mean because your dad died? I resent the hell out of the medical debt, that we live in a country that lets this happen. I hate that your dad died when he wanted so desperately to live. But this is my life, Holi. Loving him, loving you and Robin, learning how to take care of other people and myself. And we've had it so easy compared to others in similar situations. We've had this house. I'm not ignoring the pain in it, sweetheart. But Dad—and Alex—we had their love and a chance to return it in the time they were with us."

"But Robin. We could've been too late." I've dreamed it so many times in the last year.

"But we weren't. There are so many paths possible, Holi. You can't end up paralyzed thinking about them all. In this one, Alex died but Robin survived. That's the one we have."

"I don't know how not to think of what could've happened."

She puts her arm behind my head and pulls me closer. "There are so many things, sweet pea, that feel like they could destroy you. But life is about becoming. Becoming a person— the truest, best version of yourself."

She's starting to lose me. She knows it too.

"Let's go back to the caddisfly. We're taking what the world gives us and making it into something functional, maybe even beautiful. That's the goal—no wondering about whether better materials might come eventually, whether floods will wash us away. We just keep becoming something made of our connection to the world. Hopefully part of that's love: giving it, receiving it. That's it, I think—the whole story for me."

I want to be little. I want to be the kid waking up in the morning snuggled against her mom, her brother on the other side. I want everything solved with pancake mornings and snow days and dressing as blueberries for Halloween, and it's not.

But maybe life is mostly just minutes passing without drama, and that time is blessed. Not about perfection or knowing the answers. Just one minute and then the next.

I lean forward and kiss her cheek. She holds my head close for a minute, breathing me in, like I'm still her baby.

Dr. Galaxy calls around four to tell me that Elsie's doing okay. Yes, she's broken something. No, it won't kill her. Yes, she needs to be in a rehab facility for a few weeks once she's released from the hospital. Yes, I can visit her and he'll tell me when.

No, she won't be coming home again.

No, I shouldn't feel like that's my fault.

That's it then. Sitting with her in the guest room and unveiling her own possessions to her—that's over. Giving her my arm, helping her to bed, ignoring the whiff of smoke when she'd come out from her nap—it's done. If I'd been downstairs instead of pawing over the treasure she'd buried as carefully as any pirate, maybe I would've stopped her.

I wish I'd known.

Now, though, now it's time to do my job. It's not one she'd want me to do, not one her kids would sanction either. I'm not even sure *I* want to do it.

I pull the bulging manila envelope from my bag and lay it on my desk.

In the burn box in her house is a picture of Elsie, Martha, and a wild thing. Two of them made it out into the world. One of them did not. This, I think, is that story.

Oh, Elsie.
   This is what happened to you.

Robin left for work around 5 a.m. I know this because I had three chapters left at that point. I heard the squeaks of his bed as he rose, and the flush of the toilet, and the opening and closing of doors—fridge first, front door last. I looked out the window in time to see him flash by on his bike.

By seven, Mom's up too, the smell of coffee rising from the kitchen as she packs up for work and school. She doesn't call to me as she leaves, thinking she's letting me sleep in. That's for the best. I don't want to see anyone, talk with anyone, leave my room and walk out into the world.

My phone flashes siren red with everything I've avoided. Dr. Galaxy checking in again to say Elsie remained stable. Lucy letting me know that I'd need to meet with her to go over what was left to sort in the attic and make a timetable. Maya asking if we could meet up. Mouse asking if I'm doing okay. And, finally, Noa.

Time is short.

I make tea. Water in the kettle, filter in my mug, leaves and flowers unfurling as the hot water covers them. I lean into the steam and breathe deeply. Mint and rose petals. I cry.

Back upstairs I open my laptop, then leave it open and turn to my phone instead. **Yes**, I say to Maya. To Lucy, **Yes, I can meet you at the house, when?** To Mouse, **I think?** And to Noa?

Hey are you around tomorrow?

I can look up obituaries while drinking tea because I can multitask. I can drink tea while feeling like someone punched me in the chest. I can drink tea while trapped in a tornado made of ugly things people do, the things that punch someone in the chest over and over and over until no chest remains to punch.

People die in all sorts of ways, ones that you expect and ones you don't. Hurts happen that are simple—like getting dumped—and that are more complicated than calculating the gravitational pull of stars many light-years away. They happen constantly, even as I lift a mug with a picture of a grinning bear and touch the brim to my lips.

The closest newspaper to Eastley, Maine, digitized its archives a few years ago. Discovering that is the easy part. The hard part is searching for an obituary without a date beyond the year, in grainy black-and-white pages filled with auction results and details of military service. I see a whole family die from carbon monoxide poisoning, and a woman give birth to triplets at home during a snowstorm, and a boy's goat win the state championship. I see chicks for sale and hams for sale and pills for "change of life" issues for sale. I see Scout meetings and Elk meetings and Farm Bureau meetings. I see the obituaries of grandfathers and grandmothers and mothers and fathers and brothers, and finally, on November 1, 1947, I see an obituary for Bridget Boyle. Cause of death: suicide.

More specifically, *suicide following a long period of melancholy and mental confusion, her body found on land burned in the Eastley fire.*

Motherfuckers.

Elsie told the whole story of 1947, of the three of them and what actually happened. Of a wild thing and a fire and never forgetting.

Elsie, what happened to your book?

I grab the scrap of paper with Monica Meyers's email address. Juliet told me to be a fan, but I think I'm past pretending. For subject, I put "Elsie McAllister."

I work for Elsie. She's not well these days. I know you're Martha—Patsy to her. I know about Bridget. Can you call me at the number below?

My phone rings while I'm getting dressed. Not just a call; this is Facetime. The caller ID shows a smiling woman with a white halo of hair and a heart-shaped face. Either I caught her on a slow day or my message struck a chord. I answer.

"I hope this is okay," Patsy says. "I'm a bit hard of hearing and find it easier to listen if I can see your face." Her expression is dialed to Business Pleasant, the look you put on to negotiate a billing issue. "I'm sorry to hear Elsie's ill. She's hearty stock, though. I'm sure she'll pull through. How can I help you?"

"You're Ruthie in *Tongues*. Elsie's best friend in real life, Martha Bower. Patsy."

"Yes to all of those." She still sounds neutral, patient.

"Why did you vanish?"

"If Elsie's told you the rest, then I'm sure you know that I left Eastley because I was a young lesbian stuck in a small rural town in the 1940s."

"But you disappeared completely. Because you wanted to . . ." *Wash the stink of the town off yourself.*

"Escape. I wanted to escape. It's not that unusual. And it saved my sanity once Elsie's biographers started hunting for Martha. I'm still not sure how this is relevant to your work with Elsie."

She's going to hang up any moment. No more easy questions. "Elsie's first book, the real one, wasn't fiction. It all really happened, right? That's why you dedicate your books to Bridget."

Patsy's not speaking. I can practically feel her finger over the disconnect button.

I rush on. "Bridget's family was poor—more than poor, her dad was mentally ill and her mom was alcoholic. So she grew up feral, spending her time outside and alone, aside from school. But you all became friends, you and Elsie and Bridget. Elsie would give Bridget her old dresses so she didn't have to wear her father's overalls. You'd embroider them to disguise them but also to make them more like presents. You all had bicycles and one day you took the ferry to an island with a monastery that grew roses. That's why you sent Elsie the rose book."

Patsy looks surprised. "You've seen it?"

"Yes, and the cards you sent her." Don't get detoured onto a dead end. "They did it, right?" Everything is so tied up in me. I can feel Bridget's fear like my own—only she fought, she fought so hard. "They murdered her, those town heroes back from the war. They raped her and murdered her and left her under the Kindly Oak."

The good boys, the soldiers who'd served their country, ones with sweethearts who shouldn't have to pay for an accident with a girl who was asking for it, a girl everyone already thought was disposable.

"Yes, it's true." Patsy's voice has a tremor woven by more than old age.

"Elsie found her," I go on, "and Elsie's father took Bridget's body to the icehouse because he was the doctor and he had to store her until an investigation could be done." Bridget had wanted to live. Elsie wrote that, about what she found when she pulled back the sheet to look at Bridget's body during the long terrible night she spent holding Bridget's cold hand so she wouldn't be alone.

"In the morning, her mother called her into the house to pack some essentials because the fire had shifted toward town. Elsie looked out her window in time to see her father and the minister driving away, toward the smoke. They had Bridget's body with them."

Patsy's gaze has shifted away from me. "All of that is true. When her remains were found after the fire had burned through, they said she'd killed herself, that she was crazy like her father, maybe a drinker like her mother. I know crazy's not the word used today, but it was then. Everyone said it, the whole town repeating the same story."

Elsie, holding Bridget's hand. Elsie, watching a man with deep scratches down his neck dig a firebreak alongside her brother in the field up the road, sharing a jug of water with him and laughing.

"Did you read it—the original book?"

"Some of it. We met a few times that first year after high school graduation, when she was writing, when we were both working as secretaries. She'd bring pieces for me to read. It ate at her, all that rage, all that loss. Bridget, her family, her sense of justice. Writing was the only thing that soothed it."

"She told me that fiction was all lies."

"Elsie never lied as a girl. About anything, ever. She couldn't stomach lies."

And *Tongues* must've felt like the biggest lie someone could tell. Those good boys now heroes, home and suffering the scars of war, their tragedies the wobbling center of the story.

"But in the published version, all that was left of Bridget was Butterfly Girl," I say. One sliver of truth in three hundred and fifty pages. "Why did she do it?"

As if Patsy would know. She sent the card because she didn't. She sent the rose book as a reminder.

"If she gave you the book to read, she's the one you should be asking," Patsy says. "She certainly never answered me. I'm sure this feels like an intellectual puzzle to you, but it's real lives and real pain for me. I've given you what I can and I have nothing more to say. I'd appreciate it if you promise not to share anything about me with the press."

"Of course. Thank you. I'm sorry—"

She ends the call.

I'm here in the present, in Amherst, Massachusetts, and I feel like someone I love has died. Not died—been murdered. By the *boys*, but by their fathers first, with their stares and their sideways comments and the disdain that Elsie meticulously cataloged in her manuscript. They made the rest okay because they'd first made Bridget not a person. They made her story disappear. They filled that space with their own and theirs was what mattered.

Elsie left Bridget along the side of the road. She hated lies and she lied. She thought women shouldn't write, but she did.

Elsie, what the fuck happened?

Noa's texted back, in response to my question about tomorrow.
Yes, what time? And where?

I text Mom to see if I can use the car tomorrow. The answer is yes. The answer would be yes no matter what I asked today.

She left me lunch in the fridge as well—in my lunch bag, with an outline of a heart on a slip of paper inside it. An actual anatomical heart. Because that's us.

It's easier to text Noa than to think about Eastley, Maine.

Come over around 9:30?

Yes. I look forward to it.

We always want questions to have simple answers. But life is fucking messy. All the problems Maya and I have had—there's no one answer for why we broke up. Is it because of Maya wanting to go out with Logan (maybe) or me being the kid from the wrong side of the tracks (marginally) or Alex's death or Robin's overdose or John Allen? Is it because I grew up without a dad? Is it because people change over the course of years, or because only some parts change and the ones that don't no longer match up to the new shapes?

The truth is that it's all of them, because I'm all of me. That's the wormy core at the center of the search for any answer involving any person. Including Elsie.

Two books exist: *Of Wild Things and Flame* and *Tongues as of Fire*. One writer. One small town. One late October weekend made of tinder and spark. Only one story published. Why?

I think the answer, at least part of it, still waits in the attic. It slumbers amidst *Misc: Costume Jewelry* and *Misc: Calendars*. As much *Misc: Correspondence* as I've gone through, there's an equal amount still waiting.

Every line of her Wikipedia entry reads differently to me now. A quote from Elsie in the section on the long road to publication, in which she states that she "never would've given up on it." Everyone thought she meant the book itself. I'd like to think *it* was literary justice—the story she'd set out to tell and still hoped to tell. That could be me projecting, though.

The claim that her editor, Joe Bell, "worked with her over the next three years to shape her manuscript into the novel that would net her a Pulitzer Prize"? That's not what he did. He oversaw the creation of a whole new book, reusing the characters and setting but cutting out the original core.

I walk to town, to the silhouettes of Emily and Robert. Today I sit next to Robert. "Fuck you, old man," I say. "Talk to me about granite, about birches, about anything but humans. Tell me about how everything will someday be okay."

He stays silent, his shadow stretching long across the lawn.

Emily, though, Emily knows the truth: when women write the contents of their hearts, they're called sentimental, while when men do the same they're called brave. She tells me through the grass beneath my feet, through the house sparrows chattering in the trees, that Elsie may not believe women have no business writing but that the business of writing may destroy the very shape of our honest hearts.

No one's home when I return. I grab a handful of peanuts and a glass of water and retreat to my room. Onto the bed, Elsie's manuscript in my hands. Much of it I can't stand to look at again because the fury and pain travel through the words and straight into me. It pulls no punches.

It's not a brilliant book, not like *Tongues* is. It's slow in places and can go from pages and pages of scenery to sudden agony. Sometimes it reads like a legal document, sometimes like diary entries written by a smart and lonely kid. But there are points where Elsie's talent shines through and illuminates the fucking beauty and tragedy and horror and love of it all. If this was her first book and *Tongues* was her second, what would've been her third, her fourth, if she hadn't stopped?

I finally turn to the part that crushed me.

The monk did not follow us through the hedge. Beyond the boxwood wall, the carefully trimmed bushes grew to our waists and a trellised tunnel of climbing roses grew at the far end. Some rows were in full bloom, some had lost their bloom already, and on some the buds had yet to do more than swell. Their scent settled dense as water in our lungs.

"If only we could bottle this." Patsy held one to her nose.

"If you have the money for it, I'm sure you can find this smell in a bottle," I said.

She swatted at me. "Not the same," she said. "Nothing like this at all."

Their conversation goes back and forth, just two teenage girls talking about the things that interest them. It's real but a bit like a transcription of an actual conversation—slow, fun mostly for the people involved. Then, though:

Bridget had dropped to the ground, where she lay staring up at the sky, at the undersides of the roses—at the world, I supposed. She wore the yellow dress I'd told my mother I'd outgrown, the yellow sweater that went with it, her hands stroking the fabric. "It's the bees," she said. "The bees and the sky and the hummingbirds and the stars at night." For the first time in months, she looked alive, free of the darkness that had roosted in her. "The edge of my skin ends here and the grass begins there—that's what we're supposed to think. I don't think it's true, though. Maybe there are no edges to us at all."

Patsy sank to lie beside her, eyes closed. "Bridget, you may go ahead and be nine-tenths grass, but I'm sticking with fully human. Or nine-tenths human and one-tenth porpoise."

"Don't you ever think about these things? Like how the caterpillars on the milkweed are made from the milkweed itself? I feel like I could stay there watching the whole process, from when one hatches to when the butterfly leaves, because it's not just the caterpillar changing into a butterfly, it's the plant changing into a caterpillar."

"Not really." Patsy laughed and in no time Bridget joined her.

It was there, in that moment, that I realized I couldn't see into Bridget's future. Not the way I could for myself, or for Patsy, or for the other children with whom I'd grown up. Bridget's past, present, and future seemed to be, instead of a book of standard size and shape, a single page folded into a kite, the smell of roses on a spotless summer day on a small island off the coast of Maine.

This is what Elsie meant to write. Bridget, and being innocent, and loving people the way we do, and believing the world spins on magic. Elsie wrote the truest thing she knew, even though it wrote her out of family and her home and everything she'd had. For Bridget.

And then she threw that book away.

I wake to a text from Lucy. **We need to meet this morning. Chris and I are both available at 10. Let me know you get this.**

Of course today. Of course they made the plan without me. **I have something to do. Can we make it tomorrow?**

Nothing, nothing, nothing. After a few minutes I leave for the bathroom to confirm what I already know. Periods thrive on drama and mine loves to steal the spotlight of every show. What my body tells me can be boiled down to this: shower, sleep, sleep, and sleep.

What my phone tells me is: **I'm sorry, but it really needs to be today. Chris leaves this afternoon. We can pay you double time, if that helps.**

I text Noa. **Can we bump it to 12:00? I need to work a bit.**

I change into a shirt that says *Fuck You. Love The Horse You Rode In On*, because battle gear can take all forms. On with thrift-store cargo shorts, into my pocket with my watch.

From Noa: **Yes, of course. I'll see you then.** Does that mean *yes, that's fine*, or *yes, of course you're a screwup who would ask me out for a hike and then flake at the last minute*?

No matter. That train has left the station. Back to Lucy. **K. I can be there at 8.**

8 doesn't really work. 9:30 at the earliest. I thought you'd sleep in. ;)

I can think of a thousand things I'd like to say. Exactly none of them will make any of this better, though. **I guess I can make it work.**

THX Holi! You're the best!

I open my laptop and start my opposition research.

Cap lied. That shouldn't be a surprise. He does sell art directly, instead of simply brokering deals for museums. His gallery's heavy on pre-Columbian figurines and pottery. On his website's "About" page, the picture of Christopher McAllister Harkness—gallery owner and member of NAADAA—shows a much younger man in a pale linen suit. Just an average guy who wants to get his hands on his mother's priceless keepsake.

Lucy also has a website. *Lucy Harkness: Writer, Editor, Journalist.* No forthcoming memoirs about living with a famous mother, no cashing in on the name. Just a handful of short stories published in literary journals I've never heard of. Her headshot's of a younger woman as well, an eighties version of an MFA student, I'd guess.

I skim one of her linked stories. It's not bad. It's just that . . . some writing reads like a marble statue: beautiful, hard, cold. No oxygen applied, no epinephrine injected can change its inert nature. In *Wild Things*, everything is in motion: the girls on their bicycles, the ocean against the shore, the bees in the rose garden. Bridget, Bridget most of all, because Elsie returned to Bridget all the life she'd lost. This swirling, unique, wild energy—messy as fuck and jumbled up and so totally alive.

That's what Lucy's stuff is missing. Poor Lucy. She's like a scientist trying to get the proportions exactly right, as if she can measure out meaning in quarter teaspoons or extract it from sterilely crafted paragraphs.

Paul Harkness shows up as a pediatrician and founding member of Northfork Community Health Center in upstate New York. It's a place that provides medical care for all, regardless of their ability to pay. According to his bio, he's also on the board of the local women's shelter and the food bank.

If someone other than Elsie gets the book, I know who I'd pick.

Lucy and Cap are waiting in the living room when I arrive. He's on the couch, legs up and bare feet crossed. He's wearing a tasteful blue tee that likely costs the same as twenty shirts at Goodwill. Lucy sits upright in Elsie's chair. She's a cloud of linen, a waft of vanilla perfume, a fantasia in white upper-class aging. I'm positive that she and her brother are both main characters in the shows playing in their heads, and headaches in the real world.

If I had to guess, I'd say they've been fighting. Her cheeks are red, and on closer inspection, his position appears distinctly posed.

"I'm so glad you could reschedule for us," Lucy says, and it hits me: they may be about to fire me.

The ladder is pulled down from the trapdoor. Two hours is plenty of time to make me explain the organization upstairs.

"We're so grateful for all you've done for Mom. It's been such a relief to know you're with her, and you've saved her twice now, haven't you?"

"Twice?" Cap sounds pissed, though I don't know if it's at her or at me.

"This time and when Mom had to go to the doctor. Right,

Holi?" Lucy gives me a smile that's a little tight, a little brittle, and yet open enough for her bleached teeth to shine.

"Taking her to the doctor wasn't exactly *saving* her." Apparently, Cap's gotten up on the wrong side of the bed and I'm the floor he's stepped onto. "I mean, right?" His smile shows more teeth than his sister's.

Lucy plows ahead. "Holi, we've been working on a plan for how to manage the work now." Each time she says my name I feel like she's trying to establish that yes, she does remember who I am.

Cap smiles at me again. "We're certain that Mom's no longer capable of making decisions for herself. Rational ones."

"She's been sharp the whole time I've been here."

Lucy gives me a sympathetic pout. "I know it seems that way, but she fell going outside, alone, so she could smoke. With an oxygen tank. That's not the act of someone thinking clearly."

No, it's not. It's the act of an addict. "She smokes. For like, her whole life, I bet. If she couldn't quit in all that time, you really think now, when she already knows it's gonna kill her anyway, she'll suddenly be able to stop?" That doesn't mean she can't think clearly. It just means maybe people need to stop pretending and figure out how to keep her safe.

"We can't trust her with her affairs anymore. Not even with her possessions." Cap is nothing if not dedicated to his approach.

Lucy's phone rings. For a moment we're all connected by surprise at the noise. She taps it and Dr. Galaxy's face appears.

He looks exhausted, even in miniature. "You didn't start without me, right?"

I suddenly have the sense of him being the baby of the family while also being the only adult. At least when it comes to practical matters.

"We could've handled this without you," Cap whines. Okay, maybe it's not a full-scale whine, but the irritation is bubbling over.

"I'm more aware of what Holi's been doing than either of you are. Thanks so much for taking the time to do this, Holi."

I still have no idea what *this* is, but I'm glad he's here.

Cap tries to break in again. "All we need her to do is to explain what's been sorted already and what—"

Dr. Galaxy cuts him off. "And what she still has left to do. Mom needs to have the whole picture so she can make some decisions."

"Mom can't make any decisions, Paul. We've talked through this again and again and you refuse to see the signs." Lucy scratches at her wrist, leaving a red welt.

"For fuck's sake, stop picking at yourself," Cap snaps. "Two thousand shrinks and you still can't stop."

He sounds annoyed, but the look he gives her isn't angry. Neither is how he reaches toward her, only to stop halfway. I can see the kids they were, hating and worrying about and loving each other in equal measure.

Lucy takes a pillow from the couch and places it on her lap. In a horribly obvious way, she starts to pick at that instead.

"Our mother isn't incapacitated," says Dr. Galaxy. "There are no medical indications she is."

"How can you say that?" Lucy tosses the pillow aside as abruptly as she picked it up. "God, how can you be so naïve?" She grabs the phone and heads for the trapdoor. Cap and I glance at each other and follow.

The attic looks both smaller and emptier. Nothing is missing. It's just like the rest of the house, lonelier without Elsie there.

Lucy pans the phone screen around the space. "Have you been up here? Do you have any idea how much crap she's stored away?" She kicks at the nearest box. I flinch. "Kindling, Paul. She has a box in a hot attic labeled *Kindling*. You want to know what it's full of?"

She hands me the phone. I hold it awkwardly, away from me. Once she has the box open, she shows her brother what's inside. "Fucking highly flammable pinecones. Tell me how that's the act of a sane woman."

I cough. Faintly, just enough to get them to turn toward me. "When was the last time she was able to get up here? Like ten years ago? More?"

They stare at me blankly.

"Either she put it up here a long time ago, or one of you did it for her recently. Are you saying that Elsie's been sick for decades and it's only just now that you're worried about it?"

Lucy takes it like an actual blow to her gut. I can't see Dr. Galaxy's reaction. I'm bracing to be told to get out and not to come back.

Instead, Cap says, "She does have a point." He's the last ally I expected. "It's not like she labeled it *Memorabilia* and tricked us into carrying it. *I* sure as hell wouldn't have brought a box of kindling up here for her."

Lucy points at me. "But *she* left it here—"

Now I'm the one feeling punched. She's right; I should never have left it. If not for what I'd found, maybe I would've brought it downstairs. Or maybe not. I can pretend I'm responsible all I want. That doesn't mean I am.

"We haven't been fair to Holi since we hired her," Dr. Galaxy begins.

"Since Elsie hired me. She's the one who picked me. Since

then, you"—I point at his tiny face—"have offered me more money to work seven days a week and babysit her. You"—I point at Cap—"offered to pay me ten thousand bucks to pass on any manuscripts I found."

Lucy takes a sudden breath and I can feel her reconfiguring herself into someone blameless.

"And you, you treated me like untrustworthy help and offered me money to stay away. But Elsie's the one who hired me and she's the one I've been working for and she's not here to defend herself or to sort through her own things."

I didn't mean to get as loud as I have. The silence freezes everything once I stop. They'll fire me now, I know they will. All the same, if I've gone this far, I may as well go the rest of the way.

"She's been here mostly alone, trying to hold on to the little bit of time she's had left at home. You three don't get it. You see clutter and crap—I did too at first—but it's not. A box of party decorations is full of all these memories. I have to assume they're of you. Birthdays or whatever."

I can see that now. This attic holds so much more than the awards she tossed into boxes like trash. So many other things she stored with care—things I can never understand because I wasn't part of that life, but maybe her kids can. If they bother to look.

"My dad died when I was three. I don't have lots of memories of him, and my parents were so broke that he didn't leave much beyond his library. What we do have, even the silly stuff—it's worth so much to us. Your mom has reasons for everything up here. You can fire me if you want, but I think she wants me to finish going through it for her. For you."

I don't want to cry. I want to open everything and

235

understand it all. I want to tell Elsie's kids that her reputation is based on the wrong story.

I want to ask the question that I thought was only about her book but that I now understand is about her whole life. *Elsie, what happened to you?*

Dr. Galaxy speaks through Lucy's phone. "We're not going to fire you, Holi. I promise. We need your help—Mom wants you to finish the task and so do I."

Lucy stares down the length of the attic, her eyes rimmed in red.

Cap toes the box of pinecones, takes one in his hand, looks at the phone, at me. "Please let us know if there are other dangerous things up here. I'll take this out when I go."

Noa has dots of sunscreen caught on the edges of her nose. She has a hat too, a green baseball cap with a lizard and the word *Canyonlands* across the front. As we pull into the tiny parking area, I wonder how I look to her, because she looks damn near perfect to me.

It's funny. I wanted to do this so much, but now that we're here, I'm not sure what to say. *Hey, I'm living inside a tornado at the moment and I don't know if I'm going to land like Dorothy in someplace strange and new, or if I'm going to crash to the ground and be destroyed. It's like I've got too much control in some places and hardly any in others, and I don't know what to do, and I want everything to be simple. You know? Just simple.*

"You come here often?" Noa asks when we've gotten out of the car.

"Used to. Especially when Robin and I were little; our mom would bring us here on weekends. Then when we got older, we'd come out here together a lot." I don't mention that this is the first time I've brought someone new without Robin's company. It makes everything different, from sun to tree to sky.

We start downhill. Draining rainwater gurgles along in seasonal streambeds on either side of the dirt road, the forest sporting fading green leaves still a few weeks from turning flame red. We're not talking, but the silence feels right, not awkward. We walk past the snarled husks of old sugar maples, the stands of new pines growing up through the tree graveyard of an old logging site.

The first stretch of water we meet is a thin finger—dry marsh to one side, a muddy slick stretching all the way to the nearest island on the other. The smell rising is of shallow water and mud and late-summer decay, not exactly the sensory delight Noa may have expected. But beyond it, where the water opens out, the world unfolds in postcard splendor. Seventeen miles long, millions of gallons of clean water. This reservoir is the secret heart of the state and makes up a not insignificant part of my own.

Farther in we go. Tree canopies break the sky into fragments as we leave the shore for the woods. The road switches to crumbling blacktop, then back to dirt, before we finally reach a larger cove. At the edge, Noa stares out toward the distant shore like a fisherman counting the days until home. Perhaps she is. I realize that I don't even know how it might feel to be so far from home. Does she look out at the water and wonder how she could've ever left Amsterdam?

"There's a better view up there." I point to a small trail that cuts along the edge of an unused sand pit.

"Show me," she says.

September on the hill is tall grass and goldenrod and asters and scrubby sumac everywhere. Three old apple trees fight a losing battle with time on the rim. Half a dozen apples hang from them. Beneath one, a porcupine snuffles over fallen fruit.

Noa crouches to look at it. It looks back at her, then continues eating. It's huge, old, experienced and not fearful of us in the least.

"You've seen them before?" I ask.

She tilts her head to look up at me. "Yes, but never like this. So close."

"They like the apples. They like all of it, the whole field."

They're not alone. Native bumblebees work the flowers with enthusiasm, only a month or so left to their lives. The swallows that use the nesting boxes set up for them have left for their winter homes, but the hawks have yet to mass in the skies, where they'll ride thermals up and away, gone till spring. Ducks are migrating through and they congregate in flocks on the water.

When I was sixteen, Alex came home from rehab with a theory that in certain places, at certain times—and with just the right music, because she was Alex—we could access points that travel through all of time. Where time becomes a sort of mystical accordion, compressing and releasing, its tune woven from the living and the dead, past and future and the brief breath of now. This is one of those places, I came to believe.

Only now I look at Noa and think maybe that's too simple. Here, this place is change more than it is stillness, not a pin in a layer cake of time. The field, the trees at the edges growing taller until they fall; the bumblebees who die off as the weather gets cold; the swallows who make the long journey away, the ones who won't come back and the ones who will; me, rings added to me from the passage of another year, just like the gnarled apple trees.

I'm changing, I see that now, even though I've been trying so hard not to. At some point I stopped seeing anything but the pain in the past, the potential pain in the future. I learned to hold very still in the hope of not suffering.

Maybe Robin's not the only one trying to figure out how to be alive.

We follow the grassy wheel ruts along the edge of the field to a cluster of stunted trees. A massive honey locust shadows them, a thorny protector guarding a secret. At its feet lies a well. A stone slab's been placed on top to prevent fall-ins, human and animal. A few steps away, in the heart of this little thicket, remains the stone foundation of a house removed in the 1930s to make way for the reservoir. I explain it to Noa: Five towns dismantled, only the roads and cellar holes and stone walls left behind, all so Boston could thrive. For the people then—tragedy. For the Nipmuc people who came before—tragedy and atrocity. Now, for the turkeys and the fish and the moose and the eagles and me—beauty. Home. Love and loss, layer upon layer.

Noa crouches to place her palm on the stone covering the well. I crouch as well, our shoulders touching. "Mom used to bring Robin and me here when we were kids, and we always thought the well was incredibly deep. A bunch of us were here once, though, and moved the cap and found out it only went down about eight feet." Shallow, much as my conversation feels now.

She glances away, across the field, out to the water and the islands. Beyond that, maybe. I don't know what she sees. We all wear glasses with lenses made from the monsters under our beds and the heroes who rescue us, and from when and how we've seen the world, and from why it came to us that way.

"If we go down to the shore," I say, "we can walk along it because the water level's low."

I'm falling short as a tour guide, but Noa grins and says, "Lead on."

We follow the shoreline back. We travel on sand and loose rocks, navigate the skeletal stumps washed ashore. "Everything's gone of the towns?" she asks.

"Everything. Houses, barns, trees, graveyards. They stripped it all. People imagine stuff is left standing underwater, but it's not."

"It's a melancholy place."

"It is." I can feel it when I'm here, a steady buried ache. "It's cool too. When you look into the old cellar holes, ferns and trilliums and things have grown through them and made them beautiful. What they were is vanishing. They're becoming something else."

"Like us." Noa bumps me with her shoulder. That could be anything. Suddenly holding my hand, though—that one's hard to ignore.

I'm not sure how to do what I want to do. Standing on the shore, just the two of us and a thousand rocks and the scent of grapes drifting on the breeze, and not a bit of space to hide from anything, including the blush that springs up. Inside me everything still spins—the world, galaxies, tilting and turning. Nothing is simple.

But sometimes maybe it is. Maybe galaxies align, maybe two girls see through to each other on a sunny day and in that moment are just alive, together.

"Um." I step closer to her. She doesn't back away.

The first time Maya and I kissed, we were magnets connecting, no planning involved. Lack of planning isn't stopping me. Feeling like I'm about to cheat on Maya is.

We're not together. We haven't been for a long time.

Still.

"Is it weird? That I want to . . . I mean, do you . . . ?" My face becomes the sun: that hot, that explosive.

And yet: "Not weird." And she wrinkles her nose again, and leans toward me, and the magnets take hold. It feels like speeding down the hill on my bike: inescapable and perfect and dangerous, that space where only bodies exist.

Softly chapped lips and where do noses go and oh yes, this please.

"Was that what you meant?" she asks.

I nod, not sure what to say. "Thanks." Thanks? Really, thanks? Should I shake her hand too?

I don't have to think about that either because she kisses me again. It's a current and I'm pulled right into it. My hand is on the back of her neck and I'm not sure how it got there; hers are on my back. I want some part of my life to always be this, this afternoon and the water and the light and this kiss.

We both pull away. I stare into her eyes. My skin's suddenly so full of nerve endings that even the slight breeze against the hairs on my arms feels like overkill.

"That was kind of great." I utterly fail at words. A great writer would have a sonnet at hand.

"It was." She puts a hand to either side of my face, palms so much cooler than my cheeks. "Kind of great."

"I haven't ever kissed anyone but my ex. I mean, outside of family." Words are the sidewalk that I'm stumbling drunkenly over.

"Me either."

I'd assumed that speaking multiple languages and wandering the world on her own meant she had more of everything, including exes. "I thought you would have—because of being away from home so much . . ."

Noa shrugs. "It wasn't what I was looking for. I wanted to feel like myself again. Do you ever feel like things change so much, so fast, that the center of you is lost? Most of my travel was me figuring out that my center wasn't gone, just moved. And I had to move with it."

My center's been AWOL for a while now. "I wish I could be that brave. I thought going to New Zealand with Maya was the answer for me, but . . . I don't think staying is helping, but I don't know how to leave. I don't have friends everywhere like you."

"You know me, which makes you travel friends with the people I know."

"Travel friends?"

"People with information and couches, who'll eventually be regular friends. Once you start traveling, your travel friends become a huge network because everyone you meet has at least one or two of their own."

"You make it sound easy."

"It is; it can be. You need to trust—yourself most of all."

Trust is the opposite of easy. Trust is believing that Robin doesn't need me to count his pills and how many hours he sleeps, that Death isn't stalking the people I love.

But maybe easy is also her hands, mine, our bodies, the ways in which water and desire are the same.

Goodbye is this: two girls, one sidewalk, one wisp of moon on the horizon, a hug like a lifetime wrapped in a minute, a kiss made of sunlight and here and then and always and maybe never again.

I know I'm asleep, I can feel the dream like wool between my fingers, but I still don't wake up. Bridget is with me, her long straight hair in a tangle along her neck, oak leaves rustling above us. She takes my chin in her hand and pulls me around to face the field. The color's gone from the land, from the sky. Bridget's mouth moves in words that the wind carries away. I move closer to hear, but it's just the sound of bees buzzing.

Or it's my phone, vibrating away on my desk. Dr. Galaxy, of course.

"Yeah?"

"Holi, did I wake you?"

"No, not really." I was just dreaming about your mom's murdered friend who was written out of her own story in order to make more room for her killers. That's all.

"Oh, good. I worried about that. People your age tend to sleep."

Yes, we do. In our coffins, with soil fresh from Transylvania, or hanging upside down from trees with our clawed feet holding fast. That's the way he said it—as though we were a different breed. Isn't he a pediatrician?

"Anyway, my mother has asked me to see if you can come visit her. I suspect she wants to thank you. We all do."

You all *should*. You put your mom in a frigging eighteen-year-old's hands because you were all too chicken to take responsibility for her safety.

"When?" My pocket watch tells me it's 8:05—a.m., I hope.

"She said ten-thirty. She has quite a bit of physical therapy, you know. It tires her out. I can give you directions to the facility."

All I have planned is working at her house. And . . . yesterday with Noa becomes today without Noa, a sudden empty spot. "Yeah. Okay."

Robin's door is cracked open. I stick my head in. "Hey."

He's got his bass out, unplugged, and he's playing something I don't recognize. "Hey, I didn't know you were up."

I explain Dr. Galaxy and going to see Elsie.

"You need a ride?" he asks.

"Nah, I've got it."

"So it's okay if I take the car?"

"Depends on what you're doing." I mean it as a joke. Robin's life revolves around work and home and sometimes letting Betts or, lately, Noa in. At the thought of Noa my internal wiring scrambles, not knowing whether it's supposed to be conducting happy or sad or any other emotion.

"Gonna catch up with Hedy," Robin says.

"You're going to fucking what?" I'm not confused or sleepy now. Just 100 percent steaming furious.

"See Hedy. What's the big deal, Hols?"

"The big deal is that she blew you off! You were in the hospital and she never came then or after or even sent stupid flowers!"

"Wait, just stop. First of all, flowers? Hedy would never do that in any situation. And second—"

He looks terrible. Guilty, I think. Disappointed? "Hedy didn't ditch me, Holi. I told her I didn't want to see her or talk to her."

I'm on a roller coaster, coming into a loop, and my restraints have vanished. "What? You did what? You let me believe—"

"I didn't *let* you believe anything. You didn't even ask."

"But you could've told me!"

There's that moment when you've been watching someone inflate a balloon and it hits you that the balloon is going to pop. You can feel it in your spine, you want to cover your ears, but that's not going to help because it's not just the sound of the explosion that you're dreading.

Robin is the balloon. "Do you know what this is like, Holi? To have people look at you like you broke their hearts, to know they don't trust you anymore? I fucked up and I hurt everyone. I'm your big brother, I'm supposed to look out for you, only here you are watching over me. I didn't want Hedy to see me because I didn't want to see how much she hurt. How much I'd made her hurt."

"But that's messed up." I think of Hedy's quiet voice and intense eyes and how much she cared, really cared, not just about Robin but all of us. How much I've hated her in the last year. "That was a shitty thing to do—more than shitty." To all of us. "Alex died and then you left us, Robin. *You* fucking died and I saw it. I came home from the hospital and picked up all the wrappers on the floor that the EMTs left behind."

"I know that! Don't you think I do? Don't you think I'm reminded of it every time you're texting to check on me, not turning out your light until I'm in my room? I'm trying to do the right thing now. I know how much I hurt Hedy—"

"You don't know. You can't know because you're not any of us."

"Just like none of you are me."

There it is, cold smooth reality. We don't get to live in someone else's skin. All we have to bridge the gaps are words, and only if we listen to each other.

"I think I need things to change," he says. "I need us to change."

We already have. So much. I already can't go back to how I was before.

I want to go back. I want to go forward.

I want.

I want.

I want.

I'm filled with anger. Some of that is fear, I know, and some of it is shame at people seeing my hurt and how it made me different.

And some is love.

Robin says, "Hols, I gave Cass some old Horse Caves demos, and I heard from her yesterday. She and Blue invited me to sit in on some gigs with them. Maybe join the tour the whole way through."

My heart stops. "You're not going to go."

"I am. I—"

"Mom won't let you."

"Mom said I should."

Mom's all swept up with Martín when she should be keeping an eye on Robin—

No, that's not right. Not fair. It makes my insides hurt, like everything has been sucked out suddenly, a drought on fast-forward. Robin and me and Mom, we're the stayers. Only . . . what if we're not?

Puck, always with a phone full of numbers, an aura full of open doors and other people's giggles and rapt stares across crowded rooms as he played his guitar. Is Robin still Puck? Am I still me?

I check my pocket watch. I have plenty of time and not anywhere near enough. "I have to go," I say.

"I can give you a ride so we can talk more." He takes a step toward me; I take a step back.

"I think I need the fresh air. Some space, you know?"

I can see that he does know, and how much he wants me to tell him everything's okay. I want that too—to say it, to have someone say it to me so I can believe them. But whatever okay is, it's not where I am now.

At the bike rack outside the rehab center, guilt swarms me like seagulls surrounding a lunch on the beach. Elsie's face as the EMTs carried her away has bumped Robin from the forefront of my thoughts. The easiest thing to do right now would be to enter her room, smile, ask how she is and what work I should do, and leave. I could hand the book over to Cap and be done with it all. This choice shouldn't be mine.

The smell in the building as I enter stirs a mammalian response in me. Dad died in the hospital. The flu ran right over him, fire-fast, and he was gone less than a day after he was admitted. I never even saw him there. The time I spent at the hospital with Robin, though, everything was permeated. My hair, my clothes, my skin. Nothing worked to remove it.

I check in at the desk. "Room 310," the receptionist tells me. I soothe myself with the feel of my pocket watch in my hand. I do not fit among the beige walls and the beige plants and the nurses hanging out at their station, side-eyeing the girl with green hair and hairy legs and bike shorts and mask. The look I give back holds a bit of pity for anyone who's learned to blend in with beige.

I locate 310. As I pass the room next door I glimpse an old, old man by himself, sitting up in his bed and staring out the window at the scrubby field stretching away toward the strip malls and the busy road.

Elsie's alone too. She's too small to dent the pillows propping her up. She looks at me. I look at her. Dr. Galaxy may have been wrong when he told me she wanted me to come; whatever the expression on her face is, it sure as hell isn't delight.

It's up to me to start the conversation, I guess. "Does it still hurt?" Instead of *I'm really sorry but I had to call. You know that, right? That I couldn't have fixed you. I was hired by so many people, for so many reasons, but not that one.*

"That's not why you're here." Her attitude rides on, but it comes via a voice I strain to hear.

"Why then? I know you don't want to thank me, no matter what Dr. Galaxy says."

I don't catch it until she sucks in a breath—even more audibly than usual. "Is that what you call Paul?"

Crap. "Not to his face." Does that even help? "It's . . . he was wearing a tie with stars on it . . ." No, that's not helping.

She looks straight at me. "I thought it was because he always has his head in the clouds."

She starts to laugh. Not a stunted giggle but a loud bark. God, did they give her Oxy? *America's Treasure Develops Opioid Addiction Following Negligent Care by Oblivious Caregiver.*

"He's very nice," I offer.

"He's pleasant. A dreamer. He's the one who should've written. Not Lucy. I don't think she's capable of loving it."

I almost start in with *Well, according to you, women,* but I don't. My nerves have been fully cheese-gratered by my conversation with Robin and now with what I'll tell Elsie. It's not banter time.

I pull a chair up close to the bed so that neither of us has to speak above a whisper. "I found it. That's what you wanted, right? For me to find it and keep it hidden?"

A real writer could probably capture her expression. I'm not a real writer, though.

"You have it?" She is an old woman, very sick, and my lungs strain in sympathy for hers.

"Not with me. It's safe, though. I would never let anything happen to it."

"No one else has seen it? No one else knows?" One hand clenches the blankets, its skin so thin that the bones of her knuckles look bare.

"No. I promised you."

The hand relaxes. My insides do not.

"Why didn't you publish the original book? For Bridget." Because Bridget is who I think of, can't stop thinking of. Bridget by the ocean, *like a sea captain's wife, like a tern waiting for flight.* That's what Elsie wrote. That was what Bridget deserved. "It was true, right? It was the story you set out to tell."

"That story was important only to me. And Patsy."

She's a tiny music box, her wind-up time rushing toward its end. I should stop. But time will continue whether this conversation does or not.

"It could've been important to so many other people." Bridget in the wolf tree watching a cicada grow its wings. Bridget riding a bike on the island where the roses grew.

I think about the woman in the author photo, barely older than me. Elsie set out on a quest to avenge Bridget by telling her story. She gave up everything for that quest. Lived with all that anger, all that isolation, all those rejections, and then . . .

"It was Joe Bell. Wasn't it? You changed the book for him. Did what he told you." She could've said no. She could've done something else, waited. "You gave up."

"I did not give up." She hisses at me like a snake. "Joe knew it wasn't good enough. *I* wasn't good enough."

I didn't fight for *Dragon Girl* at all. I have no box of rejections. Just one guy's casual criticism was enough to make me stop.

"No one would've published it in its original form. Is an unseen book even a book?" Her hand continues to clench and loosen, and I'm not sure whether it's anger or pain or part of a full-body effort to keep breathing.

"Then publish it now. You could get anything published now! You could finally have justice."

"There is no justice. Bridget is gone."

"Patsy isn't." I keep expecting that something I say will make her pause, will make her change her mind.

I keep being wrong. "At best, it would be an old woman's vanity project. At worst, they'll say that I'm senile and my children took advantage of me, published an inferior manuscript for the money. It would serve no purpose."

"Please, Elsie. Don't ask me—"

"You promised." She grabs my arm, her hand traveling along it until she finds mine. "You promised you would do what I asked."

"You can't. It's not fair."

"You promised me." Unlike her children, Elsie does not offer me more money. She knows what she's asking goes far beyond that. "It's why I chose you. Because I knew you would understand. As a writer."

There is a word for this feeling, but its language lives somewhere other than our tongues. It's frightened and incandescent and furious and damaged and loving and maybe two thousand more things. It's what I've wanted to hear from her every day since I started. But, "Why do you say that?"

"Because you listen like a writer. There is no skin between you and the world. I see it."

"So you know I can't—"

"I know you must. I wasn't brave enough to do it myself. At night I'd think the fire would come for us—me and the book. I put it in pinecones. I dared myself to fall asleep with a cigarette. This is the only task I have left. Please." Like a chest dragged from the deep on a creaking chain, that word.

"Elsie—"

"Ladies, it's time for Elsie's meds." The nurse entering the room is a big Black woman with a Jamaican accent, wearing scrubs covered in ice cream cones. She puts her hand on my shoulder. "Sweetheart, you come by and see your gram any time, okay? Visiting is the best thing you can do for her, but I need to look after her now."

Elsie grips my hand, pulls me toward her. I bend close. "You promised," she whispers.

Outside, the rain's left behind a change in the air. Not cold, not really. Just the understanding of the coming dark days. I head back up the big hill into town. I want to be snuggled in a giant comforter in a quiet place, where all I have to be is warm and safe. I want someone else to give me all the answers, about Robin and life and what to do with my life and what to do with Elsie's book. No one can do that for me, though.

Scratch that. Maybe someone *can* help with one answer.

Juliet's sitting in her home office. She's in fleece bottoms and a ratty shirt with kittens on it. The shirt is a joke. Mouse accuses her of being a crazy cat lady and salts her life liberally with cat paraphernalia. Juliet tolerates it.

"Good afternoon, Holiday! You're just in time to consider the Western literary canon with me. I think I'm ready to kick the habit completely. What's your take?"

"I guess I don't have an opinion at the moment."

She looks at me intently, less of a professor now and more a mother. "That's valid. Mouse is working. You can head over there if you want to catch her."

"Actually, I was hoping to talk to you."

She's wrapped her hair up in a messy bun, and her feet are bare, and on my Juliet list goes *little toes have hunched backs and big toes are hairy as a hobbit's*. "Pull up a chair. What's up, kiddo?"

I drag over the rickety chair on rollers that looks stolen from a 1950s office. "If I ask you a question, can it just be between us? Can I trust that you won't try to track anything down?"

She makes a duck bill with her lips. She does that when perplexed. "It depends on what you're talking about. If you're committing murder, for example—"

"No, it's . . . If you had something that would make a big difference if other people knew about it, but someone also didn't want anyone to know, how would you know what the right thing to do was?"

She shifts back in her seat and blows on the tea in the mug she holds close to her lips. Add to list: *one hand trembles slightly, enough to wiggle the top of the tea*. "Can you give me more than that?"

"If you found something, and it would be the kind of thing that would . . . would change people's thinking about something forever, something big . . . is it more important to do what the owner asks, or to share it? Especially if . . ." I look at her like I'm seven and begging her to understand why I cut Mouse's hair off. "If the owner will be dead soon."

To her credit, she holds steady, except for the slightly deeper breath she draws. "I see. Assuming the owner is the creator—not a plagiarist, for example—well, that's very hard, isn't it?" She stares out at the street as a commuter passes on an electric bike. "Hmm. If a painter stashes away a few paintings that aren't up to their standard, that they think are foolish dabbles, and someone finds them and insists they become part of the painter's body of work, without the painter's permission, is that right or wrong? What if the painting were intensely private, the artistic equivalent of a sex tape? Does the public have a right to it merely because the painter is a public figure?"

It's clear that she knows what I'm talking about, so I just wait for her to say more.

"As a member of the public, I might think I was owed that piece. As a scholar, I'd desperately want it to expand my understanding of the artist's work, their process, their life. As an art dealer, I'd want the payout waiting for me. The question is whether those desires outweigh the rights of the artist. Whether the artist owes us their life—their intellect—entirely and without limits." She glances down at her cup as though she'd forgotten she was holding it. Maybe she had. "Holy cow, that's a tough one. Had I known it was coming, I would've made Irish coffee."

We both laugh.

"Seriously, I think lots of things aren't meant for other people. Writers, for example, might write entire books that were what *they* needed, not what they wanted to share with the general public. I can tell you that if someone went through my manuscripts and decided they knew what was best to do with them, I'd be pissed as hell. If I lose control of them, I lose control of my own narrative. My story, my power in the world. Would I feel the same if I weren't long for the world? Maybe more so then, because I would have so little control over so many things, and so few chances to change anything. On the other hand, it could be that I'd be freer to put things out into the world, things that I'd hidden my whole life. I might want to say things that I'd always been scared to say."

"It's hard to imagine you being afraid to say anything."

She snorts. "Show me someone who's never been afraid to speak and I'll show you someone either lacking imagination or born into power." She pauses, swirls her tea and stares into it. "I won't pretend that I don't have a good sense of what you're talking about, Holi. That's not fair to either of us. Depending on what you have, it could be anywhere from a curiosity for academics to something that shifts an entire reputation."

A corset engulfs my chest, the laces pulled so tight it's hard to breathe. Yes, no, yes, no. Does it belong to Elsie or the world?

Juliet's phone rings. I jump at the sound.

"I've gotta go," I say. "You take your call. Thanks for talking."

She touches her fingers to her lips and blows me a kiss. I wave goodbye.

Maya's texted me three times and called once while I've been with Elsie and with Juliet. I can continue to put her off until I'm home. And clean. And have eaten.

I know why I'm dragging my feet. Does she?

I could wait a little longer, hoping life will magically calm down. I have no reason to believe it will, though, so I text to ask if she can meet me at Groff Park. She immediately says yes. I get back on my bike and proceed to the next stop in Holi's Really Hard Day.

She's sitting on top of a picnic table, wearing jeans and a tee from the CSA, her hair held back with little pink butterfly clips. I can feel her excitement radiating from yards away, her anger from the other day tucked away for the time being.

I stand in front of her. "Hey." My voice sounds funny to me.

Not to her, unless she's ignoring it. "Hey! I was emailing with a farm in Ireland and they want me to come for a few weeks. Like, right away. Only I said I needed to wait for you to be done with your job. Our visa applications for New Zealand are already in, so we're just going to be waiting on them anyway, and the tickets to Dublin are super cheap. Ireland's beautiful—you'll totally love it, I promise."

It feels like she memorized this speech and now, in the moment, she's not sure it's the right one. I'm pretty sure it's not.

"What's wrong?" she asks.

I run my fingers round and round the rim of my pocket watch in my pocket. Crap.

I don't want to do this. I want to be on the other side, at some point in the future where we call each other from wherever we each live and talk about everything, the way we used to, the way I think we've forgotten how to do.

She understands before I say anything. She's always been way ahead of me. Knowing when we started being in love, and when we started not being in love. Of course it's not simple like that. I don't know what happens to love over years and years, a lifetime, but I don't think it switches on and off. It's like one of

Mouse's weird experiments with decay, where the body slowly vanishes and then something else is there. It could be beautiful and sad like bones, or beautiful and happy like an oak seedling, but it's never just gone.

"You're not coming." She's looking at her hands, not me. The coldness isn't really cold. She's trying not to cry.

"No. I'm not."

"Because of the money?" She gives me a quick glance, trying to steer us onto a familiar path.

If I say yes, that's easy. So much has already been about money, like all the things I haven't done with her family because I don't want to struggle to be part of a secret handshake club that would tolerate me for Maya's sake.

Not this time. "It's just . . ." Just, just, just. It's *just* this little thing, *just* that one, *just* ignore the big one. "It's like we're in this fake place all the time, where we're broken up only we're also not."

"So if we were back together again it would be okay? Because I think I made a mistake before. I keep thinking it—"

"It's not that. I mean, it is, but I don't think it's about you breaking up with me. I think you did what we both needed, even if I couldn't admit it at the time. Everything hurt, and everyone was dying or dead, and I wanted this—us—to be something sturdy. Safe, I guess. I think you knew that's what I was doing and that it wasn't right for either of us. I love you—I think I'm always gonna love you. But I can't go with you. I'm sorry."

I want to sit on the picnic table next to her. She'll put her leg over mine, her ankle between mine, and I'll squeeze it with my feet while we wait for the fireflies to come out. Only the lights of the fireflies have been gone since August. Fallen leaves would collect on us as we waited, then snow, and finally we'd cease to be ourselves. What we need to do is walk away now, and some July night next year, maybe we'll be able to wait for the fireflies again. As friends.

She won't meet my eyes. I feel like shit. There's no going back to normal anymore, because normal was an iceberg that ended up in the warming ocean that is me.

"Do you want to talk about it?" I ask. I don't. I don't want to talk about anything. I want to go to bed and stay there for the remainder of my lifetime and probably a few generations after that.

She shrugs. Shakes her head. "I just want to go home."

I watch her walk away, up the grassy hill. She gets into her mom's Tesla and sits for a minute or two or ten, then turns on the car and drives away.

We are done.

I'm finally done.

It's time for me to go home too.

Deep down, so deep that I can feel it more than understand or see it, I am relieved. Whatever will come, for the first time in a long time, my feet are on the ground.

Robin came home after I was in bed. I heard him in the bathroom, heard his bedroom door close, and then silence. He's gone again when I get up this morning. It's just as well—I'm not sure I'm ready to talk with him. I'm not sure I'm ready to talk with anyone, which is why spending the day in Elsie's house feels perfect.

Except, of course, that one of the looming issues in my life is whether I'm going to do her bidding.

About two thirds of the attic has been cleared at this point. I could start anywhere there. Without Elsie to oversee the contents, no one but me cares what comes downstairs when. Therefore, I should feel no guilt at all if the box I choose is all the way at the back. *EPHEMERA*. An inch below her label is mine: *Old Correspondence*. No matter what it's called, I think it contains a murder weapon. Bridget was killed a second time. I know the who, but not the how. I should find it here.

The box is full of letters—mostly from friends, from other writers. The first time I opened it and saw some of the names, I imagined the letters would be grave and full of importance and beautiful lines, but the few I read were pretty mundane. Boring or not, this time I'm here to read them all.

The top of the stack are births and deaths and *remember when* and *I miss you*. Some are from Patsy. I read these slowly, expecting revelations, getting the sorts of things that friends send to each other when their lives are rubble and hope.

I miss her so much. Don't you? I think about riding around Barnacle Island and how happy she was in that dress of yours. It was always like that with her, feverish happiness or utter despair, or that place that seemed more between worlds than anything.

I don't mean to write you like this. I start out with a mental list of things that you might enjoy. The funny poodle owned by the woman in the apartment below—it's a tiny thing and she dresses it in pink sweaters with bits of feather trim or little beads, as though it's a spoiled and ridiculous child. The woman dresses herself quite sensibly.

These are the things I should send. Instead . . . I miss her. I miss you. I miss the roses along the beach, and the gulls—even the gulls—and the Kindly Oak, the way it was before that day. Write me.

Patsy wrote these to the Elsie of the picture on the book jacket. Is Bridget just outside the frame, in her place between worlds? Is she always there?

I keep going. Notes from Joe Bell paperclipped to early reviews of *Tongues*. The one from the *New York Times*, with a scribbled *Well done!* on the margin and a handwritten letter attached.

I think we've done it, Elsie. I know it was a slog. I know you'll never forgive the fights over punctuation—just accept that I'm in the right next time—and the endless rewrites. But this book will be a sentinel of truth over the years to come. I have complete faith in that.

No mention of *Wild Things*. I keep going. I can smell the answer I'm looking for like I can smell hidden roadkill at the height of summer.

And finally, here it is: in another letter from Joe Bell, three years before *Tongues* was published.

> *I understand your attachment to your original manuscript, Elsie, but as your editor and, I hope, your friend, I'm asking you to look at it as a reader would. The girl, Bridget, would she choose to have herself memorialized as you have made her? Unkempt, of questionable sanity, meeting a sordid end? Who would such a story serve? It would be a book read by few, mostly deviants who are drawn to the lurid bits. And to be honest, I'm not sure you are the writer to do this tale, or the girl, justice. I think you know that as well. Perhaps in the future, after you have a few published works under your belt and can distance yourself appropriately, you may have the skill and perspective required for it.*
>
> *Meanwhile, the pieces are already there for the better book. The love Frannie has for her brother—indeed, the love the family as a whole has for one another—could easily become the focus. You make note of a young man who returned from the war and died in the fire, with a question as to whether his death was suicide. I think we need to revisit that incident and its potential. It promises a more universal story, the sort that truly speaks to all readers. You could keep the girl's perspective, possibly younger. A touch of hero worship for her older brother and her brother's friend; a hint of a girlish crush? It would be a wonderful lens through which to view the larger, more important events that transpire.*
>
> *Trust me; there's greatness here, waiting to be tapped.*

And please, Elsie, consider me an ally in your goal of preserving your friend's memory. We will find room in the final work for her.

How could Elsie have trusted him? He literally wrote Bridget off as being of "questionable sanity." Elsie's original manuscript showed Bridget's mind as it was, not as Joe Bell believed it should be. The final draft erased her.

But he did what he promised. He made Elsie famous. He convinced—pushed? manipulated?—her to write the Great American Novel.

I am so close to ripping up the letter. It's history, like all the other documents here, but it's history I'd like to shred. I hate Joe Bell. I want to dig him up from his grave and grind his bones into dust, until the earth swallows them completely. I want him to be as forgotten as Bridget is.

He made Elsie doubt her writing and the story she wanted to tell, then used her talent as a pen to make something *he* wanted. She was so young and had no family and carried all this trauma, and the only relief she'd had, according to Patsy, was writing *Wild Things*. Here he came, with all the privilege of a successful white man in the fifties and the power of being an established editor, and there she was, a woman who'd had rejection after rejection from people who called her work disgusting. He told her that she wasn't good enough, but that if she did what he said he could make her a real writer. And that *then*, maybe, she could give Bridget her justice.

The realization hits me like electricity from a downed wire. Did Elsie see that in me from the beginning? A girl who destroyed her book on the word of a man who wanted to use her for something else?

The anger that inflated me like a helium balloon escapes through a jagged hole made by John Allen and his hands and my finger on the delete key. I can't cry. I can't even tell what I'm feeling, other than shaky and lonely in Elsie's abandoned house and wishing Bridget were alive and sitting here with me. Not just Bridget. Alex too, and Robin from before Alex died, and Hedy, and Maya—all of us, happy.

Maybe I do cry a little.

I'm as close now as I'll ever get to the reason she never wrote again. It was like Patsy said: Elsie hated lies and she told the biggest one she could, and she discovered the world loved it. How could she not hate herself, hate her writing, hate the awards and the fan mail and that one misplaced scene, that last scrap of Bridget shoved in a corner? How could she trust herself to write anything else?

I've found what I was looking for, but I keep going. Deeper in, searching through letters from other writers, unique long-hand, unique styles. Names I recognize, plenty I don't. But no sign that any of them knew Elsie as more than the writer of *Tongues*.

Elsie, why were you so alone?

I pause at a long letter written on thick cream paper with a monogram—CKB—centered at the top. The handwriting is sharp as lightning, all zigzags, broken further by stern punctuation.

Elsie dear,

I wish we had had more time. Isn't that always the way, at least once you've left childhood behind and mortality begins to unveil herself? I understand, of course. You have all the things that one might desire: husband, children, home, and more than a little fame and fortune. It will always make sense to me that you chose that over the life of a vagabond such as myself.

Even now I think, Elsie, that you might have loved this life as well. Once one sees the world like this, in all its moments of intimacy and despair, it changes you. Makes you more alive, I suppose, more aware of how brief it all is. And it is brief. I know that now. I'm left counting days instead of years, in this hospital in Paris, with just the tree outside the window to keep me company.

I often think of what you told me, that every cigarette you light is a bead on a rosary of regret. So it has been with me, one drink at a time. We would have been a pair, loving the world, hating ourselves. I think it would have been fun.

I've enclosed a picture for you. I bought the film off the stringer who snapped it all those years ago, before he had a chance to recognize what he had. I never had a reputation to uphold, but I didn't want you hurt. I destroyed the negative after making one print. Over the years it became a compass point for me, a reminder that we are never just one thing. Inside the frame, everything we were to one another for that brief window of time; outside, the entirety of the lives we've lived.

Anyway, a picture.

I have one more thing to say, and I wish I had long before now. Your work healed people, but it destroyed part of you. Elsie, what of you, of the artist in you? You still have time to change course. Not for your readers, no matter how they idolize that single book; not for Bridget, whose suffering ended so long ago; but for yourself. In the entirety of

your life, does that one piece of you not deserve freeing? It's
not too late.

> *Yours always and in love,*
> *Charlie*

The picture is clearly not CKB-caliber work. It's a black-and-white snapshot of two people. Charlie—tousled blond hair, brown bomber jacket, slouchy charm—looks like someone who grew up with a summer house and early mornings rowing on a misty river. They're both standing, Charlie staring straight at the camera, Elsie providing her profile as she gazes off into the distance, an unlit cigarette between the thumb and forefinger of one hand. They're outside a cafe, a wrought iron table behind them, just two people, surrounded by so many others. Two desperately alive people, holding each other's secrets.

The internet tells me that Charlie died long ago of liver cancer. Unmarried, unfriended, alone in a French hospital, having worked until almost the end.

I reread the last paragraph of his letter. I can feel it now, the weight of *Wild Things*—of Bridget's life—balanced against the weight of *Tongues*. All those letters, all those people, all those relationships between readers and the book that Elsie couldn't love. Elsie has more than one albatross around her neck. Charlie was right: she deserved to write for herself. Not for Bridget, or for Joe Bell, or for me.

I came into the attic today wanting to know why and how she could've given up *Wild Things*. That's not really possible to know, though, is it? Just like I can't understand why she saved—or even had—so many napkins, I can't say what made her decide that writing the book the country wanted was better than publishing the book she needed. Joe Bell, sexism, wanting to be considered a good writer, wanting to *become* a better writer, wanting fame, wanting to prove herself, hoping to gain the skill and credibility that would make it possible to write Bridget's real story later . . .

Maybe the more important thing to understand is what happened once she did give up her book.

I think it broke her inside. I think she always remembered what she gave up. The regret eventually dwarfed everything else until she became a woman smoking herself to death all alone in a house that could be crushed beneath the weight of a lifetime packed into boxes.

I like to think I'd make a different choice. But who we'd like to be and who we are only sometimes match up.

I spend most of the afternoon at Elsie's. Without her, the downstairs feels like an off-season hotel, shuttered and lifeless. The attic remains a Sunday morning flea market, ready to open as soon as the tarps are pulled off the tables. Did she truly imagine that at some point she'd want to bring the two—two!—cuckoo clocks down again, wind their clockwork hearts, and watch their painstakingly painted birds do musical battle every hour? Here they wait, soon to be homeless and hoping to attract an odd bird afficionado.

Maybe the why of the cuckoos is as big as the why of the book. As she slides down her overstuffed pillow at the hospital, what does she think about? Children in snowsuits, literary acclaim, coffee table books, trinkets and Gettysburg and the Red Sox? Charlie, drink in hand? Reading Joe Bell's letters without seeing the future he was selling her? Patsy and their shared and unshareable grief? Bridget, in the Kindly Oak, among the roses, on the shore?

Who controls the narrative of Elsie's life? Does the public own it because they've locked her one published book deep in their collective heart? Would publishing her furious and flawed first book, the true one, finally wrestle control free for her?

Or is *the true one* my way of saying I own her life? Choosing for her, going to her kids with the manuscript—that gives her life to *me*: past, present, and future. Hands me the power to tell the story of who she is, which is really the story of who I want her to be.

My grandfather—a gentle man with big farmer's hands and imposing eyebrows who loves ice cream and his family and philosophizing—likes to tell me that the hard thing isn't *knowing* what the right thing to do is, it's just *doing* it.

He's right. The right thing can be so frigging hard to do.

By the end of the day I've finished, if not the full cataloging, then at least the mapping of this vast archeological dig. A few more days and I'll be done. No ten-thousand-dollar reward collected. No further thoughts on writing dragged from Elsie's reluctant lips.

I've packed everything I need in my backpack. Joe Bell's letters, Patsy's, Charlie's. Anything that makes an obvious reference to Bridget and *Of Wild Things and Flame*. The single lines written on envelopes and recipes, memories of Bridget tucked carefully away.

The attic has finally begun to make sense to me. If you can't bear to take the final step of destroying your secrets yourself, one alternative is to bury them deep in the mundane. Place settings and pitchers and pinecones. Memories clipped to objects they have no relationship to.

I have the book of roses as well. The book has done nothing wrong in its long life. It can expose no secrets to biographers, net no windfall for fortune-hunters. I'm commuting its sentence. I think Patsy will take it.

My last stop is the living room. I pull out volume M of the encyclopedias. The book within has clearly been read many times, but the pages fall open to the dedication, not the main text.

Bridget, is this all that's left of your story now? Dedications in sweet sapphic romance novels, fragments of a literary puzzle collected from an attic. Then again, how much immortality do any of us get? Never enough, not for the people who love us.

I check all the other encyclopedia volumes, just in case. I'm prepared for a whole collection of illicit reading materials, with the best saved for X. There's nothing. Just elands and geodesic domes and semaphores. All thrilling in their own ways, I'm sure.

I hoist my bag, shut the door and head for home.

Once home, I can't settle. The only solution is to hit the road and ride until I physically cannot ride more.

That's my plan at least, the one that's gotten me halfway to the middle of nowhere. Up the twisty curves that motorcycle jockeys always misjudge, up farther than that, turning to go past the lake where a few mothers and toddlers dig in deserted sand. Farther, farther, where the houses are sparse and McMansions are nonexistent, where signs notifying residents that broadband has finally arrived dot the sides of the roads. Where a tornado once flattened saplings on a hillside, where I could scream and nobody would hear me. And I want that so badly, to scream and scream at this life and its trajectory that feels more like a Gordian knot than a line leading anywhere.

When I hit a pocket of cell phone reception and pause for a swig of water and a quick message check, I have a text. From Noa. A photo: clouds from the view of a plane window. I've never been on a plane. Never seen the clouds below me instead of above.

I take a good look around. I've been here before, at this crossroads. Literally, four directions wait for my decision. Home, known, rare, never.

Which road?

It's up to me.

✤✤✤

I don't know what to text Noa. Something that says *I'm not waiting for you* and *I want to round a corner and see you there*, with a dash of *I totally don't have my shit together* thrown in, all in just one line. I'm not sure it matters half as much as I imagine it does. I probably don't need to send anything more than a heart.

Maya texts before I can decide. **I'm so pissed even though you're right. I wish you'd said it before now. I wish it had all been different. I don't understand when things stopped working.**

It's tempting to try to talk about it with her now. To explain what happened to me. But that's my own story and I don't owe it to anyone, even if I love them. And the real answer to why things stopped working is so much more complicated than that.

I know. Do you know when you're leaving for Ireland?

Monday

So soon! Are you excited?

She doesn't respond. I don't try again. I've needed space to figure things out. Maya does too. It sucks, but maybe it's like a forest fire: until everything burns to the ground, the seeds waiting in the soil won't have their chance to grow.

To Noa, I say, **Send me a picture of how the sky looks from the ground when you can <3**

I open up my notebook. I have written so many lists. So many. I've been trying so hard to write. Elsie wrote one book in a rush, feeling like nothing existed beyond that one thing. But then she wrote another over . . . years.

Which means she wrote two amazing books in two very different ways. Maybe there isn't just one way for me either. Maybe for every writer who sits down and knocks out two thousand words a day, there's also one who writes twenty-five words. Or one who waits a year, two years, ten, to be ready, and then writes like a holy spirit moves them.

If that's true, and I'm not saying it is, then maybe the problem isn't that I've been failing because I destroyed my one true book. There's not even a problem, in fact. I might just be growing a book in the way that works for me. Maybe not, but I think there's a chance.

Robin's working again tonight. After dinner, Mom leaves too, this time to see Martín. I'm starting to wonder how often *studying* translated to *booty call* over the years, but I'm also content not to go any further down that road.

Alone in my room, I open my laptop, stare at the screen for a minute. Instead of opening a Word document, I search for a file. It's a video Maya made for my sixteenth birthday. She'd asked Mom and Robin and Alex and Hedy to donate photos and footage. I haven't looked at it for a long time, not since Robin was in the hospital.

It's a mix of pictures and more video, from birth on. Me and Dad, me and Mom, me and Robin—so many of the two of us, from tiny people in a plastic pool to us standing in the same field I showed Noa. Me and Maya, me screaming "It tickles!" as she writes her name on the tips of my toes. All of us—Robin, Hedy, Alex, Maya and me—in a laughing selfie before we hit Secret House. All of us again, passing the phone back and forth to film as we dance in a field off the bike trail, more than a little stoned.

It doesn't seem like me at first, that happy laughing girl. And that girl never would've thought she'd become me. But here I am, my caddisfly self, making a home with all the things life tosses me.

By the time I've closed the laptop, I've got a feeling in the base of my spine that isn't about writing. It's about finding my skin and slipping back in. The late-night sounds of the town drift through the window as I slide out of my clothes and into my bed.

Holiday, what of you?

For my next visit to Elsie, I wear black pants and a white shirt. I slick my hair down, noting how the green has faded and the roots show through. It's almost time for a decision on that as well. I take out most of my earrings and the cuff, leaving only a pair of hoops. I don't look like who I was two years ago, or six months ago, or even the last time I dyed my hair. That's okay. For today, for right now, this is me.

I hold my hand up to the mirror, palm to reflected palm.

"Hello, friend," I whisper. "It's good to see you here."

Elsie's propped up a bit higher tonight. She doesn't look *good* quite as much as she looks less bad. She's surprised to see me, at least for a moment.

"I didn't ask you to come."

"But I came anyway." I slide the chair over to the bed and take my seat next to her. "How are you?"

She's surprised again. "Why are you dressed like an imposter?"

I suppress a snort of amusement. "Um, because I felt like it?"

Only now I see the trouble. She thinks I've come to tell her I gave the book to her kids already. Because she knows they'll have offered me money, or because I want to be famous, or because I think I'm doing her a favor. And that's not a silly fear.

I lean closer to her, put my hand on hers. The skin is cold and waxy. I cup her knuckles, willing them to be warm. "I'm here to say that I will do what you want me to do."

There's bone-deep relief in the way everything about her slackens. It's like she's been bracing for battle.

"But I have conditions. I won't do it while you're alive. I know that seems silly to you." She's trying to speak but the floor is mine. "You've had it for most of your life. You can stand the fact that it exists for the rest of it. I'll keep it safe, and never tell anyone, and if you never change your mind, I will burn it on a funeral pyre when you're gone." Because it will be like that, like burning a body. "This way, if you do change your mind, you can still publish it. But the default will always be that I do what I promised. Okay?"

She pulls her hand away from me and reaches for a tissue from a little floral box on her bedside table.

"I'm even throwing in some freebies," I go on. "I've collected all the letters. Everything that mentions it. From Patsy and Joe Bell. One from Charlie Kirk Brushmeier and also the paper you tucked behind the picture of the Kindly Oak. Do you want to see any?"

She's tired. Whatever energy she had when I came in has vanished. She shakes her head ever so gently.

"I took Patsy's book too. Just in case you don't want anyone to wonder why you've got lesbian romances stowed in utterly destroyed encyclopedia volumes."

She cracks a bit of a smile. Even that looks tiring. She taps the tip of her pointer finger on my wrist. "You keep it. It's what you like."

I narrow my eyes at her. "I'm eighteen years old. Much too young for that book."

"Not forever," she whispers. "Sooner than you think."

"I don't think I'm ever going to be old enough to want to read that book, Elsie McAllister."

Finally, she breaks a smile. "Piss and vinegar."

A nurse comes to the door. She's the opposite of yesterday's nurse in just about every way: skinny, blonde, eighties bangs and plain pink scrubs. "You need to leave now," she says with a frown. "Visiting hours are over."

Elsie rests her cold hand on mine. "You promise," she says.

"I promise."

She squeezes.

I give her a grin. "You have any suggestions for the next color?" I point at my head.

The nurse taps her wristwatch. "It's time to go."

Elsie gives her that drop-dead imperial look, then turns to me, crooks a finger. I lean closer. She's laboring to breathe again. She looks at me like she's storing away details to use in a future manuscript. "Electric. Ocean. Blue. I would. Have. If I. Were. Brave."

I nod. "Good choice." I walk to the door and stop by the nurse. She's about a foot and a half shorter than I am, short enough that I can see her gray roots. "Be nice to her. She's America's Treasure."

I hear Elsie's barking laugh as I walk away.

I ride the long way to work this morning. Past the Common, the tiny branch library, the church. Past the fields, past the barns, past the hill where Alex died. Once upon a time this trip was forever long. I did it first in the kid wagon Mom would pull me in, then the tag-along, Robin peddling his big-kid bike with hand brakes and three speeds. Now it's no longer a challenge to my legs, lungs, or imagination. Just my heart, I think.

The boxes won't all fit in the guest room, so I start a corner in the living room. By noon, I've moved everything I've cataloged downstairs and I decide to take my break at the bar in the kitchen.

At some point Elsie had three little kids waiting for lunch here every day. Did she have a nanny, or was she flipping grilled cheese sandwiches and chopping celery sticks while chain-smoking? She could've traveled the world with Charlie but chose to be here. She could've written more books like *Tongues* and people would've bought them. She could've said fuck you to Joe Bell and all her adoring fans and published *Wild Things*. She could've hit the talk show circuit and told everyone what had been done to Bridget and who did it. She could've answered Patsy's card.

Gordian knot, baby. It's hers, though. Not mine or anyone else's to cut apart.

❀ ❀ ❀

I'm coming out of the bathroom before leaving for home when I hear the slider squeak. I hurry down the hall to find Dr. Galaxy putting a travel bag down.

"Oh," he says. "Holi. I didn't expect you'd be here."

I see his red eyes and I know.

He doesn't have to say anything. It's not as though anyone should be surprised.

And yet, somehow, I am.

He gives me an awkward wavery smile. "I'm sorry to tell you—"

"She was okay last night."

"She had a stroke. It can be a complication. It's . . ." He wipes beneath his eyes. "She didn't suffer. That's the important thing. She just went to sleep, Holi."

I want . . . I don't know what I want. For her not to have fallen. For her to have been able to come back here. For me to have sat down with her and her Red Sox cap and listened to the game.

Tears gather in his eyes. "I know this must be hard for you too, Holi. You've spent so much time with her recently. She thought very highly of you."

I steel myself and give him a very chaste, lean-in hug. He snuffles on my shoulder for a moment, and I look at the rotary phone on the wall and suddenly I also want to cry.

"I'm so sorry," I say, but it's not really for him. It's for Elsie, and not because she's gone. I'm apologizing for choices she had to make that ate her up inside, for having a shit dad and a shit town, for all the burning—of cigarettes, talent, time, soul.

"I really appreciate that," says Dr. Galaxy, and something

shifts and we're unhappy strangers trying to think of what else to say to each other in the house of a deceased woman. I'm tired and sad and confused and I want to be home.

"She was a pretty special person," I say. "I think I should . . ." I motion toward the door.

"I can be in touch with you about finishing things here. The arrangements . . . I'm afraid the funeral will be private, because of crowds. There will be public events, I'm sure. We'll make a statement. She had something, let me . . ." He leaves the room, returns after a minute. "The other day she asked me to give this to you." He hands me a sealed envelope. "Is there anything else—anything more I can do for you?"

I look at the boxes in the corner, the dry and quiet room, the mantel. No. The rest is up to me.

Over the next two days I eat bunny crackers from the box and peanut butter from the jar. I sleep all night and most of the afternoon. I let the shower have a break. I let myself have one too. Fulfilling my promise, opening the envelope—I ignore those tasks completely. Dr. Galaxy told me that I should take a week off before coming back to finish work. I may take the rest of my life off instead.

After the family released their statement, Elsie's neighborhood became an impromptu shrine, her driveway filling with flowers and candles that need constant putting out so that everything doesn't go up in flames. Since her original home in Eastley burned to the ground, the Kindly Oak has borne the brunt of the fanatic love and mercenary greed her death has unleashed. I saw one picture of it—the limbs sawed and broken away, the ground around it now apocalypse-barren. Love? Yeah, fuck that.

On the third day, I come downstairs to find Martín on the couch, drinking coffee and reading what looks like a guide to trains.

"I don't need babysitting, you know."

He sets his book on the side table and smiles at me. "Come, sit." He pats the couch beside him.

We both sit. I become aware of just how strongly unwashed I smell. He, politely, doesn't hold his nose.

"Are you missing her?" he asks.

"Elsie? Kinda." I think about the feel of her arm on mine, the sound of her breathing as I drove her to the doctor, how she told me there was no skin between me and the world. That's what I'd wanted, though I hadn't understood it. Not to have someone tell me I wrote well, not to get a good grade . . . I wanted someone to look at me and say *Writer* in the same way a birder might raise their binoculars toward a flash of red and say *Cardinal*.

And Elsie did. We do that all the time to each other, right? *Daughter, friend, girlfriend, sister.* I've been called all of those things and they've shaped me. And when I've lost the people who called me these things, even temporarily, part of the hurt's been losing who I am to the person who's gone.

But *writer*—that's all me. Elsie named it, but it was mine from the start.

"I do miss her," I tell Martín. "I didn't think I would but I do."

"You saw her life in a very intimate way, I expect."

You have no idea, my friend. I want to tell him. I want to tell someone, everyone, *She gave you something that destroyed a part of her. She was so much more than the one book you loved.*

Instead, I smile and say, "Archeology." I still want answers, but about myself, not Elsie. "Do you ever think about giving up? On writing?"

He laughs. "Who doesn't? That's part of the deal. The trying, the struggle, the pain, the discovery. Learning which conversation you seek to have with the world and how to achieve that with the words you have."

"Don't you ever feel like you've failed at it?"

He studies my face. "When I was younger, yes. I so often felt like a failure. Everything felt much more binary, either good or bad. Now, though, I understand that you're always building. Writing is also a conversation with other writers, with readers, with your own history and the history of the world. The stories that weren't quite ready for the previous generation, the ones whose writers were gone too early—they wait to be written by those yet to come."

My stomach rumbles.

He picks up his book again. "Take a shower, Holi. Get dressed. Life needs you in it."

Robin and I are collecting firewood. The state park picnic area is empty aside from us. I was surprised when he agreed to come. We've been keeping a porcupine distance from each other since our fight. Of course, he hugged me after I told him and Mom that Elsie had died. He brought me fries from the diner. That's what being a sibling means, I think: being able to be so angry with someone and still ready to drop everything and run to their aid.

We work in silence for a while. It takes a lot more wood

than you might think to make a fire strong enough to burn more than a ream of paper on a damp gray day. I appreciate the time. I have a lot of thoughts to organize.

Once finished, we sit by the firepit on logs that serve as makeshift chairs. Behind us is a pond slowly evolving into a marsh. Squirrels race back and forth through the dry leaves on the ground. An acorn drops on my right foot. We've fully taken the turn from summer to fall. Every living thing in the woods knows what to do when the seasons change. Why don't I?

I light the tinder. Robin snaps brush into bite-sized pieces for our newborn fire. It grows rapidly, clean and free of smoke. I pull my backpack forward, then set it back down.

"I've thought about what you said," I tell him. "About why you cut Hedy out. I still don't think it was fair, but I also understand, I think. I can't imagine what it felt like, feels like for you to have everyone looking at you the way we have. I've still hated you sometimes."

"I've hated me too."

"But I don't want that."

"I know. It's just how it is, though. It's not just myself—I've hated everyone at some point. You, Mom, everyone. I've felt like I'm drowning here at times. Everything I love is so tangled up with everything that hurts so much."

"I think I get it now, why you want to go with Blue and Cass. Why you should go."

I swear he looks like he might cry, and if he does, I will too, so I push on.

"But I worry that you'll get sad, that you won't sleep enough, that you'll forget to take your meds or just stop them on purpose."

"If I get sad, I'll call my therapist. If I get really sad, I'll come home. I've gotta be able to live on my own, Hols. This way I'm doing something I love with some good people."

"Plus you have a thing for Cass."

When he grins, I can see Puck there. What you need to know about Puck, though, what I don't see until right now, is that he isn't immortal. He grows older with the rest of us. He becomes something new too.

"I love you, Robin Goodfellow."

"I love you, Holiday Golightly. But do me a favor and do what you wanted to do before it rains on us."

I open my backpack. "Should I say something?" I pull out the letters from Joe Bell. No regrets about starting with those.

"I don't even know what you're up to here, so your choice."

"I promised Elsie I would do this and I want her to know that I have. I want her to know it was right to trust me."

I put the first letter in the fire. The flames take it effortlessly. Just like that, history vanishes, page by page, until Joe Bell's entry in the encyclopedia of Elsie's secret life is nothing more than ash.

"It's weird, you know? That she's—was—this person people thought they knew, only she was like the rest of us."

"Totally messed up?" Robin gives that lazy sideways smile of his.

"Well, yeah. But I was thinking that no single person in her life could see all the parts of her."

Next up: the letter from Charlie. I want to put it in my pocket and take it home. But no, it's not mine. I lay it in the flames.

I wish we had had more time.

If Christians are right, Charlie and Elsie are meeting up for a drink and a smoke in Hell. If Mom's right, they've become something new already. All of them—Elsie, Charlie, Bridget, Alex, Dad, everyone who has already lived and died—exist as nothing and everything now.

I take a deep breath.

Patsy's cards. Her book. Not the rose book—that I've already mailed to her agent to forward to her. *Hers and Hers*, with its happy cupcake lesbians on the front. It existed as a conduit between Elsie and Patsy when everything else failed. A private one. The fire keeps it that way.

All that's left is *Of Wild Things and Flame.*

I thought deciding would be the hardest part of this. Only now, in the warmth generated by burning wood and other people's thoughts, I truly understand what my grandfather meant about the pain of doing the right thing.

"Sometimes things suck," I say.

Robin scoots over next to me. "So much. So so much. But other times they don't."

"It's brain damage, right? That makes you talk like this?" It's funny only because it's part of our sibling language.

He squints at me. Motions me closer. Says carefully and with great clarity, "Fuck. You."

I take a stack of pages from my bag.

"Are you sure I should be around for this?" he asks. "Are you doing something illegal?"

"I'm doing exactly what the owner of the materials asked me to do. On her deathbed, and before her deathbed, and on the very first day I met her. There's not really any ambiguity here."

I put the first group of pages in the fire. Face down, so that I don't have to see the words burn. I spread them slightly with a stick and close my eyes.

I'm on a dirt road on an island in the sun, the smell of roses drifting through the air from a place I can't yet see. My friends haven't yet caught up to me. I'm free to pause at the edge of the road to watch a rabbit nibble on the grass there. It lifts its head, twitches its nose, and is gone in the brush. Part of me goes with it, into the spaces known only by wild things, and only for their briefest of times.

I hold my brother's hand. He squeezes it tightly.

The embers have just about given out and we're almost ready to leave when I remember the envelope. I open it to find two sheets of paper—white, unlined, unmonogrammed—folded separately inside. The first holds a handwritten note.

> *For Holiday Burton. Writing is a vocation I recommend no woman choose, as it may well cost her things it never asks of men and in ways she cannot imagine. However, once writing has chosen her, no woman should be forced to enter its arena sans sword and shield. Consider this the means to prepare yourself for the ring.*

The second sheet cradles a check. I turn it over. The only thing I see at first is the date: September 6. I'd only been working a couple of days at that point and . . . already, she called me a writer.

Robin looks over my shoulder and makes a slight noise, almost like a choke. "Holi."

I look at the amount.

It's not real, right?

I return to the date. It means she made a decision about me before I'd even been there a week. Before I found the manuscript. Before she'd asked me to burn anything. It's not hush money.

There is no skin between you and the world. I see it.

My throat pulls tighter, tighter, tighter, until maybe even air will be too much to pass through it.

"That's a really big check," Robin whispers.

"It is," I whisper back.

"You must've been a really spectacular labeler of boxes."

"The very best."

"Hols. What are you going to do? Now, like, with your life?"

That

is

the

question.

EPILOGUE

I text Robin. It's hard to line up our schedules while he's on the road. I text, he's asleep, he texts, I'm asleep. We're getting better, though.

I start. **You there?**

Absolutely

Did you take your pills?

Of course

Did you eat something?

Yes

Did you take a shower?

What kind of monster do you take me for? Are you finished? Let's talk about something else

Like what?

Like are you having fun? Are things good? What's new?

Since yesterday? Not all that much

But my laptop is open on the table and the file open on it is not empty. Elsie was right. Sometimes it catches hold of you and there is nothing else you can do. I'd forgotten how that felt.

Robin sends a sleepy emoji. It's 2 a.m. for him.

Was the concert good? It's the kind of conversation you have when you don't want to let go, even if it's just until the next check-in. At the same time . . . I look at the laptop screen again.

Awesome. I'd forgotten how it feels. Applause and shit. Connection.

Do you is as far as I get. The pull string dangling from the light over the table begins to sway in slow lazy circles. I look, I always look, out the window at the barge trundling by. The jaded swans cluster by the dock to wait. Across the water a woman and a small black-and-white dog walk the trail there. Beneath me the floor rocks ever so gently as the houseboat shifts in the wake.

I erase what I started and try again. **I miss you. It's pretty awesome here. I'm so frigging lucky.**

Lucky that Elsie's kids didn't cause any trouble over her check—which they had to endorse since she died before I cashed it. Lucky that Noa's sister hadn't already rented her home out to someone else. Lucky in a million ways.

It's a little hard though. Not being home. Not being with you and Mom.

You're living in flipping Amsterdam on a houseboat on your own. The rest of us will still be here when you get back. Shine on, little sister.

You too. You must be beat. Get some sleep. It's good for your brain.

Yah. I gotta crash. Cass and Blue say hi. Blue wants to know if you've got her, whatever that means.

I watch the swans fan out across the water, sooty black coots scattering before them. Later today, I'll walk through the park where the feral parakeets fly. I'll stop at the market to pick up bread and fruit and come back to read in bed while night turns the water to ink and the city to light.

Tell her I think so. <3

<3

I wake my laptop and look at what I've written so far. It's not much yet, but I can feel the rest waiting like muscle coiled from the tip of my tailbone to the top of my spine, eager to unwind.

AUTHOR'S NOTE

There is no single origin for *Sometimes the Girl*. I tend to magpie stories together, collecting shiny things until suddenly I see the pattern in them. For years I've kept the history of Maine burning in the fall of 1947 at the ready. I wanted to write about home, about the places that have shaped me. I had unfinished business with some characters, but no sense of what that business was.

The biggest piece, though, was the one I was most afraid to touch. In 2015, *Go Set a Watchman*, Harper Lee's first novel, written before *To Kill a Mockingbird*, was published. What happened next fascinated me. Because *Go Set a Watchman* was understood to be the original draft of what became *To Kill a Mockingbird*, and because elements of that first draft contradicted its beloved sibling, a narrative arose that seemed as driven by reader need as by plausibility. In it, Harper Lee was an elderly woman taken advantage of for financial gain, who would never have agreed to a late-in-life publication of such a book.

My interest wasn't in Harper Lee. I've never read *Go Set a Watchman*. Lee's biography is largely unknown to me. The truth of why that book was published—whether she'd been duped or made a fully informed choice or something else

288

entirely—is her story, not mine to assume. The same goes for other famous writers whose work has been published posthumously, sometimes against their documented wishes.

That said, I did want to explore what it might cost a writer to not just leave behind their original draft but to distort their vision completely—and in doing so become famous. More than that, what would they then owe the public? Their entire intellectual life? Nothing at all? In such a situation, might choosing to publish the original work be the braver, harder thing?

To explore these questions through fiction, I needed one character to provide a lens and another to look through it. Elsie and Holi stepped forward from the never-ending dinner party in my brain to volunteer.

Much like Holi, I've craved the answers to questions like why Elsie McAllister stopped writing. And much like Holi, I've discovered those questions almost never have simple answers. I do believe, though, that when we think about the questions we ask of other people's lives, we often find what we're looking for in our own. Holi could just as easily have been asking *Holiday, what happened to you?* The answer to that question, of course, would have been *so many things*, just as it was for Elsie. Just as it is for all of us.

QUESTIONS FOR DISCUSSION

1. How does Holi's perception of herself—who she is, what she wants, what she's capable of—shift over the course of the story? Give one example of a change that stood out to you.

2. In the past year and a half, what has changed about Holi's relationship with Robin and why? In what ways might it be starting to change for the better?

3. What do you think of Holi's relationship with Noa? How does it compare to her relationship with Maya?

4. What aspect of Elsie's personality or backstory surprised you most and why?

5. How do nature and music nourish Holi? What do you turn to when you want to feel a sense of connection to the universe?

6. Discuss the passage in Chapter 36 where Holi reflects on Alex's belief that "in certain places, at certain times . . . we could access points that travel through all of time." Have you ever been in a place that made you feel this way? What

do you think of Holi's speculation that a place's power may be "change more than it is stillness"?

7. Why do *you* think Elsie stopped writing? How does your take compare to Holi's?

8. What do you think of Elsie's pronouncement that fiction is a lie?

ACKNOWLEDGMENTS

Writing is an acknowledgment of our existence, however brief, in the world. We write about ourselves, people we love, people we hate, the times we live in and the ones we wish we did. Even when writing about the ice moons of Jargon Nine, we're reconfiguring the worst of our nightmares and the best of our daydreams and the comfort of a picnic we had on a good sunny day to fit in the frozen wilds. Artists reflect our humanity. Right now, the world sorely needs reminders of what it is to be human. Writers, light your beacons, be they lighthouses, campfires, or stars. My faith in you is as boundless as your creative hearts.

Writers need editors, always. Joe Bell is nightmare stuff. Amy Fitzgerald, whose thoughtful and supportive editing helped shape the story in your hands, is anything but. I'm deeply grateful to her for her care, enthusiasm, and skill. Many thanks to the whole Lerner team as well. Translating a manuscript into an actual beautiful book that people can find and read is no small feat, and they do it with style.

Writers also need champions. I'm blessed to have one of the best in my fearless and compassionate agent, Alice Speilburg. If Elsie had had Alice in her corner, you better believe there would've been more books with her name on their spines and less flammable material in the attic.

Even though the act of writing is solitary, community makes the experience and the stories so much better. Many thanks to my writing soulmate, Abi, and to Margot, Nancy, and Cathy, who treat me like a real writer even when I feel like a pumpkin in a beret set in front of a laptop. Thanks too to my mom and brothers for their endless support. Many thanks to Don and Barbara for all the happy stories they've shared over the years about growing up in Maine.

Thank you, a thousand times thank you, to my kids. As adult creative beings, you rock my world. And while neither of you are Holi or Robin, the two of you together have taught me so many things about what sibling relationships can be, in good times and bad.

I also lucked out when it came to finding the perfect spouse for a writer. Jonathan, you're not just an excellent patron of the arts, you're also an excellent human being without whom my life would be a much smaller and bleaker place. My work is better because of you, my life even more so.

The kind of immortality offered in the pages of a book is often a fleeting one, an illusion of permanence, much like life itself. Whatever I have to confer with this book, though, I give to you, Wish. I believe we all echo on in the places we loved and were loved in; I believe you do so now.

And finally, always: love you, Pop. You taught me how to grow carrots and how to watch for the secrets of a forest and how to recognize my own compass and follow it. Your echo fills my life as steadily as the beat of my own heart and always will.

ABOUT THE AUTHOR

Jennifer Mason-Black is an author of books and short stories, including the young adult novel *Devil and the Bluebird*. She lives and writes in Massachusetts in a place where there are far more trees than people and where foxes dance with owls on midwinter nights.